# DEATH BY COFFEE ... AND PEANUTS

"I don't know what you mean," I said, pulling my arm from his grip.

"Brendon's death was an accident."

"Was it?"

Mason's expression hardened. He looked like he was going to tell me off and then suddenly his face softened. He glanced around to make sure no one was listening before speaking.

"Do you really think someone could have killed him?"

"Don't you?"

"I . . . I don't know."

"Doesn't it seem funny to you that he would forget his EpiPen the very day he comes in contact with peanuts?" I remembered the conversation he'd had with Heidi. "I'm sure you've thought the same."

He nodded and then frowned. "It just doesn't seem possible. Why would anyone kill him?"

"You tell me," I said. "Who would have a reason to kill your brother?"

**Books by Alex Erickson**

DEATH BY COFFEE

DEATH BY TEA

DEATH BY PUMPKIN SPICE

DEATH BY VANILLA LATTE

DEATH BY EGGNOG

**Published by Kensington Publishing Corporation**

# Death by Coffee

## Alex Erickson

**KENSINGTON PUBLISHING CORP.**
http://www.kensingtonbooks.com

KENSINGTON BOOKS are published by

Kensington Publishing Corp.
119 West 40th Street
New York, NY 10018

All Kensington Titles, Imprints, and Distributed Lines are available at special quantity discounts for bulk purchases for sales promotions, premiums, fund-raising, and educational or institutional use. Special book excerpts or customized printings can also be created to fit specific needs. For details, write or phone the office of the Kensington special sales manager: Kensington Publishing Corp., 119 West 40th Street, New York, NY 10018, attn: Special Sales Department, Phone: 1-800-221-2647.

Kensington and the K logo Reg. U.S. Pat & TM Off.

ISBN-13: 978-1-61773-751-0
ISBN-10: 1-61773-751-8
First Kensington Mass Market Edition: June 2015

eISBN-13: 978-1-61773-752-7
eISBN-10: 1-61773-752-6
First Kensington Electronic Edition: June 2015

10 9 8 7 6

Printed in the United States of America

# 1

"One caramel latte," I said, setting the drink on the counter. I smiled brightly at the older woman who'd ordered it. She glanced at the cup, gave me a solid glare, and then snatched it off the counter with a grunt. She carried the cup to the corner table by the window, sat down, and sniffed her coffee like she fully expected it to smell awful.

I watched her show with my smile somehow still in place. When she'd ordered the drink, the woman had acted like she was being forced into it, which was stupid. Who would force someone to drink coffee?

She shot me a withering glare from her seat, as if she could hear the thoughts passing through my head, and then took a tentative sip out of the cup. Her eyebrows rose in surprise before she scowled at her cup and took another, longer sip. The more she drank, the angrier she looked.

"All righty then," I said, turning away.

When my best friend, Vicki Patterson, had called me up out of the blue and asked if I wanted to move to Pine Hills and start up a combination bookstore and coffee shop, I'd been ecstatic. I'd been working at a retail job I hated, selling clothes to women as big around as my leg. Her call was my way out. We loved books. We loved coffee. What could possibly go wrong?

Vicki had moved to Pine Hills a few months before her call. We'd grown up in California together, where celebrities walked the sidewalk, where you couldn't take two steps without tripping over someone's runt of a dog, so her move to a small town in the Midwest caught me completely by surprise. We'd spent nearly every second of our lives together before she left. We'd gone to the same high school, attended the same college. Losing her had felt like losing a part of myself. When she'd called, I'd just started to get used to life without her.

"There's absolutely no bookstore or coffeehouse in town!" she'd all but squealed into the phone. "It'll be perfect, Krissy! We can live close together again!"

How could I say no to that?

Before I knew what I was doing, I was talking to my dad about the investment and looking for a house in Pine Hills. It would be good for the both of us. Vicki had moved away from home in order to get away from her parents, who loved her, sure, but were intent on making her follow in their footsteps. They were both actors and they didn't understand why she wouldn't jump at the chance to be a star. But show business wasn't the life she wanted. She hated being in front of cameras, hated comparing herself to the other girls, who would do just about anything to land an acting job. No matter how many times she told her folks, they just didn't get it. So she just up and moved away. It was the only way she could escape the pressure.

I glanced up the two steps that led to the bookstore portion of our store. Vicki was talking with a woman near the mystery rack, who was listening to her with rapt attention. Vicki had the requisite long legs and the perfect blond hair to get most any job—acting or otherwise, yet this was what she wanted to do. Her bright blue eyes, trim figure, and bubbly personality would have been a hit on the big screen, and I often wondered if I was somehow holding her back. I mean, who was I, really? If I tried out for a movie, I'd end up being cast as the creature from the swamp or the unattractive best friend, if I was cast at all.

Vicki saw me looking, gave me one of her winning smiles, and then turned back to the woman. She held out a book to her and I noted it was one of my dad's first.

I heaved a sigh. Vicki wasn't the only one who had a somewhat-famous parent. My dad used to be a mystery writer before he retired, and it was on his minor success that we were able to open our little store. I don't think we would have gotten a big-enough loan, otherwise.

The bell above the door tinkled and I turned to our newest customer. A middle-aged woman stepped inside and looked around the little space in wide-eyed wonder. She was short, a little on the dumpy side, and was graying at the temples. Her gaze fell on me, causing her entire face to light up. She rushed over to where I stood behind the counter; her purse was clutched so tight to her chest, I was worried it would explode.

"Welcome to Death by Coffee," I said, cringing just a little. I abhorred the name, but Vicki had insisted on it.

"Kristina Hancock?" the woman asked. She leaned forward, giving me a look that made me worried that she was looking for a bit more than just a cup of coffee. She appeared ready to devour me, clothes and all.

"Yes?" I answered hesitantly. I was pretty sure I'd never seen this woman in my life. My name wasn't any big secret or anything; but being new in town, I found it unsettling to have someone already know who I was when I didn't have the slightest clue as to her identity.

"Daughter of James Hancock?"

I groaned inwardly. Of course. That was how she knew me. I should have known. "Yes," I said, somehow managing a smile.

"Oh, my." She fanned herself with her purse. The skin under her arm flapped alarmingly as she did. "I'm such a big fan of your father's. I mean, when I saw the name on the door, I was positive it had to have something to do with him. And then when I saw you . . . Oh! You look just like him!"

Sure, if I had a beard and was bald and was sixty pounds heavier, maybe.

The woman blinked her eyes rapidly as she continued to fan herself. I didn't know what to say to her. I never wanted to name the store after my dad's most popular book, but Vicki had insisted. He'd supplied us with most of the money we needed to get started with the store. He'd even donated over half of the books we were selling. He hadn't written a book in at least five years, yet people still treated him like royalty.

It was part of the reason why I wanted to get away so badly. Like Vicki, I didn't want to live on my dad's reputation. I wanted to be my own person, find my own way.

Vicki, unfortunately, didn't quite see it my way.

"Just think of it," she'd said, trying to convince me it

was for the best. "His fans will surely love the name and will come flocking in because of it. Can we really risk losing such easy advertising?"

I, on the other hand, wasn't so sure. I could handle using my dad's reputation to at least get us started, but the name? I mean, Death by Coffee? Really?

Of course, she wouldn't listen to reason. She insisted it would be for the best. My dad was the only real celebrity we had. Her dad's only claim to fame was a cameo on *The Walking Dead*. He was zombie #12, I believe.

"Do you have any of your father's books for sale here, hon?" the woman asked after she'd sufficiently fanned herself off.

"We do," I said. "And they're signed. If you'll talk to Vicki, I'm sure she can—"

"Oh no, I don't need them," the woman said with a wave of her hand. "I already have his complete works, all signed, of course. I met him in Austin a few years back. That's Texas, you know?" She leaned in closer. Her impressive bosom rose up beneath her chin and threatened to spill out over the counter. She lowered her voice to a whisper. "Do you know if he's working on anything new?"

I kept my smile plastered on as I answered. "I don't think so. I'll ask him the next time I talk to him."

"Do that." She leaned back, allowing her breasts to jiggle back into place. "My name's Rita Jablonski, by the way." She held out a dumpy little hand.

"Krissy Hancock," I said automatically, taking her hand. It was damp and oddly squishy.

She gave my hand a single weak pump before scanning the menu. "I suppose I should have some coffee," she said.

"Yes, just plain black coffee. I can't abide that flavored stuff. It's bad for my digestion."

My face was starting to hurt from all of the smiling, but I refused to stop. I was afraid of offending Rita somehow. We weren't getting many people stopping by, despite the fact we'd just opened Death by Coffee that very morning. I would have thought the people of Pine Hills would have been thrilled to have a place to buy a book or two or get a morning coffee and a cookie, but it appeared I was wrong. A part of me was certain it had something to do with the name.

I poured Rita her coffee and carried it back to the counter. She hadn't clarified whether she wanted it for here or to go, so I put it in a to-go cup in the hopes she'd take the hint and would go away. I handed it to her with a polite "Thank you for stopping by."

Rita took off the cap and sniffed the coffee. She didn't turn to leave.

"You know, I've always wondered why we never had a bookstore in Pine Hills," she said, glancing toward where Vicki was ringing up a sale. "It's a shame, I tell you. The library is a mess these days. No one seems to want to read real books anymore. They have their new-fangled electronic devices and call that reading." She snorted before taking a sip of her coffee. "This is good."

The door opened and an older couple stepped inside. I perked up, hoping they would distract me long enough that Rita would leave, but one look at them told me I'd have no such luck. The woman was dressed in what I could only describe as schoolmarm. Her dress sagged on her roundish frame. Even the flowers looked sad. Her hair was pulled tight to her head in a steel gray bun.

The lines on her face gave her a severe look that warned that she wasn't someone to be messed with.

Her scowl practically burned when she glanced at me before she scanned the rest of the store. The man at her side—her husband, I presumed—looked like a rabbit surrounded by savage wolves. His sweater looked old and worn, like it was the only article of clothing he wore. He was balding in a way that made me wonder if he spent time pulling his own hair out, or if his wife did it for him. He didn't look anywhere but at the woman in front of him, as if waiting for her to give him some command or another.

"That's Judith and Eddie Banyon," Rita said. "They own the diner down on Pine, J and E's Banyon Tree." She glanced at me. "It's like a play on words, you know."

"Ah," I said.

"Their diner was the only place in town where you could get a good cup of coffee—at least until now."

Judith continued to scan the room, not budging from the front of the store. Her fists were clenched, as were her teeth. I was afraid she might have a stroke or something if she didn't relax.

Finally she gave an exaggerated huff, turned, and stormed back out the way she'd come. Her husband looked up long enough to give me a quick apologetic shrug before following her out.

I watched it all with a feeling of dread. One day open and I'd already alienated the local diner owner. I guess I'd better learn to cook for myself if I wanted anything other than fast food. Speaking of which, I didn't recall even *seeing* a fast-food restaurant in town on my way in. They'd probably all been scared away by Judith's scowl.

The older woman in the corner heaved herself up the

moment the couple was out the door. She gave me a dirty look before she took off after the couple, leaving the remains of her coffee behind. I could hear her calling out Judith's name as the door swung closed.

"And that was Eleanor Winthrow," Rita said. She took a slow sip of her coffee and sighed in contentment. "She's Judith's best friend."

"Is she now?"

"Oh yes," Rita said, turning to me. "She often checks out new places for Judith and reports back to her. Her husband died ten years ago—an aneurism, if you can believe that. Ever since he died, Eleanor has followed Judith and Eddie around like a lost puppy."

My smile grew strained. I really didn't need the play-by-play of all my customers, though I did have to admit it was nice to learn a little about the people in town. I didn't know anyone.

"Excuse me," I said, extracting myself from behind the counter, rag in hand. I headed to the table Eleanor had so recently vacated and took my time in wiping it down. I hoped Rita would wander off to bother someone else. However, when I was done, she was still standing there, watching me. With a sigh I returned to my spot behind the counter.

"Brendon Lawyer," she said with a nod of her head.

I followed her gaze and found myself looking at a man across the street. He'd apparently just come out of the building behind him—the door was just swinging closed. I couldn't read the lettering on the windows, thanks to the sun reflecting off them, so I wasn't sure what the building was exactly. He looked both ways before crossing the street, with briefcase in hand.

"A lawyer?" I asked as he approached the door. The man was dressed like one, in a three-piece suit magnificently pressed. You could cut yourself on those lines. A giant class ring on his right hand caught the sun, nearly blinding me, as he reached for the door.

"Of course not," Rita said with a flippant wave of her hand. "That's just his name. He thinks he's a bigger fish than he really is." She snorted as if she found it preposterous.

Brendon entered Death by Coffee and strode to the counter. He glanced disapprovingly at Rita before scanning the menu board. He was clean-shaven, though he'd nicked himself below the right ear, leaving a tiny cut. His hair was black and slicked back to shiny perfection. His jawline was as severe as his clothes, and if the lines on his face were any indication, he spent quite a lot of time scowling.

"Coffee. Black. Two sugars. To go." He looked away.

I went to get his coffee, slightly miffed at his abrupt manner. Whatever the guy did for a living, I hoped it didn't involve dealing with live people. He'd spoken all of six words to me—well, barked them more like—and I already disliked him.

When I returned with his coffee, he snatched the cup off the counter, tossed down some money, and then walked away without waiting for his change—all of two cents. Even though he'd asked for his coffee to go, he took it to the corner table I'd just cleaned.

"You should come to our writers' group meeting!" Rita clasped her hands together.

"Uh, what?" The abrupt change in subject caught me off guard. "I don't write."

"Sure you do." Rita playfully smacked me on the back of the hand with a giggle. "We meet Tuesday nights at the local church." She pointed out the window. I looked at where she was pointing, but all I saw were the stores on the main drag. She gave me another giggle. "You can't see it from here."

"I don't know," I said. "I just moved in and have yet to unpack. And like I said, I don't write."

"Everyone will love to have you." Rita opened her purse, seemingly oblivious to my refusal. She removed a coffee mug and held it out to me. "Here," she said. "I brought this for you."

I took the mug from her. "Um, thanks." I tried hard to sound enthusiastic.

The mug was white with PINE HILLS WRITERS written on it in large block letters. I set the mug behind the counter, where it wouldn't get broken.

"It's no biggie," Rita said with a smile and a pat of my hand. "I hope to see you on Tuesday." She glanced at her watch. "Oh, dear, I best be going. I don't want to keep you too long, you know."

*Too late,* I thought as she grabbed her coffee from the counter where she'd set it. She waved once and then waddled away.

"She seems enthusiastic."

I glanced over to see Vicki smiling at me.

"She seems something, all right."

"Think you'll go?"

I shrugged. "I don't write."

Vicki laughed. "I don't think that matters to her. I caught a little of your conversation. She seems taken with the idea you'll be just like your dad."

"She'll be disappointed."

"Excuse me, miss?" I looked up to find a short, balding man in a tweed jacket standing at the counter. He was holding his hand over his nose like he smelled something terrible.

"Yes?" I asked, taking a deep breath. Everything smelled fine to me.

"There's a cat in here."

I looked past him to where a long-haired black-and-white cat sat on the table that I assumed was his sitting spot.

"That's Trouble."

"It sure is," he said. "I'm allergic."

"No," I said with a smile. "The cat's name is Trouble. He's our resident feline."

"I'll go get him," Vicki said. She hurried around the counter, long legs scissoring toward where the cat was busy washing his nether regions on top of the man's newspaper. All eyes followed her.

Well, all male eyes, anyway.

"He's supposed to stay up in the bookstore," I said, trying my best to sound apologetic.

The man's eyes were watering. He frowned at me a moment before turning and walking out of the shop, leaving both his coffee and paper behind.

"And there goes another one," I said with a groan.

A loud blast of sound came from the back corner. Brendon Lawyer snatched his phone from his belt, barked something into it, and then slammed it back in place. He snapped his briefcase closed, stood, and then gathered his things. He left the shop without a glance.

"And another."

Just as Vicki reached the table, Trouble jumped down, flipped his fuzzy tail at her in an "I've got this" sort of way, and then strolled back up the stairs. His work, obviously, was done.

"Sorry about that," Vicki said, returning. "He has a mind of his own sometimes."

"Tell me about it." I plopped my chin in my hands and looked out over the meager crowd. "This was a bad idea."

"Nonsense." Vicki patted me on the shoulder. "It's only been one day. Business will pick up soon. You'll see."

I sighed. "I'm sure you're right." I just wish I could believe it.

"I'm always right." She glided her way back up toward the bookstore, presumably to tell Trouble to stop acting like his namesake.

I spent the next twenty minutes trying to pretend I wasn't worried. I cleaned the counter, brewed fresh coffee, and washed clean tables twice, just to have something to do. A few more customers came in, seemingly more interested in the newness of the place than actually wanting to buy anything from it. At least a few of them ordered coffee before leaving.

I was in the process of making a red eye—an extra-large helping of espresso to go with the coffee—for a brown-haired girl whose arms and chin were covered in scabs and who carried a skateboard under one arm, when I heard the sirens.

I looked up in time to see an ambulance, quickly followed by a pair of police cruisers, come to a screeching halt outside the building across the street. Traffic came to a halt and everyone in Death by Coffee rose and crowded around the large plate glass window fronting the store to gawk at the scene.

The cops and paramedics leapt out of their vehicles

and rushed inside the building. Nothing seemed to happen for the longest of time before a pair of cops returned. They ushered the gathering crowd back away from the entrance.

"Is someone hurt?" Vicki asked, coming to stand beside me.

I shrugged and continued to watch.

As soon as the path was clear, the paramedics returned. They carried a stretcher between them. Someone lay upon it, face covered by a plain white sheet.

There was a collective gasp as everyone realized the person was already dead. You don't cover the face of the living.

Just before the paramedics managed to maneuver the dead man into the ambulance, his right arm fell free of the sheet covering him. Even from as far away as I was, I could make out the overly large class ring on his finger.

Brendon Lawyer, the man I'd so recently served, was dead.

# 2

Of course, I couldn't be sure it was actually Brendon Lawyer who had died. There could be any number of people in Pine Hills who wore a class ring just like that one. As far as I knew, it was a local status symbol that half of the town wore or something given to everyone who works in the building across the street. I hadn't been in town long enough to know.

It was tempting to head over and ask someone. It seemed like everyone else in town had converged on the spot. I had a feeling deaths like this weren't all that common here. This wasn't New York, or even Cincinnati for that matter. Pine Hills was perhaps a tier above a small town, making a sudden death all the more shocking because everyone probably knew one another by sight. News of the death would be spread across town within an hour.

The police were having a hard time keeping everyone back, though I doubted there was much to see. If the guy had been shot or stabbed or something, I had a feeling there'd be more panic. People would be running around, screaming, hands waving in the air, making it harder for the police to do their jobs. As it was, the crowd was simply trying to push forward to get a better view of what had happened.

I could only assume Brendon Lawyer had suffered a stroke or maybe an aneurism like Eleanor's husband. Natural causes. That's what I kept telling myself. The guy had died of natural causes and everything would get back to normal in a day or two.

"What do you think happened to him?" Vicki asked. She had Trouble in her arms and was stroking him as if he was the only thing that was keeping her calm. He had a look on his face that said he was none too happy about the attention; but whenever Vicki held him, she could get away with just about anything. I, on the other hand, would have had gouges in my arms that would have required stitches.

"I think someone died." I didn't want to voice my opinion on who I thought was dead, in case I was wrong. It would be just my luck to start a rumor that would turn out to be wildly inaccurate. I didn't need that sort of attention, especially being so new.

We watched the scene for a little while before going back to work. There wasn't much to see out there, anyway. A few of the onlookers had given up on catching sight of something exciting and had come over for some coffee and gossip. I had to admit that while the circumstances weren't ideal, the death sure had increased business. I spent the next half hour filling orders and bussing tables without a breath in between.

Vicki, likewise, was busy up by the books. Whenever she got a moment, she'd come down and help me out. She'd fill a few orders and then would return to the books, pushing my dad's novels more often than not. And despite her rushing around, not a hair was out of place. I, however, was drenched in sweat and my hair was plastered to my forehead like it had been glued on.

I wasn't jealous. Really.

"Excuse me, ma'am?"

I looked up from where I was scrubbing a table to find an angel standing before me.

Okay, maybe he wasn't an actual angel, but I swear to you that when I first laid eyes upon him, he was glowing. It might have been the sun, or the way the lights caught his sandy brown hair, which verged on the edge of blond, that caused it, but that knowledge did little to diminish my first impression of the man. His eyes were a deep blue and he had dimples that I could lose myself in for days.

"Um, yes?" I glanced away before he realized I was staring. I hurriedly brushed hair out of my eyes and tried to tidy myself up as much as I could without a shower. I sucked in my gut, tucked in my shirt, and silently wished I would have started working out before now. I kept promising myself I'd get in shape, but something always came up, like a good cupcake or a movie that I just had to watch. I wasn't fat or anything, but compared to Vicki, no man was ever going to give me a second glance.

"I'm Officer Dalton. Are you in charge here?"

I came crashing back down into reality. "Yeah," I said, looking down at the badge on his chest. The glow dissolved around him as realization set in. This man, this angel who'd been so kind to bless me with his presence, was a police officer.

Craptastic.

"I'd like to ask you a few questions, if you don't mind," he said, almost shyly. He might be a police officer, someone who was supposed to be in charge of any given situation, but he seemed downright cute with his sheepish smile and kind eyes. I couldn't see him throwing anyone down and cuffing them. Well, maybe in someone's dreams, perhaps.

I felt the flush rush up my cheeks and I glanced around the room to hide it. There were still quite a few customers left and they were all watching us. I feared what would happen if I were to be questioned in front of them. I hadn't done anything wrong, yet I couldn't help but feel that one wrong move would destroy any hope of Death by Coffee surviving.

"I can handle this," Vicki said, coming up behind Officer Dalton. She raised her eyebrows at me and mouthed, "Wow," just before he glanced back at her. She smiled sweetly at him.

Officer Dalton looked around the room, surprisingly unhypnotized by Vicki's good looks. "Is there somewhere we can talk that would be a little more private?"

The thought of being alone with him was enough to make my temperature rise. I had to fan myself and clear my throat before I could even think to speak.

"The office," I said, gesturing toward one of the two doors behind the counter. I doubted he'd want to go back into the kitchen, with the dirty dishes, or in the stockroom upstairs, where the only place to sit was on unpacked boxes of books and cups. "We can talk there."

There was a collective groan from the crowd. I swear one of the ladies sitting by the window had moved a few seats closer while I wasn't looking. They'd just have to get their gossip somewhere else.

I led Officer Dalton to our dinky office, sort of wishing the space was bigger. Maybe the stockroom wasn't such a bad idea. At least there we could talk without knocking knees.

I prayed Vicki did a good job with the customers in my absence because, quite frankly, I'd been just about running myself ragged working with just the coffee. She was going to have to run both sections, which had to be near impossible.

Officer Dalton closed the door behind us. I offered him one of the two computer chairs crammed into the room with the tiny desk and filing cabinet. The space was more of a closet than anything. In fact, I think it was a closet at one time, but it was the only place where we could put a computer without sticking it in a sink.

We both sat.

"What is this about, Officer?" I asked, taking my cue from the movies.

"Call me Paul," he said, clearly not going by the script. "Everyone else does."

"Okay, Paul." I felt the blush creep farther up my neck. I felt like a girl talking for the very first time to a boy she liked. I wasn't sure when I'd last felt that way. "I'm Krissy. Kristina. Hancock. Krissy Hancock." This time my face erupted into a flush that burned.

Paul gave me another flash of those dimples of his before opening a notepad. "I just have a few questions for you, Mrs. Hancock. You're not in any sort of trouble."

"I'm not married," I blurted out. I promptly wanted to die.

"Noted," Paul said with a smile.

"Just call me Krissy."

He nodded, cleared his throat, and then launched into the questions.

"Did you know a man by the name of Brendon Lawyer?"

*I knew it!* I choked back the exclamation and nodded. "Sort of," I said. "He came in for coffee earlier today."

"Was he with anyone else?"

"No, he came in alone."

Paul flipped a page. "Did he buy anything to eat while he was here? I noticed you sell donuts?" He made it a question, telling me he hadn't looked too hard.

"Cookies," I said. "Homemade. And no, he didn't buy anything other than a coffee. He asked for it to go and then sat down to drink it." I wasn't sure why I added the last.

"Did he eat anything at all while he was here?"

I thought back. "I remember seeing a briefcase. I suppose he could have brought food with him, but I didn't pay too much attention to what he was doing. He didn't stay long. He got a call and then rushed off after only a few minutes."

"Did you see where he went?"

"Back to his office, I think." I tapped my chin before nodding. "Yeah, I'm pretty sure he went back to his office, though I didn't actually see him go in."

"So you don't know if he made another stop?"

"Sorry."

Paul scribbled something into his notepad before asking, "Do you happen to use peanuts in your cookies?"

The question caught me a little by surprise. "Peanuts? Why, no."

"Is there any chance his coffee came in contact with some sort of peanut product?"

"Not from my end," I said. "If Mr. Lawyer had brought a lunch with him, then I guess he could have had some peanuts then. Why?"

Paul wrote something else down in his notepad before looking up at me. He was all seriousness. My heart rate picked up and I had to force myself to keep from looking too nervous. My foot wanted to jiggle up and down, so I planted it firmly on the floor, where it had nowhere to go.

"Did Mr. Lawyer leave anything behind when he left your store?"

"No," I said. "I cleaned the table myself just a few moments after he'd gone and I didn't see anything. Did something come up missing?"

Officer Dalton sat back in his chair and flipped his notepad closed. "His EpiPen."

I frowned. I'd heard of an EpiPen before, but wasn't sure what it was for. I asked him as much.

"It's used by people with severe allergies," he said. "If they are experiencing an attack, they jab themselves with it." He used his pen to demonstrate, poking himself in the outer thigh with it. With a frown he looked at the mark he'd made on his otherwise clean tan slacks. He clicked his pen closed and looked back to me. "Mr. Lawyer's EpiPen was gone. He went into anaphylactic shock."

My hands went to my mouth. "He had a peanut allergy?"

Paul nodded. "He was extremely allergic to peanuts. Though from what I've gathered, he could eat most other nuts. He was alone in his office and his EpiPen was missing. Right now, we think it was an accident. He might have left the device at home and then came into contact with peanuts somehow during the day. I was hoping you could shed some light on what he might have eaten."

"I'm sorry," I said. "I don't have peanuts here and I didn't see whether or not he brought anything to eat with him."

Paul gave me a reassuring smile. "It was a long shot," he admitted. "Someone is talking to his wife and I'm sure she can fill us in more."

We fell silent. I couldn't believe someone I'd just served had died. The guy had a wife, maybe even a kid or two, and was now gone forever. It hit me just how bad of a name Death by Coffee really was. No one was going to want to eat here now.

"I take it you are new in town?" Paul asked suddenly, drawing me out of my contemplations. He cleared his throat and looked at his hands instead of directly at me. "I haven't seen you around before."

"Just got in yesterday," I said. "Would have been in sooner, but my U-Haul broke down on the way. I still haven't unpacked." I paused. "We just opened up the store today."

"Hell of a way to start out, right?" Paul gave a nervous laugh before clearing his throat again.

"Yeah." Vicki was going to die when I told her what had happened. So much for a positive outlook.

Paul sat there a moment longer before suddenly standing. "I'll get out of your hair," he said. "Thanks for your cooperation. If you learn anything more, please let us know." He held out his hand.

We shook. His hand was firm, but surprisingly soft. I was guessing he didn't do much hard labor, but he kept himself in stunning shape due to his job. I had to force myself to let go of his hand, lest I drool on it.

This time Paul led the way as we left the small office and returned to the store proper. He nodded once to Vicki before glancing back at me. He gave me yet another winning smile before leaving. He crossed the road and stopped to talk to an older woman in a police uniform. They spoke for a few minutes before they each got into a squad car and drove off.

I stared dumbly after them. I was trying hard to remember if there was any way I could have gotten peanut extract in Brendon's coffee. I was terrified I was somehow responsible for the man's death. He'd come here just before he'd died. Did that mean his coffee had been laced with peanuts?

"What did he want?" Vicki asked, coming to stand next to me. Her hair was still perfect and she hadn't broken a sweat the entire time I was gone. All eight tables were sparkling clean and the customers seemed happy. They watched me with eager, curious eyes.

I led Vicki behind a stack of to-go cups where no one could see us. "The guy who died came here for coffee before he, well, you know . . . died." I spoke at a near whisper. "He had an allergic reaction and went into some sort of shock." There was no way I was going to try to pronounce the word Paul had used. I'd end up sounding dumber than I really was. My tongue did strange things on big words, even if I *knew* how to pronounce them.

"A reaction to something in the coffee?" Vicki asked, a little too loud for my liking.

I glanced around the cups to see some of the customers look at their coffee cups as if they might contain poison. At least four of them got up and left.

"I hope not," I said. "He was allergic to peanuts. We don't have any of those here."

"Oh." Vicki was quiet a moment. "What about the hazelnut coffee?"

I sucked in a breath. Could I have accidently given him the wrong kind of coffee? I was almost positive I'd served regular black coffee, but I supposed I could have made a mistake.

"I don't know if that would affect his allergy," I said. I'd have to look it up sometime. "Besides, he wanted regular coffee, none of the flavored stuff."

Vicki slowly nodded her head and then burst into a grin. She nudged me with her elbow. "He's cute, though, isn't he?"

"Who? The dead guy?"

"No, silly, the police officer."

Visions of dimples and blue eyes swam in my head. I very nearly swooned.

"I suppose," I said, clearing my throat. "Paul isn't bad."

"Paul, eh? First-name basis already." She waggled her eyebrows at me.

"Shut up. He's okay."

"Right," she said with a laugh. "The last time I saw you look like that was when my dad introduced you to Jason Momoa at the movie premiere. I swear you floated all the way home that night and wrote 'Krissy and Jason forever' in your diary about a thousand times."

"I did not!" I'd settled on writing his name over and over, but I wasn't about to tell her that.

"You should go for it," Vicki said. "He wasn't wearing a ring."

"That doesn't mean anything."

She winked. "Of course, it doesn't."

"He's investigating a murder!" I said, putting as much indignation into my voice as I could. I knew Officer Dalton had said he thought it was an accident, but murder sounded much more dramatic. "I shouldn't be thinking about whether or not the man is available."

Vicki only smiled before walking off to take care of an elderly man holding a few paperback books upstairs.

I looked across the street at the now-empty building. The lights were out, telling me that anyone who worked inside had left with the crowd. Even Death by Coffee was emptying of guests now that the excitement had died down.

Or because they thought the coffee might kill them. Either way, the place was definitely dying down.

I thought of Brendon Lawyer and how he'd been rude and abrupt to me while he'd been here. But even then, he hadn't deserved to die.

Could I have been responsible?

I looked away, wondering if I should do something. A man died after coming to my place. I couldn't sit back and let that go. I might have to talk to Officer Dalton again sometime to make sure my coffee had nothing to do with Mr. Lawyer's death. In a grim sort of way, I actually sort of looked forward to that conversation.

With a sigh that might have been just a little dreamy, I went back behind the counter to double-check my labels. If something I'd served had peanut extract in it, I planned on finding it. I never, ever wanted something like this to happen again.

## 3

"In our top story tonight, Brendon Lawyer, of Lawyer's Insurance, was found dead in his office earlier today of an apparent allergic reaction to peanuts."

I cringed, waiting for the news anchor to go on and talk about Death by Coffee, how it was instrumental in his death. The screen went to the Lawyer's Insurance building with ambulances parked out front as the anchor went on. I didn't recall seeing cameras there, but I suppose it was possible they had been.

"Mr. Lawyer is survived by his wife, Heidi, his father, Raymond, and his brother, Mason. While the police are currently classifying his death as an accident . . ."

I stopped listening as I studied the picture that popped up of Brendon standing beside a woman I assumed to be his wife. Neither Brendon nor Heidi was smiling. In fact, they looked as if they didn't want to have the picture taken together at all.

Heidi Lawyer might have once been beautiful, but apparently her life hadn't been easy. She was dressed in a black dress and heels, though she looked uncomfortable in them. Her hair hung around her shoulders, almost limply. She had lines on her face that spoke of an unhappy existence, eyes deep-sunken and sad. Thinking back to how Brendon had spoken to me, I could see why she might not be the happiest of people.

The screen cut back to the anchor, who threw it over to sports. I clicked off the TV, not really interested. I'd only wanted to see what they had to say about the death and was thankful my coffee wasn't mentioned.

I heaved a sigh and looked into the empty carton of Rocky Road in my lap. I'd eaten the entire thing in one sitting. No wonder I could never get in Vicki-like shape. My cat, Misfit, was curled up at my feet, though he was giving me the stink eye for not offering to share. Normally, I let him eat off my spoon.

"Why is this happening to me?" I asked him. As far as I could tell, there'd been nothing in the shop that could have caused Brendon's attack. I suppose Eleanor Winthrow could have had some peanuts with her coffee and left crumbs lying around, but I'd cleaned the table. There was no way he could have come into contact with anything in Death by Coffee. I was sure of it.

Then why did I feel so responsible?

I kept thinking that if I'd stopped him from leaving, he'd still be alive. I could have offered him a gift card or maybe offered a refill of his coffee. Perhaps he wouldn't have come in contact with the peanuts that had killed him if I'd delayed him even by a few seconds. I mean, I could have been one of the last people—perhaps even *the* last person—to see him alive. If that didn't totally suck goats, I didn't know what did.

"What a day, huh?" I said to Misfit, who swished his

tail at me. I heaved myself up and headed for the kitchen.

Misfit followed me, which he usually did any time he thought I was going to get him something. He and Trouble had come out of the same litter seven years ago, though you might not know it by looking at them. They both had the same long hair, same white feet, and same white underbellies. They both even had the same white spot on their upper lips, right beneath their left nostrils, which made it look like they'd gotten milk splashed on their faces. But where Trouble was black, Misfit was orange as, well, an orange.

I'd chosen the orange fluffball, while Vicki had taken Trouble. Of the two, Trouble tended to be far friendlier when it came to other people, hence him being chosen as the store cat. Vicki didn't mind gathering him up and taking him home every night. I, on the other hand, would rather scrub toilets for a living than try to get Misfit into a cat carrier or on a leash. He knew how to use those back feet of his. He could strip flesh from bone in point-two seconds flat.

As soon as I entered the kitchen, he leapt up onto the island counter. I'd chosen this house specifically because of that little island, knowing it would be where I'd spend most of my time. Well, that and the quiet little cul-de-sac seemed like the perfect place to relax after a hard day's work. I didn't live at the end of the road, like I'd have liked, but was close enough for it not to matter. There was little to no traffic here, and that's exactly how I liked it. It was a pleasant change from the busy streets of California. I never would have thought it before, but I definitely was liking the small-town-girl life.

A stack of puzzles sat on the floor beside the island.

They'd been one of the first things I'd unpacked. There were word puzzles, Sudoku puzzles, and the traditional picture puzzles. I've spent more hours than I cared to admit putting puzzle after puzzle together. They always helped me think.

Beside the stack of puzzles was an open box labeled MISFIT. I removed a bag of treats sitting on top of his food. I opened the bag and shook out a few pieces in front of him.

"No more than that," I said. "You're putting on weight. I really don't want to have to put you on a diet."

He glared at me before he began the process of making a mess of the counter. I sometimes wondered if he actually ever ate the treats I gave him or if he simply liked to crush them up and spread them all over the place just to annoy me. It always seemed like there were more crumbs left than there were actual treats.

I reached for the box of puzzles, thinking I could start on one, but was distracted by the ring of the house phone. I altered my reach to answer it, curious as to who could be calling me. As far as I was aware, no one but Vicki and my dad knew my number.

Except maybe the police, of course.

I hesitated before answering. What if Officer Dalton was calling to tell me I was a suspect in the death of Brendon Lawyer? I'd let the word "murder" slip earlier. Could that have gotten me into trouble somehow?

I picked up the phone, ready to be read my rights. Why they would do it over the phone and not in person didn't even occur to me at the time.

"Hello?" I asked with a cringe.

"Oh, my Lordy-Lou!" someone shouted in my ear. "Someone died in your store today!"

"Uh, hi," I said, not recognizing the voice. It's pretty hard to when they're screaming so loud, your earpiece rattles. "Who is this?"

"It's Rita, dear. Rita Jablonski." She took a tiny breath before launching into her rant. "This is just awful. I mean, to have someone die in your place? It's terrible. Terrible, I tell you. How will you ever recover? Do you think the coffee had anything to do with it? Am I going to get sick? What about your father? Do you think he's going to come to town?"

My head was spinning at the onslaught. Rita Jablonski talked like the world was about to end and she just *had* to get in the very last word.

"He didn't die in my shop," I said.

"But rumor says—"

*"Rumor is wrong!"* I didn't mean to shout, but I really wanted to cut her off before she could launch into another spiel. "He came in for coffee and then left. He died in his office."

"Oh." She actually sounded disappointed.

"And there's no reason to believe he was killed by anything from Death by Coffee, either." *Despite the name,* I thought, but didn't add.

Rita sighed heavily into the phone. "Oh, well. I was hoping for something of a mystery, something your father could solve for us. Wouldn't that be exciting? They might even do a special on the television about us."

I rolled my eyes. "My dad is a *writer.* He makes stories up for a living. He's not Castle."

"Oh, well, I know that. . . ."

"How did you get my number, by the way?" If Vicki gave her my number, I was *so* going to kill her.

"It was easy enough to find." Rita laughed, but didn't explain how she'd done it.

There was a knock at the door. Thank God for the interruption. Even if the police were out there, ready to arrest me for the murder, it would have been something of a blessing right then.

Rita was talking, but by this point, I wasn't listening. I cut her off and smiled faintly at her shocked huff.

"Look," I said. "I've got to go. Someone is at the door."

"Oh, all right," she said, sounding put out. "I suppose I'll see you tomorrow. Don't forget about the writers' group. We'd love to have you."

I hung up with a shake of my head. The knock at the door came again. It sounded almost rhythmic, like it was to the beat of a song I didn't know. I hurried to the door and opened it without looking through the window to see who it was.

A man stood smiling there. He was wearing, I swear to God, black-and-white tap shoes, a pink suit with white lapels, and his hair looked like something out of a British pop band. His skin was the color of caramel and there was a slight upward slant to his eyes.

"Hello?" It came out tentative. Someone dressed like that couldn't be normal, especially in a small town like this.

"Hi!" he said, reaching out for my hand. I didn't resist, too stunned to think straight. He kissed my knuckles, but didn't let my hand go. He squeezed my fingers, like meeting me was the highlight of his day. "I'm so glad I could finally meet you."

*"Okay?"* I said, drawing out the word. With a little

bit of twisting, I managed to remove my hand from his grip.

"I'm your neighbor!" he said excitedly. "Jules Phan." He gestured toward the house next door. "I'm so sorry I didn't get in today to see you at your new store. I was meaning to, but you know how things are. Busy, busy, busy." He chuckled happily.

"Sure," I said.

"Do you have a few minutes to talk? I'd love to get to know you."

I sighed. I was *so* not ready to deal with this. If the guy knew where I worked, then he also knew about Brendon Lawyer and his death. I didn't feel like defending myself to a man I didn't even know.

"I'm tired," I said. "I really am not in the mood for an interrogation, okay?"

The smile slipped from his lips and he took a step back. "I didn't mean . . ." He stopped and trailed off before giving me a strained smile. "I'm sorry to bother you. Maybe we'll see each other again, sometime soon."

Jules spun and hurried away. He got into a tiny little car that was just as pink as his suit, started the engine, and backed out of my driveway. He only drove a few yards down the road before turning into the driveway next to mine.

Watching him go, I felt bad. The guy seemed harmless enough, friendly even. Maybe he really had just come over to talk. There was no reason for me to be so rude. The stress of what had happened earlier was quite clearly getting to me.

I promised myself I'd go over and apologize later. I just didn't have it in me to do it tonight.

I closed the door and returned to the kitchen. Crumbs were spread clear across the counter. I had a feeling Misfit had batted them there on purpose. He looked proud where he preened, licking his paws.

I took a moment to brush away the worst of the mess, though some of it had stuck, thanks to the kitty slobber that acted like glue. Once the counter was clean, I headed into the living room to grab my purse. If it hadn't been for Rita's call, I would have forgotten about the coffee mug she'd given me. I stepped around a couple of boxes with the words LIVING ROOM written on them in marker and took my prize back to the kitchen. I had yet to unpack most everything I owned and had no desire to even attempt it tonight.

Maybe it wouldn't be such a bad thing if Death by Coffee failed and I was forced to move back home. I was already packed, meaning it wouldn't be too much of a hassle. I could find a job easily enough and I was sure my dad would help me out until I was settled.

But Vicki would be devastated. This was what she'd always wanted, what she'd worked so hard for. If the store failed, she'd be forced to go back to acting and actually would have to put some heart into it. She used to go to movie auditions and would read her lines half-heartedly. The only time she ever took an acting job was when it was for stage acting, which didn't sit well with her screen-acting parents. This was her last shot to be free of their influence. She looked at failure here as the end of her life.

A bit melodramatic, yeah—but if you met her parents, you'd understand.

I set the mug on the island counter, well away from

Misfit. He eyed it with interest and I was pretty sure I saw his paw twitch toward it.

"Don't even think about it, mister," I warned him with a shake of my finger. "We just got here, and it's a gift. I won't have you breaking it."

He glowered at me a moment before leaping from the counter. He fluffed his tail at me and then strutted down the hall, toward the laundry room, where I'd set up his litter box. I had a feeling he was going to make a mess on the floor, inches from the box, just to spite me.

I had half a mind to follow him and fight with him about using the litter box as intended. More often than not, he would leap out and do his business on the floor, no matter how many times I tried to force him to stay in the thing. A few times I'd even tried to throw him into the box as he was going, but he'd simply shut off the waterworks, step back out, and then let it rip, preferably on my shoes if he could manage it.

Tonight I didn't have it in me to fight him. If he made a mess, I'd clean it up later. It wasn't like I was expecting guests.

I rooted around in a box marked KITCHEN until I found my ball-peen hammer. I carried it back to the island and sat down with the empty mug in front of me.

And then I just sat there.

It sort of hit me all at once. Someone had died. Someone I'd talked to mere minutes before was dead. I mean, the guy could have walked across the street, sat down, and then keeled over instantly, meaning I really might have been the last person he'd spoken to face-to-face.

It was a real struggle not to break down and cry or pick up the phone and call Dad. He was the one person

I knew I could lean on. I felt responsible for Brendon's death; and if I let it eat at me, I would probably have a complete mental breakdown or something. Stuff like that had to wear on you, didn't it?

But what could Dad do? He could tell me not to worry about it, that it wasn't my fault. I *knew* deep down I had nothing to do with Brendon's death, but it was hard to keep believing it when the police had been in to question me. I was just lucky they'd chosen to do it at Death by Coffee rather than at the station.

"Calm yourself, Krissy," I said. "There's no reason to panic."

Misfit came sauntering back into the room just then. He sat down on the floor next to me and swished his tail on the linoleum. He was watching me with keen interest, as if waiting for me to have that mental breakdown.

"You'd like that, wouldn't you?" I asked him. "Well, sir, it isn't going to happen."

He gave a little kitty huff and then walked away. The last tail swish clearly stated he believed it was only a matter of time before I totally lost it.

I shook my head and picked up the mug. I studied it a moment, turning it slowly over in my hands. Finally I set it down, held it tight with my left hand, and then struck it right above the handle with the ball-peen hammer. The ceramic cracked, but didn't break. I studied it again, checking it over to make sure I hadn't damaged it too much, before striking it in the exact same spot.

A little sliver chipped off and fell onto the counter. I picked it up, tossed it into the trash, and then carried the mug over to the sink. I gave it a good scrubbing and then filled it with water to make sure there were no leaks. Once certain, I emptied it out and set it aside to dry. I'd take it with me to work in the morning.

From there I went into the laundry room to check on the mess I was positive Misfit had left for me. Sure enough, there was a puddle next to the empty laundry basket. Before long, I was going to have to line the room with pee pads, like I'd had to do at my last place. I think the cat didn't like the feeling of litter between his toes, so he simply chose to avoid it altogether.

I cleaned up his mess, brought him into the room, and dropped him into the little box, which earned me an indignant snort before he bound away, spraying litter all over the room. I groaned and went in search of my broom, but couldn't find it. I gave up and went to my bedroom, instead.

Boxes sat along the wall. The top ones were open. My clothes were folded inside by type: jeans in one box, sweaters in another. I looked from the boxes to the closet and decided that after the day I'd had, I deserved a day off from unpacking.

If only I'd waited to break it off with Robert until after I'd moved, he could have helped me unpack. *Then* I could have kicked his lying ass to the curb. It would have made this mess a whole hell of a lot easier to deal with.

Of course, that would have meant staying with him that much longer. Two years were enough. The guy couldn't keep his hands—or lips—to himself back home. I could only imagine what he would do in a new town with a fresh batch of women to hit on.

I turned away from the boxes and plopped down on my bed. Thinking of Robert made me think of home, of my little apartment that had cost more than this entire house. People were always rushing from place to place there, too busy to pay much attention to anything other than themselves. It was always hectic, always tiring, and yet nobody had died on me there.

I fell back onto my bed and closed my eyes. I really needed a shower after my day at work, but I wasn't so sure I had the energy for it. I was tired. More than that, I was completely exhausted, worked to the bone, on my last leg.

Okay, maybe it wasn't that bad, but right then, it sure felt like it.

Misfit hopped up next to me and curled up in the crook of my arm. I thought about pushing him away and finishing up a few chores around the house, but you know what? I was done. Sleep would do me some good.

I cuddled up close to the fluffball, careful not to put an arm over his snoozing body lest he turn my arm into a scratching post, and let myself drift off to sleep.

# 4

A scream tore through Death by Coffee. I dropped the cup of coffee I'd just been making and very nearly leapt out of my skin. Had someone else been struck dead by a coffee I'd just made and served? Was there a body tucked beneath a table, stashed there by the peanut murderer?

I spun, unsure what disaster I'd encounter, to find Rita Jablonski standing at the counter, hand over her heart.

"Your mug!" she wailed. "It's ruined!"

I sagged against the wall, breathing hard. That woman was going to give me a heart attack someday, I was sure of it.

"It's fine," I managed. "I did it on purpose."

Her eyes widened and she staggered back a step. "You broke the mug I gave you *on purpose*?" Her lower lip trembled. She was acting like I'd gone and slaughtered her family. *"Why?"* I swear to God, a tear actually rolled down her cheek.

"I did it because of my dad," I said. I'd stopped trembling and was now getting irritated. Who cared what I did with my own property? She'd given me the mug, so I could do with it as I pleased.

Rita caught her breath and the hand over her heart fluttered in front of her face. "Is there something wrong with him?" she asked, panicked. "Is he sick? Should I get on a plane now? I'd never forgive myself if he passed away without me seeing him one last time."

I stared at her dumbly for a moment before managing a weak "What?"

"Isn't that why the mug broke?" she asked. "I can only assume you got a call about him being ill, which caused you to drop the mug, just like you did that coffee there." She nodded toward the puddle I was standing in. "You know, you really should be more careful."

The customer I'd been making the coffee for stood beside Rita with a vaguely amused look on his face. He cleared his throat and motioned toward the coffee machine behind me.

"Oh, sorry," I said. "I'll be right there."

I moved out of Rita's view and put together another coffee—black with a shot of espresso—and carried it to the counter. I took the man's money and then scurried back for the mop before Rita could say another word.

It wasn't that I didn't like the woman. I mean, she was one of the nicer people I'd met in Pine Hills. She was just too excitable and nosy for my tastes. It was as if she had to be involved in everything and know exactly what was going on in every corner of town.

When I returned to the counter, Rita was still there,

looking worried. She was wringing her hands together and biting her lip incessantly.

I sighed, knowing I'd have to explain. "My dad's fine," I said. "He's not sick or dying or anything."

"Oh, thank the heavens!" Rita exclaimed, raising her hands above her head and looking to the sky. She took a deep breath and let it out in a relieved sigh. "Then why on earth would you destroy a perfectly good mug?"

"It's something my dad does," I said, resigned to have to spell it out for her. "He always drinks out of chipped mugs, saying that doing so reminds him that not everything that's broken is useless. You can repair and mend almost anything and treat it as if it were new. I've decided to carry on the tradition."

Of course, I was pretty sure Dad accidently chipped his mugs on the faucet while doing the dishes. He always did complain about how low the faucet hung over the sink and would often bang dishes on it when he was trying to scrub them. There was no way in the world I was going to tell Rita that.

Fresh tears filled her eyes, but these ones appeared to be happy tears. "That's beautiful." She sniffed and began fanning herself off.

I really struggled not to roll my eyes at her. I mean, *really?* "Thanks." I forced a smile.

Rita leaned up against the counter and looked into my mug as if making sure it could actually hold coffee. As soon as she saw what was inside, she recoiled back as if she was afraid it would leap out and attack her.

"Something's wrong with your coffee."

I sighed. Again. It seemed to be a reoccurring theme around her.

"It's a cookie," I told her, wishing I didn't have to explain every last element of my life to her.

"A cookie? Why on earth would you put a cookie in your coffee?"

"For flavor."

Her face folded in disgust. "That sounds . . ." She shuddered, unable to go on.

"I like it," I said, sounding a bit defensive. "The chocolate is better than any creamer you could add and the cookie itself is sugary enough to take away the bitterness. And afterward, I can scoop up the cookie with a spoon."

Is there anything better than a soggy cookie soaked in coffee? I think not.

Apparently, Rita didn't think so. She shook her head and took two quick steps back as if she thought the cookie might swell up and explode all over her sweater.

"I think I'll skip my coffee today," she said. "I've suddenly lost my appetite for it." She paused and looked thoughtfully at the mug. "Not everything broken is useless, huh?" She glanced at me and then turned and walked out of the store. I knew she was thinking about going and chipping all of her mugs. Chances were good she'd end up breaking them all beyond repair. I was pretty sure she'd be in blaming me for the mess in the morning.

I picked up my mug, looked inside at the cookie, and then took a long sip.

Ah, bliss.

Like it had been yesterday, Death by Coffee was relatively slow. I'd served a handful of customers and we sold a couple of books, but people didn't seem all that interested in the place. I kept telling myself that once word spread about our little slice of Heaven, people would begin flocking to the store. If all went well, we'd finally be able to afford to hire someone. If that happened, we could stay open later. Right now, we closed at five, which was really too early; but with just the two of us, it had to be done.

Of course, Brendon Lawyer *had* come here before ingesting his lethal dose of peanuts. If any word of Death by Coffee was spreading through town now, it wouldn't be the good kind.

I slumped onto the counter and sipped at my coffee. Even the chocolaty goodness couldn't raise my spirits.

Vicki shouted from the bookstore and the sound of four fluffy feet hitting the hardwood followed. Trouble was being trouble again. I didn't even bother to look to see what he'd done this time.

Instead, I focused on Lawyer's Insurance. The building wasn't large, which wasn't much of a surprise. Pine Hills didn't have very many big buildings at all. I'd driven around before coming in to work and the biggest place I saw was the church two blocks over. It was one of those old monstrosities that could hold the entire town in case of a disaster.

My eyes were drawn to a woman standing outside across the street. She kept looking at her watch and was pacing back and forth like she really didn't want to be there. At first, I thought maybe she was waiting for them to open; however, as soon as the thought crossed my mind, someone walked past her and entered Lawyer's Insurance. I decided she was waiting for someone to come out.

And then she happened to glance toward Death by Coffee.

I think I let out a little gasp of surprise. Some of my coffee sloshed out of my mug as I leaned forward to get a better look. Without taking my eyes off the woman, I grabbed the washcloth from beneath the counter and began wiping up my spill.

I recognized the woman immediately. I'd only seen her once before, on the television, but I was positive it was her. Why was Heidi Lawyer waiting so impatiently outside the building where her husband had died?

I knew there were a thousand reasons why she might be there. I mean, she could simply be waiting for her husband's things to be brought out to her. But if she was there to pick something up, why hadn't she gone in to get them herself? Wouldn't she want to make sure nothing was left behind?

A moment later the doors to Lawyer's Insurance opened and a man stepped out. I could tell he was angry, even as far away as I was, thanks to his red face and posture. He glanced back at the doors as they closed and I caught the sound of his angry voice as he yelled something at those inside. He turned back to Heidi, put a hand on her arm, and leaned in close to speak to her. She listened to him, nodding the entire time, and then responded. Whatever she said seemed to calm him down because he smiled and they turned to head across the street.

All at once, I realized it might be a good time to stop staring. I drained the rest of my coffee, looked longingly at the cookie inside, and then set the mug behind the counter in the hopes I'd get to it before it got cold.

The bell above the door jingled and Heidi Lawyer walked in, holding tight to the arm of the man with her. All it took was one up close look and I knew I was looking at Brendon's brother, Mason. While Brendon had been all severe lines, Mason leaned toward softer edges, but they were otherwise similar in features.

Heidi waited by the door a moment, whispered something to him, and then walked to the back corner. She sat down and stared out the window, toward where her husband had worked, completely oblivious to the fact she was sitting in the same chair Brendon had sat in minutes before he'd died.

"Excuse me," Mason said, startling me. I'd been staring at Heidi and had completely forgotten about him—despite the fact he was standing right there.

"Sorry," I said, practiced smile falling into place. "Welcome to Death by Coffee. How can I help you?" *God, that sounds so rehearsed.*

Mason smiled. Unlike Brendon, he apparently knew how. "Two black coffees, please." He studied the case of cookies a moment before adding, "And two chocolate chip for here."

I rang up his order and then headed back to get his coffee and cookies. My mind was racing, wondering why he was with Heidi so soon after his brother's death. He could be consoling her, sure, but it appeared there was more to it than that. He'd been the one to go into Lawyer's Insurance, not her. What was going on between them? When they'd touched earlier, it had looked a little too familiar for what you'd expect between a widow and her dead husband's brother, especially only a day after his demise.

I set his order onto a tray, remembering at the last moment to smile. "Here you are," I said.

"Thanks." Mason paid in exact change and then carried the tray to where Heidi sat waiting. He leaned in close to say something before sitting across from her.

I couldn't take my eyes off them, though I knew I should. As soon as Mason had sat down, Heidi's red-rimmed eyes had softened. She gave him a weak smile before picking up her cookie and nibbling at it. They talked in low voices, each glancing across the street every few moments.

There was absolutely no way I was going to be able to stand there and *not* know what they were talking about.

I grabbed a washcloth and cleaner from beneath the counter, thankful there were no customers to interrupt my eavesdropping, and headed out to wipe down the tables. I started with ones farthest from the two, as not to appear as if I was trying to listen in. I hurriedly wiped the outer tables down before moving into hearing range.

"He never forgets it," Heidi was saying. "Do you know how it looks that it came up missing on the very day he . . . ," Heidi trailed off, shaking her head.

"I know," Mason said, sighing. He glanced my way and frowned before leaning forward and lowering his voice. "Accidents happen all the time."

Heidi's face hardened. "You and I both know this wasn't an accident."

I dropped my bottle of cleaner.

Both Heidi and Mason looked my way. A frown crept onto Mason's face, while Heidi's eyes brimmed with tears.

"Sorry," I said. "It slipped."

I scooped up the spray bottle, finished wiping down the table, and then hauled ass back behind the counter. I could feel the flush on my cheeks and knew I had to look ten shades of guilty.

Could I really have heard what I thought I'd heard? Were they actually talking about Brendon's death as if it hadn't been an accident? It didn't take a genius to figure out that they'd been talking about Brendon's missing EpiPen.

The realization that I might be staring at two murderers hit me so hard, I very nearly yelped when I bumped into the coffee machine. I'd met Brendon Lawyer. He wasn't a nice man. Could his brother have offed him because he was always treating people like they were beneath him? Could he have beat his wife to the point where she'd finally had enough and poisoned him with peanuts?

It made some sense. Brendon didn't buy anything to eat here and I hadn't seen him carrying a bag from somewhere else. Could his lunch have been in his briefcase, prepared by Heidi herself? How hard would it have been to slip some peanut shavings into his ham sandwich while removing his EpiPen at the same time?

Heidi noticed me staring again and leaned forward to whisper something to Mason. He turned, shot me an irritated look, and then rose. Heidi followed suit and they both stormed out of the store. I was guessing I wouldn't be seeing them here again.

Mason glanced back as the doors swung closed. The look on his face caused my heart to skip a beat. There was an unspoken threat there, as if he was warning me to leave them alone. I got the distinct impression that if I didn't, I very well might be the next one to die.

# 5

Needless to say, I wasn't worth much for the next few hours. I couldn't get my mind off Heidi and Mason and what they'd talked about. I very well might have overheard them talking about a man's murder for goodness' sake!

During that time I screwed up two orders and dropped a third before Vicki stepped in and took over.

"Take a break, Krissy," she said. "You look wiped."

While "wiped" wasn't exactly the word I would have used, I didn't object. I handed her the mochaccino I'd been making and scuttled off into the quiet of the office. I closed the door and sat down in one of the chairs, thoughts racing.

Could Brendon Lawyer actually have been murdered?

I normally liked letting the police do their jobs while I kept my nose far, far away from their business, but this had happened right across the street from me, to a man whom I'd just served. They might have classified it as an "accident," but after hearing the Lawyers talk, I wasn't so sure.

It was a mystery.

That was a bad thing.

Mysteries have always intrigued me. I think it had a lot to do with the books my dad wrote. He used to let me read each and every one ahead of time. I would do my best to see if I could figure out the killer or where the missing link was, and often I would help him improve upon the novel. I liked mysteries. They were like puzzles. You took seemingly unconnected pieces and found ways to fit them together so you could see the whole picture.

But my love of them was also what got me into a lot of trouble in my youth. I'd see mysteries in everything and would often insist on trying to solve them whether they needed solving or not. There was this one time when I could have sworn the school librarian was sneaking smokes in the bathroom. I could smell the smoke almost every time I went in there and she would slip into the bathroom at least two times every class period. I'd been so sure of myself, I took my theories to the principal, insisting something should be done.

Turns out, the librarian had an extremely overactive bladder, which caused her to have to go suddenly at least a dozen times a day. Apparently, it was the janitor who smoked and the smell was drifting up from the basement, through the ventilation, and into the bathroom. The janitor got fired; the librarian was embarrassed; and I was scolded by not only the principal, but by my parents, for interfering.

Still, the error didn't stop me from continually sticking my nose where it didn't belong. Even now, I couldn't help myself.

So, what did I have? Brendon died when he ingested

peanuts of some kind. He didn't have his EpiPen with him, something someone with an extreme allergy never would have done. His wife, Heidi, was seen with his brother, Mason, the day after his death. They were both at his workplace, though Mason had been the one to go in. He'd seemed agitated; yet when he was with Heidi, they both seemed to calm down. And then there was the whole bit about Brendon's death not being an accident.

I knew there had to be more to the story, but I felt as if I was getting a pretty good picture of what was going on. If Brendon was as big a jerk as he seemed when I first met him, then perhaps more than one person had a reason to want him dead. Heidi could have enlisted Mason—who, as far as I knew, could have been mistreated by Brendon as much as Heidi was—to kill his own brother. Could money have been involved? Could the police trace it back to them if they indeed were the killers?

The door to the office opened and Vicki poked her head in. "You doing okay in here?"

I rose to my feet. I could think about this all day and make no headway. I needed to do something.

"Yeah," I said. "I just needed a few minutes to clear my head."

"Well, I hope your head is clear and empty because someone is here, ready to fill it full again."

The smirk on Vicki's face told me I wasn't going to like my visitor.

I smoothed down my shirt and followed Vicki back out. She gave me a quick little wave and a grin before returning to the bookstore. I think she actually giggled on her way up.

"I'm so sorry," Rita said as soon as I appeared. "I

didn't mean to act so rude earlier. I was so stunned by what you'd done, I didn't know how to react. It took a little while for it all to sink in and I realized how brilliant the idea really was. But then I realized how horrible I treated you and knew I just had to come back in and apologize before I could go on with the rest of my day."

"It's okay," I said. I looked around for something else to do, but Vicki had cleaned and organized my entire section while I'd been in the back. Unless I wanted to pretend to be busy—I didn't—I'd have to face Rita and her ramblings.

Then again, maybe it wouldn't be so bad. She seemed to know everyone in town. Maybe she knew something about Mason and Heidi that the police might not know. There was nothing wrong with innocently milking the resident gossip for information, was there?

I leaned on the counter and forced a friendly smile. "It is terrible about Mr. Lawyer, isn't it?" I asked. "His wife must be devastated. I saw her picture on the news last night."

Rita huffed. "As if. From what I've heard, she was filing for divorce before all of this unpleasantness went down."

"Really?" My theory that she might have paid someone—Mason, more than likely—to kill her husband had just gained more traction. A divorce might have left her with very little, while his untimely death could make her rich. "Did he leave her lots of money?"

"Some," Rita said. "Despite Brendon's attitude and his choice of clothing, the business is small-time. He wasn't struggling or anything, but he wasn't as rich as he tried to pretend."

"I see." I wasn't sure if that meant anything or not. I suppose if Brendon and Heidi were going to get a divorce, he could have found a way to set it up so that she would receive next to nothing. Maybe she'd killed him because she found out about his plans, whatever they might have been.

Rita glanced around the room to make sure no one was listening before leaning up against the counter. Her chest tried to make another escape onto the counter.

"I heard from Georgina, who heard it from Andi, that the Lawyers were heard fighting a few weeks back. It was loud enough that the cops were called." She leaned back and gave me a self-satisfied nod. "Or so I heard."

I didn't bother to ask who Georgina and Andi were. More than likely, they were the other main sources of Pine Hills gossip. I could just imagine the three women sitting around a table, telling each other every juicy little thing they'd heard, true or not. I suddenly wasn't so sure I was happy about living in a town where everyone's business seemed to be everyone else's business.

"So," Rita said, clapping her hands together. I jumped about a foot into the air. "Do you think you'll be at tonight's group?"

Crap. I really had no desire to sit through a writers' meeting. I didn't write, though that didn't seem to matter to Rita. She seemed to think creative genes ran in the family.

I probably should have said no, told her that I was too busy or something, but I, instead, found the idea intriguing. Maybe getting to know others in town would help me understand the inner workings of Pine Hills. Perhaps I'd learn something that would help me understand why anyone would go to such strange lengths to kill Brendon Lawyer—if indeed he'd even been murdered. I wasn't sure what I'd overheard Heidi say was an admission of guilt.

"Sure," I said. "I think I will."

Rita beamed. "Oh, I can't wait to tell Andi! She'll be so excited."

I suppressed a groan. I was sure she would be.

The door tinkled open and a woman who looked to be in her late fifties entered. Her hair was pulled up off her neck, exposing the thin gold chains that hung there. Each of her fingers had a ring of some sort—some big enough to serve as paperweights if need be. Her lipstick was a severe red, as was her tight skirt. Her eyes speared me as she approached the counter.

"Could I get a coffee?" She asked it like I might actually say no.

"Sure," I said, plastering on my "please don't make me hate this any more than I already do" smile. "Would you like anything in it?"

She grimaced. "Black, please."

What was it with this town and their black coffees? I mean, with all of the flavors I had available, you'd think someone would at least try one! Where was their sense of adventure?

I got the woman her coffee, took her money—exact change—and watched as she stormed out of the building as if on a mission to destroy some poor chap who'd tried to take her parking space.

"That's Mrs. Regina Harper," Rita said. "She's always hated Brendon."

"Why's that?" I asked distractedly as I put the money into the register.

"Well, because he married her daughter, of course."

It took a moment for that to sink in. "Wait," I said. "Do you mean that's Heidi's mom?"

Rita nodded. She crossed her arms and gave me a self-satisfied grin. She clearly thought her knowledge of the town's residents was some miraculous feat.

But her knowledge did afford me an opportunity. I couldn't let it go to waste.

"Vicki!" I shouted as I ran around the counter. "Can you watch the store for me?"

Vicki poked her head around a corner. "Sure." She hesitated. "Why? Where are you going?"

I hit the door at a run. "Not far," I shouted back. "I'll be right back."

Vicki said something else, but it was lost as the door closed behind me.

I stopped just outside Death by Coffee and looked wildly in the direction I'd seen Regina go. For a heart-stopping second, I'd thought I'd lost her. There weren't very many people on the street, but Regina was a small woman. She could easily vanish in a crowd of two if she so chose. And if she'd gotten in a car instead of walking, she'd be just as gone and I might never see her again. I had no idea what I could learn from her, outside of confirming Brendon and Heidi had been getting a divorce, but at least I would have confirmation. I wasn't totally sure how far I could trust Rita's word.

Just as I was about to give up the chase even before it had begun, I caught a glimpse of Regina's red skirt as she stepped around a pair of teens leaning against a brick building decorated with green and yellow balloons. I took off after her.

"Mrs. Harper!" I shouted. She didn't appear to hear

me the first time, so I shouted again, this time louder. "Mrs. Harper!"

She stopped and glanced back. A scowl that could melt concrete crossed her face when she saw me.

"I gave you exact change," she said. "I don't like being taken advantage of, young lady."

I was panting by the time I reached her and I hadn't run all that far. Maybe it was time I started going for a jog in the mornings or perhaps stopped eating a tub of Rocky Road every time I got depressed about something. If working out wasn't such hard work, I very well might have started already.

"No, it's not that," I managed between gasps. "I just want to ask you something."

Regina continued to scowl, but at least she didn't storm off in a huff. I had a feeling she wasn't the type of person you messed with. She seemed like someone who would use her pumps as deadly weapons if you annoyed her enough.

"Well?" she asked when I didn't speak right away. "What do you want?"

I took a deep breath, happy I could breathe again. I didn't know how this woman was going to take to me asking questions about her dead son-in-law. I might end up wearing the coffee gripped in her manicured hand if I offended her. This was a woman who wasn't afraid of confrontation.

"My name's Krissy," I said, figuring it might be best to start off with introductions. Maybe she wouldn't glower at me so much if she knew who I was. "Krissy Hancock."

Regina tapped her foot, but otherwise didn't reply.

"I was just wondering what your thoughts are on

Brendon's death." I swallowed back a surge of fear as her eyes narrowed. "He was your son-in-law, wasn't he?"

"He was." Her jaw tightened, as if admitting it was enough to anger her.

"Do you think his death was an accident?"

Her eyes narrowed even more. "What are you imply-ing?"

Okay, time to be careful.

"Nothing," I said, trying on a smile that only seemed to irritate her more. "It just seems odd he would have forgotten his EpiPen the very day he ingests peanuts."

Regina gave a disgusted snort. "He probably left it with his whore."

I very nearly choked on my own spit. "Excuse me?"

Regina Harper glared at me as if she thought I'd been the one to sleep with her daughter's husband. "Brendon Lawyer was a no-good cheater who couldn't see the value in what he had. He went around screwing women like they were there simply for his own pleasure. That man deserved what he got. Maybe now Heidi will find herself someone who actually cares about her. I'm glad he's dead."

An icy chill crept up my spine. Maybe Heidi and Mason hadn't worked together to kill Brendon, after all. Maybe Heidi's own mom had killed him, and her daughter had found out about it. If anyone could heart-lessly murder a man, this terror of a woman could.

"Is there anything else?" she asked, clearly wanting to get back to whatever it was she'd been doing before I'd interrupted her.

"No," I said. My voice came out as a squeak. "I think that's all."

Regina looked me up and down, gave an irritated

huff, and then stormed away, coffee expertly held so that it wouldn't slosh out onto her clothes, no matter how fast or hard she walked.

I sagged against the side of the nearest building, which turned out to be a place called Tunes and Loons Music Emporium. Did every store in this town have to have a stupid name? I waited for Regina to scowl her way around the corner before turning back to Death by Coffee, thankful to be alive. I felt like I'd just been flattened by a falling safe and wanted nothing more than to curl up with Misfit on the couch. If it wasn't for, you know, actually having to work for a living, I very well might have gone home and found a new tub of ice cream to empty.

As it was, I dragged myself back into work and went about filling the few orders I had. I was just thankful Rita was long gone by the time I got back and that Vicki hadn't bombarded me with questions the moment I'd walked through the door. I wouldn't have known how to answer.

The only thing I was sure of was that Brendon Lawyer hadn't forgotten his EpiPen before accidently consuming peanuts. Call it "intuition," call it a "wild hunch," but after talking to a few people he'd known best, I was pretty darn sure he had been murdered.

# 6

"Okay, what did I do this time?" I asked as I peeled the wet sock from my foot.

Misfit glared at me from the doorway to the laundry room. He swished his tail twice before turning and strutting away. Apparently, he was satisfied his little present had made his point and I wouldn't do whatever it was I'd done to make him unhappy ever again.

My nose crinkled as I dropped the sock, as well as its match into the washer. I stepped around the puddle that had just about killed me to get some paper towels. One of these days, that cat was going to learn how to use the litter box properly.

Once the floor was wiped up, scrubbed clean, and air freshener was sprayed throughout the room, I headed to my bedroom to get ready. I considered taking another shower, since my foot smelled like cat pee. I decided that since it would be shoved in a shoe for the rest of the night, a quick wipe off would suffice. It wasn't like I was planning on taking my shoes off at the writers' meeting.

Misfit sat atop the bed, where I'd very nearly set the

clothes I planned on wearing. Just before stepping into the shower, I'd changed my mind and hung them on a hanger and stuck them back into the closet. I had a feeling I would have had little wet cat prints all over the blouse and long orange hairs up and down the black slacks if I had left them out.

"Not this time, mister," I said as the cat eyed me with a hint of disappointment in his eye. I opened the closet and retrieved my clothes, one by one, giving him no opportunity to ruin them before I had a chance to wear them.

I had no idea how to dress for a meeting like this. Did they dress up and sit around drinking tea while telling each other how brilliant they were? Was it more casual and fun? If it wasn't for the fear of making Rita think I actually wanted to talk to her, I would have called and asked. As it was, I would just wing it and hope for the best.

I pulled on my blouse and slacks and checked myself over in the mirror. I looked nice, but not so nice that I'd feel overdressed if they were all wearing jeans and T-shirts. With a satisfied nod, I grabbed a pair of comfortable shoes and socks and started for the kitchen.

A soft thump was all the warning I had.

Misfit tore out of the bedroom like someone had dumped a gallon of water on him. He chose his path carefully ahead of time, I was sure. He managed to run between my legs, smacking each with his fluffy body, coating them with his orange fur. He very nearly succeeded in sending me flying face-first into the door.

I caught myself on my dresser, which, in turn, caused me to lose my grip on my shoes. They went flying across the room and slammed into the far wall, thankfully not putting a hole in it.

I thought I heard a little kitty snicker from the other room.

"One of these days," I grumbled, retrieving my shoes and thinking black thoughts about buzz clippers and a flea bath. I carried my shoes out into the dining room, where Misfit, of course, was sitting on the table, tail swishing. I'm pretty sure his eyes strayed to the box with his treats.

"Not on your life," I said as I grabbed a bag of treats, anyway. Even when he was trying to kill me, I couldn't resist him.

As he began crunching the treats up on the table, I slipped on my socks and shoes, grabbed my purse, and then headed for the door.

"Be back in a little bit," I called as I quickly opened the front door and slipped outside. Misfit, as usual, leapt from the table and tried to make a run for it, but I managed to get through the door and slam it closed before he could get there. I swear his entire purpose in life is to give me a hard time.

I walked to my car—a black Ford Focus I had gotten a deal on, thanks to my then-boyfriend, Robert. I'd considered giving him the car back when I broke up with him, but decided I loved the car too much to do that. Besides, then I would have to go buy a new one on my own. It wasn't the car's fault the guy who helped me get it was a lying ass. I was fumbling for my keys when my gaze fell onto the house next to mine.

"Damn it," I grumbled, shoving the keys back into my purse. I'd wanted to get to the meeting early to scope it out, but there was something else I needed to do first. I wouldn't feel right until I did.

I crossed the lawn and approached the front door of Jules Phan's house. It was a little bigger than mine, but not by much. The entire front was lined with a well-cared-for flowerbed. The house itself was white, looked freshly cleaned, and smelled of flowers in bloom. It looked like Mr. Phan spent a lot of time tending to his home. Maybe if he had time, he could come over and take care of mine for me, because there was no way I'd ever manage to get my place looking—and smelling— like this.

I hesitated before pressing the doorbell. It was oddly colored, looking like a red-and-white-lined peppermint. I was afraid it might actually *be* a peppermint and I'd end up getting my fingers all sticky.

"That's absurd," I muttered as I pressed the bell. A faint chime rang through the house. Immediately high-pitched yapping started up and claws hit the door from the inside. A moment later the door opened to a smiling Jules Phan and a little bundle of fur, the latter of which immediately barreled into my legs.

"Maestro, no," Jules said, clapping his hands. "I'm sorry. He gets so excited when we have guests."

The little dog wagged his tail at me before turning and leaping into Jules's waiting arms.

"It's okay," I said. "I have a cat."

"Ah." He smiled as if the thought of a cat repelled him.

I started to speak, but that's when I noticed how different he looked. The last time I'd seen Jules Phan, he'd been wearing an outlandish outfit I'd taken for his usual attire. Tonight he was dressed in khaki shorts and a blue polo, with white Keds and no socks. He looked downright normal.

"You've changed." I felt stupid the moment I said it. He looked down at himself. "I have?"

"Your clothes." I bit my lip. I really should stop talking before I insulted him.

"Oh." He laughed, which caused Maestro to start licking his face. "I have." He stepped aside. "Please come in. No sense standing outside where the rumor patrol will see us."

I walked past him automatically. He closed the door before dropping Maestro onto the floor. The little dog sniffed at me and then rushed after his master, who was retreating toward the living room.

"Can I get you something to drink?" he asked. "Please sit."

"No thanks." I took a seat on the couch. Jules perched on the armrest of a chair that looked so comfortable and soft, it very well might swallow whoever sat in it. The coffee table looked to be made of solid oak with an intricate etched design around the trim. In the corner a grandfather clock ticked the seconds by. It looked old.

"I was wearing my work uniform last night," he said, and then laughed when he saw the look on my face. "I work at Phantastic Candies. Well, I own the place. I sell candy to the kids mostly."

"Oh."

"I like to dress up for it. Makes people smile." He gave me a smile of his own. His teeth were shockingly white for someone who spent his day surrounded by sweets. I couldn't help but return it.

"Look," I said. "I don't want to take up too much of your time."

"Oh no." He waved the notion off. "I don't mind at all. It can get boring sitting here alone."

"Still . . . I just wanted to come over and tell you I'm sorry about last night. I didn't mean to be short with you. I'd been stressed and . . . well . . ."

Jules shook his head the entire time I spoke. "Don't apologize," he said when I was done. "You'd looked harried, and after I saw the news last night . . ." He shuddered. "Terrible business. I felt awful for bothering you after such horribleness."

"Well, I'm sorry, anyway. I shouldn't have spoken to you like that."

Jules gave me a warm smile. "Then I accept the apology, though I still insist it isn't necessary. Here." He stood. "Let me get you something to drink." He was up and out of the room before I could protest.

Maestro gave me a happy-doggy look, wagged his tail enthusiastically, and then darted out of the room, presumably after his master.

I ran my hand over the couch, marveling at how soft and fur-free it felt. I mean, if Misfit had been here, the chocolate brown couch would be a near-solid orange and would have been torn into tiny little pieces by now. Either Jules Phan spent all day cleaning, or Maestro was far more behaved than my cat.

"Here we are," Jules said, returning. Maestro was right behind him.

I took the bottle of water he offered me. It was ice cold and looked refreshing. I drank a little to be polite, but quickly realized how thirsty I really was. I sucked down nearly half the bottle before I could bring myself to stop.

Jules sat there and smiled at me as if he'd known all along.

"What kind of dog is he?" I asked, capping the water.

"Maltese." Jules ruffled Maestro's white fur. "He's only two."

"Ah." I looked at my bottle. I really had no idea where to go after that.

Thankfully, Jules liked to talk. "Have you met Mrs. Winthrow yet?" he asked.

"Eleanor Winthrow?" I asked to be sure. I didn't know how many Winthrows there might be in Pine Hills. Jules nodded. "She came in for a cup of coffee the other day. I'm not sure she'll be back."

He chuckled. "It's no wonder." He nodded toward the wall in the direction of my house. "She lives on the other side of you. She isn't the most pleasant of people, as I'm sure you've already noticed." He leaned forward. "Make sure you keep your blinds closed. She has a tendency to use binoculars from her armchair by the window."

"I'll remember that," I said, trying to remember if I'd left the curtains open in my bedroom while getting changed.

Jules sighed and shook his head. "It is terrible about Mr. Lawyer, isn't it?"

I nodded. "He came over for a cup of coffee right before he died."

Jules's hand covered his mouth. "Oh, my," he said. "That has to be just awful to know you'd just talked to him before he died."

"Yeah." I gave a strained laugh. "I keep thinking I might have had something to do with it. I mean, he was right there, barking orders at me, mere minutes before he kicked the bucket."

"He wasn't a very happy man," Jules said with a sad shake of his head.

I perked up at that. "Do you mean because of his wife? I heard they were getting a divorce."

Jules raised his eyebrows at me. "Really? I knew things were bad between them, but a divorce?" He shook his head again. "I guess Lance was right about them, after all."

"Lance?"

He motioned toward a picture on the wall just behind my head. I craned my neck around to look. The photo showed a blond man, with a mile-wide grin, standing behind Jules, arms wrapped around him. They looked happy together, which was more than I could say about any of my relationships. I had to admit, I was a little jealous.

"He would be here to welcome you, but he's off on business this week."

"I'm sure I'll love him," I said, turning back.

Jules smiled. "He's far more of a gossip than I am. Lance tends to listen to every rumor around town and is somehow able to sift through the lies and slander to find the truth buried beneath. He swore to me the Lawyers were going to get a divorce, but I didn't believe it. I'd seen them together only last week. While they weren't exactly the happiest of people, I could still see that spark between them. Do you know what I mean?"

I nodded. I remembered when I'd had that spark with Robert. It didn't take much more than a few late nights and one wrong word for me to realize his spark liked to spread to every available outlet, but it *had* been there.

I stood, feeling a bit down thinking about the past. "I've probably taken up too much of your time," I said. "In fact, I have somewhere to be soon."

"It's no bother," Jules said, rising. "It's just me and Maestro for the rest of the week. Feel free to stop by anytime."

I smiled at him. "I will." And I meant it. Jules Phan put me at ease. The guy was probably the nicest person I'd met in town, thus far, and didn't annoy me like Rita did. "But I do have to go."

He walked me to the front door, Maestro at his heel. He scooped up the little dog before opening the door for me.

"I hope things calm down enough so you can see how nice a town Pine Hills really is. We don't have excitement like this all of the time. I promise."

I gave Maestro a quick pat on the head. "I'm sure they will. Thanks for the water."

"Anytime."

I turned and walked to the car, thoughtful. I wasn't sure what I thought about what Jules had said about the Lawyers. Could they have still been in love—despite the fact Brendon had cheated on his wife? Then again, was Heidi's mom right about that? Could she have made an assumption based on a few late nights at work? Just because one woman thought the man was cheating didn't mean he really was.

What I needed was proof.

I got into my car and started the engine. Just as I was about to pull out of my driveway, I happened to glance toward Eleanor Winthrow's place. Two round circles poked out between the curtains. She didn't even bother to hide them when she saw me looking. In fact, I think she leaned in closer.

I restrained myself from flipping the bird and instead gave her a short little wave, smiling as if I was thrilled at the attention, and then put the car into gear. I couldn't worry about Eleanor's spying now. I had a meeting to attend.

# 7

Only a handful of cars sat in the church parking lot. I idled there, not quite sure I was ready for this. The whole reason I was going to this thing was to see if I could learn more about Brendon Lawyer and his wife, but it felt somehow wrong. I was new in town. I shouldn't be prying.

But I couldn't let it go. There'd always been a part of me that was interested in this sort of thing. I think it had more to do with my dad's stories than any sort of macabre fascination with mysteries and murder. I just *had* to know.

And maybe a little part of me wanted to be able to go to Dad and tell him what I'd done. I wasn't even sure I was actually dealing with a murder, but the pieces all seemed to point that way—to me at least. If I could figure out what actually happened to Brendon Lawyer, I wouldn't just bring justice to the dead man, I'd impress my dad.

I shut off the engine to my Focus and got out of the car.

The church was magnificent from the outside. It

was probably the largest building in Pine Hills. Large stained-glass windows were set in ruby red stones that looked to have been regularly cleaned. Whoever took care of the church took pride in his work. Well-tended hedges lined the property and flowers decorated the edge of the sidewalk. It was like walking into Heaven itself.

The door to the church was wooden and looked heavy. On the door was a handwritten sign: *Writers's group upstairs*. I cringed at the misspelling and opened the door. This was going to be an adventure.

The inside of the church wasn't quite as magnificent as the outside, but it was still a spectacle. The walls just inside were painted with scenes from the Bible. The stairs had verses written upon them, though most of the words had been worn away by years of footfalls. The stairs themselves creaked as I headed up to the second floor, where I could just make out voices coming from the first room to my right.

"It's absolutely astonishing," someone said. "I mean, who would have thought it possible in a town like this?" I could almost visualize the shudder that followed.

I reached the landing and the wooden floor groaned so loudly, the voices abruptly ceased. I'd hoped to wait out in the hall and eavesdrop for a few minutes, especially if they were talking about Brendon's death. Since my cover was blown, I squared my shoulders, took a deep breath, and entered the room.

Five faces turned toward me.

"Uh, hi," I said, feeling suddenly uncomfortable. This wasn't just a bad idea—it was a horrible one!

"Oh, my!" Rita stood and waved her hands frantically in front of her face as if she was about to hyperventilate.

"You came! You really came!" She hurried across the room and grabbed my hand. She all but dragged me inside.

"Everyone," she said, "this is Kristina Hancock. She's James Hancock's daughter."

There were murmurs of greeting that ranged from indifferent to, well, indifferent. Clearly, Rita was the only one who thought of me as some sort of minor celebrity. I'd be lying if I didn't admit I felt a faint twinge of disappointment. Sue me.

"Hi," I said. "It's Krissy, really."

Rita beamed at me and led me to a rickety-looking chair. I sat down and it creaked and listed alarmingly. I shifted so I was sitting on the very edge of the seat. That way, if the thing collapsed, I might make it to my feet before I went down with it.

Rita took a recliner next to me. Her chair looked almost new. "Now," she said, "I suppose we should have a round of introductions." She smiled at me. "I'll go first."

Rita introduced herself, which was kind of pointless, since everyone there had already met her. It wasn't much of a surprise to learn she wrote mysteries.

"Next," she said when she was done.

The woman to her right smiled at me. She had white hair fluffed up around her head like a curly cloud. She wore reading glasses perched at the end of her nose. A delicate chain ran from them to around her neck. She was sitting in a rocking chair and looked like someone's grandma. The only things missing were a ball of yarn in her lap and knitting needles in her hands.

"I'm Georgina McCully," she said. "I write romantic fiction based in the Appalachian Valley."

And around we went.

The woman beside her wasn't quite as old, but her hair was a steely gray and fine lines spiderwebbed out from her eyes. She didn't quite smile at me when she introduced herself as Andi Caldwell. She apparently wrote literary fiction—whatever that meant.

Next to her was a middle-aged man who looked as if he'd slept through the rest of the introductions. He didn't meet anyone's eyes when he mumbled his name as Adam something-or-other and that he wrote poetry. His head drooped and I think he went back to sleep.

I actually had met the girl next to him, which was something of a relief. She smiled at me in a way that told me she recognized me as well. She had a fresh scrape on her elbow and a black eye. Her skateboard lay beneath her chair.

"Lena Allison," she said. "YA."

Then it was my turn.

"Krissy Hancock, as you know." I gave a nervous laugh. I felt like an idiot. "I don't write."

There was a shocked gasp from Andi, and Georgina gave me a look that said she was quite disappointed in me. I think Adam's head moved a little at my proclamation. It was either that or he was finding a more comfortable position for his nap.

"Of course, you do, dear," Rita said. "You just haven't found your muse yet."

There was a murmur of agreement.

I was saved from any more comments on my lack of writing when someone else came through the door. She was short but fit, despite her age. I'd put her around fifty, though the years didn't sit too well on her face. It looked like she spent quite a lot of time frowning. She walked purposefully to an empty chair between Adam and Georgina. She sat down in a way that told me she was used to being in charge. Her eyes fell on me and I immediately felt uncomfortable.

"Glad you could make it, Patricia," Rita said. "We'd just gone through introductions with Krissy here."

Patricia nodded. "I see." She leaned back into her chair with an exhausted sigh.

"Any new developments?" Georgina asked her, sitting forward. Rita and Andi did likewise, while Lena simply rolled her eyes and looked away. Adam remained motionless.

Patricia scowled at the room in general. "You know I don't like discussing my job."

This was met with laughter and another eye roll from Lena.

"I still think it's awful," Georgina said. "I mean, that man might have been a terrible person, but no one deserves to die like that. He had to have suffered."

My ears perked up. Were they talking about Brendon Lawyer again? I sat forward, which earned me a frown from Lena. I guess I lost a few points in her book due to my interest in the case.

"There's really been no new developments," Patricia said. "While we currently are running under the assumption that it was an unfortunate accident, we're not ruling out foul play."

Andi gasped. Georgina only nodded.

Rita leaned toward me. "Patricia is the police chief here in Pine Hills," she told me needlessly. I could have figured that out myself.

"From what we can tell, his coffee was the main source of the contamination."

"Wait," I said, startled. "What?"

Patricia studied me a moment before speaking. "His coffee was full of the dust. There was some in his food, but not enough to cause such a lethal attack."

My mouth opened and closed a few times like a fish. The coffee had been the real cause of his death? Why hadn't Paul Dalton told me?

"There's no way," I said. "I checked all of the labels. There's absolutely no way his coffee was contaminated at Death by Coffee."

Patricia's eyes narrowed as if she suspected I was lying. I felt myself flush and started breathing in and out so fast, I felt near hyperventilating when she suddenly burst out laughing.

"You're fine," Patricia said. "I'm pretty sure it was an accident. I was just messing with you." She paused, face going suddenly serious again. "Although I will be doing a background check on you, just in case."

I wasn't so sure she was joking.

"Could someone else have put the dust in his food?" I asked, just wanting the focus off me.

"Could have," Patricia said. "His wife prepared his lunches for him. She might have contaminated his food, but that doesn't explain why there was so much inside the coffee. I'm guessing he made a mistake somehow, perhaps found some peanut dust packets and thought it was sugar."

I gave her a flat look. "You really believe that?"

She shrugged. "Not sure there is much else we can go on." A mischievous smile crossed her face. "Now, you were one of the last people to see Brendon Lawyer alive, were you not?"

"I was," I said. "I already talked to the police about this." I hesitated and then said something I regretted the moment it was out of my mouth. "I didn't kill him, if that is what you're thinking."

Andi gasped and Adam's eyes actually fluttered open. I guess he wasn't asleep, after all.

"I wasn't implying anything of the sort," Patricia said. "I just wanted to make sure I've got my facts straight."

"Her father is a mystery writer," Rita broke in, saving me from further humiliation. "I bet he could solve the case. I wonder if it would be possible to bring him in as a consultant."

I wanted to slap her. "He's not a detective."

Patricia grunted a laugh. "No need," she said. "As far as I'm concerned, it was an accident. The only other ex-planation would be that his wife did it somehow, but I just don't see it. That woman couldn't have hurt a fly swimming in her soup. She'd probably eat around the thing before giving it a little fly bath and setting it free."

"What about her mother?" I asked.

The room fell silent. Andi had her hand over her mouth as if stifling yet another gasp.

Patricia's face went impassive and she leaned for-ward. There was no playful gleam to her eye this time. "Do you have any sort of evidence that Regina Harper could possibly be involved in her son-in-law's death?"

"Well, no," I said, feeling ashamed. Just because I had suspicions of my own, it didn't mean I needed to throw a woman, whom I hardly knew, under the bus. "I was just adding to the conversation." *And maybe deflecting things away from me a bit, of course.*

Patricia grunted and sat back. "If she'd done it, I wouldn't blame her. The guy was a no-good cheat. If I'd been married to him, I would have killed him myself."

No one seemed shocked by that. I was definitely getting the picture that Brendon Lawyer wasn't popular around town. If he was as bad as everyone said, how did he ever get married in the first place?

I thought back to my own failed relationship and took the question back. We all make mistakes.

Thankfully, from there talk moved on to everyone's writing. Rita and Andi both read from their latest works in progress. I smiled throughout each, though my ears tried to crawl into my head as they leapt from one cliché to the next. Georgina and Patricia passed. Adam mumbled something totally unintelligible before Lena read from something she'd written earlier that day. It was the only decent thing I'd heard all night.

And then all eyes turned to me.

"Sorry," I said. "I have nothing."

Rita closed the meeting by thanking everyone for coming and then she turned to me with a hopeful smile.

"Do you think he'd come if we asked?"

"Who?"

"Your dad."

I bit my lip. "Doubt it," I said. "He's pretty busy right now."

Rita only nodded before grasping my hand. "I do hope you come again," she said. "And please bring something to read next time. I'd love to hear what kind of story you might come up with."

What I really wanted to do was run far, far away; instead, I gave her a smile and said, "I will." She let go of my hand and went to talk to Georgina and Andi.

Adam and Lena had already escaped by then and I was about to make my own way out when Patricia stopped me with a firm hand on my elbow.

"I want to speak with you a moment," she whispered harshly into my ear before walking off.

*Oh, crap,* I thought. Could she actually think I had anything to do with Brendon's death? Was I about to be interrogated, all because my coffee was involved? Or could it be because I'd brought up Regina Harper when I really shouldn't have?

I followed Patricia reluctantly down the hall, into a smaller room than the one we'd just left. A long table was surrounded by short-backed computer chairs. They were the only things in the tiny space. Obviously, it was some sort of conference room.

She waited for me to enter and then closed the door behind me. She turned and looked me up and down, inspecting me like I imagined a highly trained policewoman would do when trying to determine whether or not someone could be a suspect. It went on for so long, I started to fear she was reaching all of the wrong conclusions. Hadn't I read something about how cops would use silence to make criminals speak on their own, often letting something slip in their nervousness?

Well, I wasn't going to do that. I had nothing to be ashamed of. I didn't kill Brendon Lawyer and I didn't know who did.

I crossed my arms and just stood there, bearing her inspection as stoically as I could manage.

"You might do," she said.

"Excuse me?" That wasn't what I'd expected her to say.

"Are you married?"

"Um, no . . . ?"

"Seeing anyone?"

"Not at the moment."

"Is there anyone special in your life at all that would interfere with you having a relationship?"

"What are you asking me?"

Patricia smiled. "My son," she said. "He's currently available."

"Oh." My head was spinning. "I see."

"You might very well do."

"I'm sorry," I said, feeling all kinds of uncomfortable. "I'm really not looking for a relationship right now."

"Sure you are," Patricia said. "Everyone is. No one wants to be alone." She fished around in her purse until she found a business card and a pen. She scrawled a number on it before holding the card out to me. "Give him a call, okay?"

I had two choices here. I could take the card, thank her, and then toss it in the trash on the way out. Or I could refuse and get on the Pine Hills police chief's bad side. Calling her son and actually asking him out on a date was completely out of the question.

I took the card. She'd written down a number, but no name. I flipped the card over, thinking his name would be there, but instead found myself looking at Brendon Lawyer's business card.

"You two will be great together." Patricia gave me one last smile; then she turned and left the room.

It took me a few moments to gather myself before I followed after her. I was so blindsided by what had just happened, I completely forgot to pitch the card into the trash on my way out.

The parking lot was already empty as I made my way to my car. I got inside, mindlessly shoving the card into my purse, before starting up the engine. I wasn't sure what I'd learned at the meeting, but I was sort of glad I'd come. If nothing else, I'd met a few more people in town. Hopefully, they'd decide to come in for some coffee.

Then again, I wasn't so sure I could stand all of the gossip, especially if that gossip started to turn toward me and my alleged involvement in Brendon Lawyer's death. I didn't need that kind of stress on top of everything else.

With a groan I backed out of the lot and headed for home.

# 8

"I don't like that look in your eye."

"Huh?" I looked up to find Vicki staring at me. "What?"

"Leave it alone."

I turned back to what I'd been doing: staring out the window toward Lawyer's Insurance. Nothing had happened all day, yet I couldn't help but watch the place. I was positive some important piece of information would leap out at me if I watched the building long enough.

But I wasn't going to tell Vicki that. She'd spent a good portion of her life warning me off situations like this one. Well, maybe not *exactly* like this—I'd never dealt with a murder before. Some little thing would catch my eye and I would immediately want to go poking around in the hopes of finding something exciting to occupy my mind, and there she'd be, telling me to stop involving myself in other people's business.

Of course, the good thing about Vicki was, she didn't actually mean it when she told me to stop. She always supported me in anything I'd ever done, even when telling me I shouldn't get involved. I think she enjoyed watching me squirm and worm my way to an answer, even if my conclusions ended up completely off base.

Then again, someone had died this time. This wasn't me finding a lost wallet, stolen by a parrot that had snuck out of his cage, or discovering where all the tea cozies my neighbor had knitted for my dad had gone after a rather rambunctious birthday party. If I wasn't careful, someone could get hurt. And that included me.

"I don't know what you're talking about."

"Uh-huh." Vicki moved to stand between me and the window. "You and I both know what happens when something like this catches your attention."

"There's never been something like this before," I said.

"You know what I mean."

"Well, I'm just curious," I said, still trying to deny how curious I really was.

Vicki cocked her hip, planted her fist against it, and gave me one of her patented warning looks. There was the faintest hint of amusement in it. "Let it go."

"I can't."

"It's none of your business."

"I know, but . . ."

"No," Vicki said sternly. "There are no *buts* here. A man bought coffee here and then he died. There's nothing more to it than that. That is the *only* connection you should have to this thing."

"Yeah, but . . ."

"What did I just say?"

I glared at her for a moment before giving in and sighing. "All right," I said, turning away from the window. "I'll try to focus."

The problem was, there wasn't much inside Death by

Coffee to focus on. There were three people sitting at a table by the window. I'd already served them their coffees—coffees, I might add, they had barely touched. It seemed that they were like me and were expecting something to happen across the street. Every few seconds one of them would look up and gaze hopefully at Lawyer's Insurance before returning to the quiet conversation.

I leaned against the counter and scanned the meager crowd. We had eight tables set up around the room, with only the one occupied. That meant a whopping seven of them were open. What other sign did I need that things weren't going as well as we'd hoped? It definitely wasn't looking good.

Vicki joined me at the counter a moment later. The bookstore wasn't busy, either. There was a couch and pair of recliners placed upstairs where readers could sit, yet they were as empty as the rest of the store. If this kept up, I could take a nap between orders. The couch was comfortable enough for it.

"It'll get better," Vicki said.

"You've said that before."

"I know. I have faith."

I wished I did.

She was silent for a few minutes before going on. "You do know you didn't have anything to do with that man's death, don't you? You can't go running off getting involved in it just because you feel guilty."

"I don't feel guilty."

She gave me a flat look.

"Okay," I admitted. "Maybe a little bit."

"I need you here, not off and poking your nose in business best left to the police."

"I know." I rubbed at my face. "I just can't get my brain to switch gears."

"Krissy, we all have to deal with that sometimes. You just have to push through it."

I started to reply, but movement across the street caught my eye. Vicki continued talking, but I tuned her out. I wasn't intentionally being rude, I swear. I just couldn't focus on anything but the man who was walking toward Lawyer's Insurance at that very moment.

"I'll be right back," I said, cutting Vicki off. I'd have to apologize about that later.

Before she could stop me, I was out the door and running across the street. A car horn blared as I skirted around it. Mason Lawyer had just opened the door and stepped inside Lawyer's Insurance a split second before I reached him. I caught the door before it could close and hurried inside after him.

"Mason!" I called, out of breath.

He turned and frowned. "Yes?" A couple of seconds passed before his eyes widened in recognition. "What do *you* want?"

"I just want to talk to you for a moment."

The secretary sitting at the front desk leaned forward. I paid her little mind. Maybe if I asked the right questions in front of someone else, Mason's nerves would cause him to say something he didn't mean to, kind of like what the police did with silence. Sometimes onlookers weren't an entirely bad thing.

Of course, it might only cause him to clam up all the tighter, but that was a chance I was willing to take if it meant getting to the bottom of his brother's death.

"Can't this wait?" he asked. "I'm sort of busy right now."

"We can always talk in your office, if that is what you'd prefer," I said with a smirk. It was obvious he didn't want to talk to me. Maybe he really did know more than he'd originally let on.

My gaze traveled around the room in the hopes of spotting Mason's office. Instead, I found only four doors, and that included the one I'd come in. One had the universal sign of a unisex bathroom on it. The other two had names on them: BRENDON LAWYER and RAYMOND LAWYER.

"I don't work here," he said just as I realized there wasn't a place for Mason to work, unless he met his clients in the waiting room, which consisted of a couch, four stiff-looking chairs, and a round table.

Before I could apologize for the assumption, the door with Raymond's name opened and an older man stepped out. He looked so much like Mason and Brendon Lawyer, I knew they had to be related, though he leaned more to Brendon's hard lines than Mason's softer ones. He had on glasses, which did nothing to ease the harsh glare that seemed permanently affixed to his face. He scowled at the both of us, a look I was sure he practiced.

"What are you doing here?" he asked. It took me a moment to realize he wasn't talking to me.

"I came to see you," he said before glancing to me. "I'm not sure what *she* wants."

I smiled at the senior Lawyer. "My name is Krissy Hancock," I said. "I wanted to talk to Mason about his brother."

Mr. Lawyer's glower deepened. He glanced at the secretary, who was watching all of this with wide, eager eyes, and then stepped back into his office.

"Both of you. In here. Now."

Mason and I both moved forward automatically. There was a command to Raymond's voice that told me he wasn't used to being ignored. This was a man who knew what he wanted and was damn sure he'd get it, no matter how many fingers he had to walk on in the process.

He closed the door behind us and stormed over to his desk, where he sat down, opened a drawer, and removed a bottle of whiskey. He poured a little into a glass and downed it before he settled his glare on us. The look in his eye almost dared us to say something about his midday drinking.

"What is this all about?" he asked through partially clenched teeth.

"Dad," Mason said. "She has no right to barge in here, demanding information on Brendon. I'm not talking in front of her."

"I didn't barge in," I said. "And I didn't demand anything. I just want to talk."

"Why?" Raymond asked.

"Uh . . ."

I hadn't even been sure what I was going to ask Mason, outside of anything he could tell me about Brendon and his death. I wasn't with the police. I wasn't a detective. There was no way he'd accept me asking questions about a case I really had no right investigating.

"I just wanted to talk to Mason is all," I said, looking

down at my feet. I felt like a kid who'd just been caught with her hand in the cookie jar.

Raymond heaved a sigh. "Even now, he haunts me."

"Dad . . ." Mason took a step forward, but stopped at a harsh glare from Raymond.

"I don't recall speaking to you," he said.

Mason joined me in studying our respective footwear. He was grinding his teeth and his face was red. The way he fell silent so quickly told me this wasn't unusual. Chances were good he'd spent his entire life getting reprimanded by the old man. I wondered if Brendon had suffered just the same. It made me understand why he had been such a jerk before.

Raymond glared hard at Mason for a long moment before turning it to me. "Brendon worked here. He was a damn right asshole who worked hard enough to earn a place here, unlike others I know." His eyes flickered to Mason. "He treated other people like shit and didn't give a flying f . . . ," Raymond trailed off, took a deep breath, and then went on. "He didn't treat others with the respect they deserved."

"I heard a rumor he was getting a divorce from his wife," I said. My palms were sweating now. I was nervous about asking these sorts of questions, especially to a man as volatile as Raymond Lawyer appeared to be. I was afraid that if I said the wrong thing, he might leap across his desk and strangle me.

"He was," Raymond said. "But someone interfered in that. I don't know who, but I wouldn't put it past that witch of a woman, Regina Harper."

I frowned. There was absolutely no way Heidi's mom

would have convinced her daughter to stay with Brendon. She hated the man with a passion that was near obsession.

"What do you think happened to Brendon?" I asked, still trying to sort out why Raymond might think Regina had anything to do with them possibly getting back together—without having to ask him directly. I wasn't so sure I'd get an answer.

"What do you think happened?" Raymond growled. "He died." More whiskey went into the glass and the elder Lawyer threw it back in one swallow. He looked longingly at the bottle before shoving it back into its drawer.

It was then I really questioned how much of this was an act. He might call Brendon all sorts of unflattering names, but he was still the man's father. It had to have hit him hard to know his son died in an office right beside his. They worked together every day. They had to have had some sort of relationship, even if it was a strained one.

Then again, perhaps the man was an alcoholic and his drinking had nothing to do with trying to drown away the misery he felt about losing his son. Here he was, working, only a couple of days after his son's death. In fact, I don't think he'd taken a single day off to mourn. That didn't speak of a father overly upset that his child was no longer alive.

Or maybe he was using work as a way to forget. Sitting at home, wishing things could be different, didn't help anyone. I should know. After my mom had died, I'd refused to leave my house for days. All I got out of all my lonely suffering was a ruined tearstained pillowcase and a bad complexion. I didn't feel better until I actually tried to live again.

"I'm truly sorry about what happened," I said, feeling guilty for barging in like I had.

"What is it to you?" Raymond's eyes narrowed. "Who the hell are you, anyway? You're not a cop, that's for sure."

Mason glanced at me with a faint smile.

I straightened, determined not to wither beneath Raymond's glare. "I work across the street," I said. "At the coffee shop."

Raymond grunted. "So yours was the coffee that killed him."

I bristled. "My coffee had nothing to do with his death."

"Other than the fact it was laced with peanuts."

"The police say it was an accident."

Raymond snorted. His hand went for the drawer with the whiskey, but he stopped himself. "If you believe that, you're dumber than you look."

I opened my mouth to tell him off, but thought better of it. Agitating this man any further than I already had seemed like a good way to get myself into trouble. I snapped my mouth closed and clenched my teeth. I'd have to punch something later so I would feel better.

"I'm a busy man," Raymond said with a weary sigh. He looked suddenly tired, as if he hadn't slept in a week. "I would appreciate it if you would get out of here." He glanced to the grinning Mason. "The both of you."

I turned without a word. If I opened my mouth, I'd surely put my foot in it. I might feel bad for the old man, but if I kept pressing, that wouldn't mean a thing to him. I had no illusions that he wouldn't pick me up and throw me out the window if I didn't do as he said.

I walked right past the secretary, who was quickly brushing her hair out of her face and looked nervous. She'd more than likely been standing at the door, listening the entire time.

I was out the door and almost to the street when Mason caught up with me.

"Hey," he said, taking my arm. "What are you trying to prove?"

"I don't know what you mean," I said, pulling my arm from his grip.

"Brendon's death was an accident."

"Was it?"

Mason's expression hardened. He looked like he was going to tell me off and then suddenly his face softened. Before speaking, he glanced around to make sure no one was listening.

"Do you really think someone could have killed him?"

"Don't you?"

"I . . . I don't know."

"Doesn't it seem funny to you that he would forget his EpiPen the very day he comes in contact with peanuts?" I remembered the conversation he'd had with Heidi. "I'm sure you've thought the same."

He nodded and then frowned. "It just doesn't seem possible. Why would anyone kill him?"

"You tell me," I said. "Who would have a reason to kill your brother?"

I thought Mason might tell me something right then.

He opened his mouth to speak, but instead shook his head. "Whatever," he said. "Just . . . just stop bothering us." He looked troubled as he ran his hands over his face.

Mason was trying hard to keep it together, but I saw the doubt in his eyes, saw the pain in the bunch of his shoulders. He'd been affected by his brother's death, but didn't want to show it. I didn't know if they'd gotten along or not, but it had to bother him to think that someone might have actually killed Brendon.

"I'm really sorry for your loss," I said, touching Mason's arm. I wanted him to look at me. I wanted to look into his eyes in the hopes I might see something there that would reassure me he had nothing to do with his brother's death. I wanted to believe him innocent. There was something about the man that told me he was a gentle soul, though right now it was buried beneath the stress of what had happened.

Instead of looking at me, he gave a sad, wry laugh and looked toward the sky. "I'm really not so sure it was much of a loss. Brendon wasn't anyone's friend. I only tolerated him because he was my brother and was married to Heidi."

Did that mean he was interested in Heidi? They'd looked awfully close when I'd seen them together. There was absolutely no way I was going to ask him about that. At least, not yet, anyway.

"Still," I said. "I'm sorry."

Mason actually gave me a brief smile. "It's okay. We're all just a little uptight right now. I'm sorry if I've been short with you."

We stood there, neither really sure what to say or do next. I really wanted to believe Mason could have had nothing to do with his brother's death; but standing here with him, I just couldn't make myself believe it. He clearly wasn't Brendon's biggest fan and he obviously had access to the office building. Could he have worked with Heidi and slipped some ground peanuts into Brendon's coffee while he wasn't looking?

Someone had called Brendon back to his office that day. Perhaps knowing who would point directly to the killer.

I forced a smile, afraid I might actually be standing right beside a murderer. Just because I was starting to like the guy didn't mean I could remove him from the list of suspects. "I best get back," I said, gesturing toward Death by Coffee. I could just make Vicki out where she stood behind the counter, watching me. At least if Mason made a move toward me, she'd see it and would be able to call the cops for me.

"Yeah." Mason glanced back toward the building we'd just exited. "I suppose I should go, too. There's no reason to go back in today."

"See you around?"

He nodded absently before turning and walking away.

A small part of me wanted to follow him to see if he was going to report back to Heidi or someone else who could be involved in Brendon's death. Maybe he was simply heading to his car. Or perhaps he had somewhere else to be. I wouldn't know for sure unless I followed him.

I took a step in Mason's direction and then remembered Vicki. If I ran off now, she'd never forgive me. We might not be busy, but I still had a job to do.

I turned away from the retreating Mason with a frustrated sigh. My eyes fell on our storefront, at the big sign above the door that showed a large steaming cup of coffee, sitting atop an open book. The words DEATH BY COFFEE were written in white froth within the cup. With a groan I shook my head at the inappropriate name and headed back to work.

# 9

"I got you something."

Misfit jumped off the table to wind himself around my legs. I snatched him up and rubbed my face into his fur before carrying both him and my purse to the island counter. I plopped them down beside each other. Without waiting for an invitation, he shoved his face into the opening and rifled around my purse in search of whatever I'd brought him.

Knowing he'd eventually find it, I pulled off my shoes and carried them into the bedroom. My feet ached from chasing Mason across the street. Okay, maybe working long hours standing behind a counter had something to do with it, but I liked to think my pain had more of a reason to exist than simply manual labor.

Vicki had been angry with me when I'd gotten back to the store, but her ire had been short-lived. She was one of those people who could never stay angry even if they tried. After about ten minutes of sulking, she was asking me if I'd found anything out before warning me off interfering too much. After a few minutes of that, she was off working on selling a romance series to an elderly man.

Even though she'd forgiven me for running off on her, I still felt bad. Instead of buying her a gift, however, I ended up getting Misfit something. It might not have been the right solution, but it made me feel a little better, anyway.

I tossed my shoes into the closet, stripped out of my work clothes, and got dressed into my pj's. I had no intention of leaving the house again for the rest of the night. I'd had a long day and I wasn't about to make it longer.

Misfit had my purse on its side and over half of the contents strewn across the counter when I returned to the kitchen. He was on the floor, dutifully ripping into the tiny packet of catnip I'd bought him at a little pet store around the corner from Death by Coffee. I purposefully didn't look at the name of the place, fearing what the owner had come up with. I was sure it would be something horrible like Jet's Pets, Pat's Cats, or, worse, Kitty's Titties.

The cat eyed me warily as I approached, as if he thought I might steal his catnip. I gave him a wide berth, knowing I could lose a few toes if I got too close. Misfit was mean when he was high on the nip. It was one of the reasons I never got another cat. The poor thing would never stand a chance.

"Don't eat it all in one sitting," I said, knowing he'd do just that. I was *so* going to regret buying him the catnip. The hair balls would be a nightmare.

I took the long way around to the island counter and went about putting things back into my purse. At least he hadn't broken anything getting into it this time. I'd half expected to come back to find the purse itself torn into tiny little shreds. It wouldn't have been the first time.

I picked up a card and was about to shove it into my purse when I realized what it was. I'd completely forgotten about the number Patricia had given me. I should have thrown the thing away.

Then again, would it be so bad to at least make the call? It might make Patricia happy, even if nothing came of it. Maybe if she liked me, she might confide in me about the case.

"Do you think I should call?" I asked Misfit. He glared at me with one eye before attacking the packet of catnip with renewed vigor.

I truly had planned on throwing the card away, but maybe fate had stepped in. Perhaps it was some cosmic sign, pushing me into a direction that would help make my life complete. It was better to think that than to believe I was absentminded enough to forget to toss something into the trash mere seconds after deciding I was going to do just that.

My mind conjured up an image of a guy sitting alone in his mother's basement, playing a computer game or perhaps reading a comic book while he waited for my call. He'd ask me about dragons and superheroes and would want me to wait for him while he watched the latest episode of *Doctor Who*.

Now, I didn't have anything against people like that; they just weren't my type. I needed someone who could keep my mind focused so I wouldn't go running off every time a mystery presented itself. Give me someone who wanted to dress up and play pretend and I very well might end up running around town in a deerstalker hat, calling everyone "Watson." If I kept going the way I was going, someone was bound to notice and stop me—the murderer, perhaps.

I bit my lip and looked at the phone. All it would take was one call. What could it hurt? I could tell him his mom tried to set us up and leave it at that. If nothing came of it, it wasn't like I'd been all that interested, to begin with. Rejection here hurts no one.

"I'm going to do it," I told Misfit as I reached for my cell phone. Just as I touched it, it started ringing.

I blinked at it. *Another cosmic sign?* I answered it without bothering to check the screen.

I really wish I would have.

"Hello?"

"Krissy? Where in the hell are you?"

A mental door slammed closed. I went utterly still, barely daring to breathe. If I spoke, then he would know I was there.

*Too late,* a little voice in the back of my head said. *He already knows.*

"What do you want, Robert?" I asked, speaking as calmly as I could manage. Deep breaths. I just needed to take deep breaths and not let my anger show through.

"What do you think I want? I want you to come back home. You need me."

I ground my teeth together. Deep breaths weren't working. "I need you to leave me alone. I changed my number for a reason." I was going to kill whoever gave him my new cell phone number.

"Come on, Krissy. You know you can't handle living without me."

"Ugh!" I just about threw the phone across the room. If I wasn't afraid of breaking it and having to buy a new one, I might have. "I'm doing just fine without you, thank you very much. Now, can I please forget you ever existed?"

"Aw, come on," he said. "Just tell me where you are. I'll come out and we can talk things through."

"We've tried that before." I knew I should just hang up, but there was still a faint part of me that cared. I actively hated that part. "I'm done, okay? Go back to your college girls and leave me alone."

"Damn it, Krissy. Quit being such a b—"

I didn't let him finish. I pressed the END button and then quickly blocked his number before he could call back. I should have done that long before now. I *so* didn't need his drama in my life anymore. *Been there, done that.* It was time to move on.

Misfit was lying on the floor, breathing heavily. The cardboard and the plastic package were torn into bits and were soaking wet. There were a few sprinkles of catnip on the floor. Most of it was in his fur. I was going to have to give him a bath or he'd be gnawing on it for days.

Right then, I didn't have the energy for it. "Tomorrow," I told him, "you are getting a good solid bath." His head moved a fraction of an inch before he continued his catnip-induced coma.

I started to shove the card back into my purse, but hesitated. After Robert's call, I wanted nothing to do with men of any sort; yet I couldn't let this go. Robert was certain I'd find no one else. Maybe his call was a sign to remind me that if I didn't do this, he very well might end up being right.

"I'll show him."

Before I could change my mind, I dialed the number

on the card. My heart was pounding and my ears were actually ringing. It felt like I was calling a boy for the very first time.

*Has it really been so long since I've done this?*

Before things had gone south, I'd been with Robert for two years. I'd been single for a few years before that and single since. I'd barely gone on a half-dozen dates before Robert and definitely hadn't gone on any after.

Man, was I pathetic or what?

The phone rang twice before a familiar voice answered. "Hello?"

I couldn't speak. I knew that voice. I'd just heard it the other day.

"Is anyone there?"

"Uh, hi," I said, licking my suddenly dry lips. "It's Krissy Hancock. From the shop. Death by Coffee." *Ugh!* I was back to speaking in three-word sentences. *Kill me now.*

"Krissy?" Officer Paul Dalton's silky smooth voice slipped over the line. "Is something wrong?"

"Oh . . . no," I said. "Your mom gave me your number." My head thumped against the island counter as soon as the words were out of my mouth.

He laughed. "Sounds like her." He paused. "I am glad you called, though. Most girls run screaming in the other direction when she does that."

*Most girls?* How many girls did Mommy think were right for him? Maybe I wasn't so special, after all.

"Well, I'm not most other girls." *God, that sounds dumb. Why do I turn into such a moron when talking to him?* This was clearly not the best way to get a date.

"No, you're definitely not."

My breath caught in my throat. *What does that*

*mean? Is it a compliment? Am I scaring him off?* I really wished I had the ability to read minds so I knew whether or not I should be jumping up and down in joy or crying softly in a corner.

"I'm sorry to have called you, out of nowhere." Another thought hit me. "Are you on the beat?" I rolled my eyes. *Do they even call it "the beat" anymore? Dumber and dumber . . .*

"You're fine," he said with a laugh. "I'm home. And really, I don't mind that you called. In fact, I'm just happy Mom managed to get it right this time."

I made a little squeaking sound. I tried to cover my mouth with my hand before it snuck out, but I was too late.

"Did you step on a mouse?" he asked, deadpan serious.

The only thing that could have made that moment worse was if he'd been standing right there. My face was so red, I could feel the heat radiating off me. *Can I please die now?*

Paul chuckled. "I'm just teasing you." He was silent a moment before going on. "You know, if you want to continue this conversation some other time, I'm open to it."

"Are you serious?" I smacked myself upside the head. One day I was going to think before I spoke, though thinking was hard right about then. Could he really be interested in me? Or was I just reading too much into an innocent conversation?

"Of course, I am." He laughed again. "You interest me."

"Even though I might be a murder suspect?"

Okay, that was it. I was going to permanently ban my mouth from running before my brain could catch up.

What did I want to do, screw up my chances for a date by saying as many stupid things as I could in the shortest amount of time possible? Did they have an award for that? Even Misfit glanced at me at the last one.

Officer Dalton was silent for so long, I was positive he was reconsidering his offer. What would it look like if he went on a date with a suspect in what could possibly be a murder? He might lose his job and I'd somehow become the prime suspect. The media would be all over how I'd come on to him in a way to throw suspicion off myself or . . .

I clamped down on that line of thought. I was pretty sure that was the storyline to one of Dad's mysteries.

"I don't see how you could be," he said. "There's no evidence of a murder in Pine Hills, unless you're confessing to one?"

"I'm not," I said, relieved.

"Good."

"Okay."

"Okay, you'll see me?"

"Sure," I said after my silent little squeal of joy.

"Tomorrow night sound good?"

"Yeah."

"Okay." I could hear the smile in his voice. "I'll pick you up at, let's say . . . seven?"

"Okay." Broken record? Me? Never. "Let me give you my address."

"It's okay," he said with a laugh. "I already have it."

Of course, he did. His mom probably *had* run a background check on me and had passed on the information to him.

There was a moment of silence where I wasn't sure

whether I should be flattered or upset. If that's what had happened, he knew more about me than I did him. That wasn't fair!

"So . . . ," he said, drawing out the word, "see you tomorrow?"

"See you then."

We disconnected and I just about melted into a puddle beside the nearly comatose cat.

I was actually going on a date. With a cute guy. One who'd asked *me* out. I might have been the one to call him, but he'd been the one to do the asking. That definitely counted.

I had to call Vicki.

I snatched up the phone and dialed her number. She answered, sounding half asleep.

"Guess what?" I asked, all but bubbling over with excitement.

"You're pregnant?"

"What? No." I rolled my eyes. I should have seen that one coming. "I have a date!"

We spent the next ten minutes gushing over Officer Paul Dalton and his oh-so-sexy dimples. By the time I hung up, I was so giggly, I forgot about Misfit's catnip high. I scooped him up off the floor and spun him in a circle. Claws flashed out and he squirmed in my arms as if his life depended on it. I managed to set him down on the counter before losing any skin. He gave me a threatening glare before leaping down. He ran out of the room, fur and catnip flying in his wake.

I had a date. I actually had a date.

A horrible retching sound came from what sounded

like my bedroom. I was guessing I'd find the pile on my pillow.

But oddly, I wasn't bothered by it. With a shrug I grabbed the paper towels, a can of Spot Shot, and headed to my bedroom to clean up the mess. Right then, even Misfit's catnip-laced hair ball couldn't bring me down.

# 10

"So you called *him*?"

"I did." I smiled at Vicki. "I picked up the phone and called him right up." I didn't add that his mom gave me his number and I'd had no idea who I'd actually been calling. She could believe what she wanted to believe, especially if it meant I looked a little less clueless.

The bell above the door tinkled. I glanced at the door, moderately irritated about being interrupted. I was so into telling Vicki about my upcoming date, I didn't want to stop. When I saw who came in, however, I changed my mind and my smile returned.

"A red eye?" I asked as Lena came up to the counter. Her skateboard was tucked under her arm like always. Even with her new scrapes and bruises, she appeared to be in a good mood.

"Yeah," she said. "Thanks."

I went to make her drink. Vicki trailed after me.

"And you are going on a date with him? Tonight? Actually with him?"

"Of course, it's with him," I said. I couldn't stop smiling. In fact, I'd spent all night smiling. I'm pretty sure I giggled a few times in my sleep. "Who else would it be?"

Vicki shrugged. "With you, who knows?"

"Ha-ha," I said flatly. "Funny."

I made Lena's red eye a double and carried it to the counter. She started to pay, but I shook her off. "This one is on me," I said, feeling generous. We couldn't really afford to be giving things away at this stage, but hey! I was in a good enough mood. I wanted to spread some of it around.

"Thanks!" she said with a grin. She scooped up her drink and headed for the door. She waved with her free hand before dropping her skateboard onto the sidewalk and riding it off into the sunset.

Or, well, wherever she was going, anyway.

Vicki waited until she was gone before grilling me some more. "Where are you going?"

"Nowhere," I said absently. I was staring after Lena, wondering how she didn't spill her drink riding that thing like that. "I'm not abandoning you today."

She laughed, which brought my attention to her, but probably for the wrong reasons. When Vicki laughed, it sounded like bells chiming and angels singing. When I laughed, it sounded more like a drunk woman with the hiccups. Why couldn't I be as blessed as she was? It made me worry about the date and what would happen if Paul said something funny.

"No," Vicki said with a wave of her hand. "I mean tonight. On your date."

"Oh." A frown crept onto my face. "I don't know."

"Do you know what you're going to wear?"

I thought about all of those boxes I had yet to

unpack. All of my nicer clothes were still tucked away inside—more than likely so wrinkled, they'd never look right again. All I had were jeans and T-shirts, maybe a few nicer blouses, but absolutely nothing else that would go with them.

"Oh, crap."

Vicki winced. "Do you need me to loan you something?"

I took one look at her lithe body and her long legs and shook my head. Like I was ever going to fit into anything she wore. I might manage to squeeze one of her dresses around one of my legs, but that was about it.

"Then you need to go shopping!"

I stared at her. "And when am I going to do that?" I asked. "The date is tonight, and, well . . ." I waved my arms around at the nearly empty store. All two customers looked up at me before going back to their coffees and morning papers.

"Do it now," she said. "I'm pretty sure I can handle this."

I gave her a skeptical look. I mean, I had no doubt she could manage the store. I doubted we'd get much more than a handful of customers for the rest of the day, and it was unlikely they'd all come at once. But I'd already run off on her a few times now. I didn't want to make it a habit. While she might be telling me to go, I felt bad for leaving just so I could buy a dress for a date that might not amount to anything, anyway.

"I'm serious," she said, giving me a friendly shove toward the door. "Get out of here before I kick you out."

Still, I didn't move. I looked from the door, to Vicki, and then back again. My eyes passed over the Lawyer's

Insurance building, and the little devil that resided somewhere on my shoulder urged me to go ahead and take her advice. What would it hurt if while I was out, I happened to pay a little visit to Raymond Lawyer or stopped in to ask the secretary what she might know about Brendon's death?

I stomped hard on the nagging voice. I might leave, but I refused to get into the Lawyer business today. I had other, more personal, things to worry about.

"All right," I said as Vicki gave me another little nudge. "It'll only take me a few minutes. I promise I'll be right back."

"Go!" Vicki shooed me away.

I balled up my apron and tossed it onto a shelf beneath the counter. "Thanks," I said, making for the door.

Just as I was about to step outside, Rita Jablonski appeared, as if by magic. She opened her mouth to speak, but I cut her off, knowing if I let her get started, I wouldn't be getting rid of her.

"Can't now. Gotta go."

I brushed past her and legged it down the sidewalk at a near jog. Rita gave an indignant huff at my abrupt manner. A pang of guilt swept over me, causing me to turn to apologize. When I looked, she'd already gone inside.

Oh, well. The apology could wait. I had things to do.

There was a clothing store a block from Death by Coffee: Tessa's Dresses. I'd seen the dresses in the window a few times already, but had never stopped to check on the prices. I couldn't really afford much, especially with the lack of customers we'd been suffering through. As I hurried inside, I prayed the dresses wouldn't be too far out of my price range.

". . . if only you hadn't slept with him."

I froze just inside the door, unsure whether I should turn and hurry away or if I should gawk some more at the two women standing at the counter. The bell above my head clanged loudly, which sort of gave me little other choice but to stay right where I was. Running would do me no good.

Both women turned my way. I recognized Heidi Lawyer instantly. Her face was flushed and I could tell she'd been crying. She had a mascara-smeared tissue balled in her fist. She sniffed, wiped at her now-dry eyes, and then hurried past me. She was practically running when she hit the sidewalk.

"Sorry," I said, turning back to the woman behind the counter.

Even though her skin was dark, I could see the flush creep up her neck as she averted her eyes from my own. She brushed a loose strand of dyed-blond hair out of her face, cleared her throat, and gave me a clipped address of "Can I help you?"

"Was that Heidi Lawyer?" I asked, letting the door fall closed behind me. I glanced back the way Heidi had gone, but she was out of sight already. I didn't know if that meant she'd gotten into a car or if she'd entered another one of the nearby buildings. I wasn't so sure it mattered.

The woman stood there a long moment, not speaking, not doing anything but looking at the counter in front of her. Finally she said, "It was." It sort of sounded like she didn't want to admit it.

I took a few tentative steps into the shop. I had no

idea what I'd just walked in on, but I was pretty sure it had something to do with Brendon Lawyer. Had Heidi been accusing this woman of sleeping with him?

I casually scanned the racks as I approached. Almost everything in the store was a dress of some sort, hence the name, but there were a few skirts and blouses near the back. I glanced at a price tag as I passed and just about sighed in relief. It seemed like I might actually be able to afford something here that wouldn't force me to ask Dad for a loan.

"She seemed upset," I said, turning my attention back to the woman at the counter. She was pretty, not quite tall, but not short, either. Like most of the other women I knew, she was thin. It made me feel like a hulking brute next to her.

"She was." The woman sighed. "Is there something I can help you with?"

"Are you Tessa?" She nodded once. "Was what she said true?"

Tessa bit her lower lip and looked over my head. I got the distinct impression she wanted to pretend I wasn't even there. She tapped her foot nervously and then glanced around the shop, as if checking to make sure no one else was listening to our conversation. Outside the two of us, the place was empty.

"You heard that, huh?" she asked with a strained laugh. "I guess it's true." She shrugged. "But he didn't die because of me, okay? What happened to him was an accident."

"Yeah, of course," I said as innocently as possible. "I'd just heard rumors that he'd been cheating on his wife, and . . ." I trailed off, not really sure how to continue. If the rumors were true, then this woman was probably a mess inside. She'd just lost someone she very well might have loved.

"He was an asshole," she said, shattering that impression.

"Excuse me?" I blinked dumbly at her a few times, not quite sure I'd heard her right. "You two didn't get along?"

"Look," she said, leaning onto the counter. "Brendon and I saw each other a few times. We had fun. Then I broke it off for someone better. That's the end of the story."

"Why'd you do that?" I asked. "If it was fun, why break up with him?" I vaguely wondered if it had to do with his wife. Maybe he hadn't told Tessa he was married when he began seeing her.

"Why would I break it off with Brendon?" she asked with something of a bitter laugh. "Outside of the fact he was a total prick when he wanted to be? Well, how about because he was seeing another woman behind my back?"

"Do you mean his wife?"

Tessa snorted in a very unladylike way. "No," she said. "It was definitely *not* his wife."

My mouth slowly fell open. Not only had Brendon Lawyer cheated on his wife, but he'd cheated on his mistress as well. No wonder he ended up dead. If I'd been Heidi, I probably would have done it myself.

And then there was Heidi's mother, Regina. If she'd known about his mistresses, perhaps she decided to take matters into her own hands. If Heidi wouldn't do it, then her mom very well might have. She could have killed him so her reluctant daughter could finally be free of him.

"He cheated on you?" I asked, still thinking I might be missing something. "And it wasn't with his wife?"

"Didn't I just say that?" She sighed. "Practically everyone knew I was with Brendon. It was no big secret. He wasn't happy with Heidi, and she could hardly stand him, so it didn't feel like I was doing anything wrong. Once I found out he was seeing another woman, and I got to know Heidi some more, I realized what an idiot I was being. I'd had enough. I moved on. He could screw this other girl all he wanted."

"Do you happen to know who this other woman is?"

"I don't know, and I don't care," Tessa said. "I really just want to put him in the past, if that's okay with you?"

"It must have hurt to find out he was seeing someone behind your back." Especially since she'd been doing the same thing to Heidi. It had to have put a few things in perspective.

"It did," she admitted. "But I got over it. He might have had some money, and he might have been, shall I say, 'satisfying,' but he was an asshole. I don't have to put up with that. No one should."

"I see."

"Besides," she said with a bitter laugh, "I should have seen it coming. The guy was cheating on his wife. What made me think he would treat me any differently? I swear the cheating thing must run in the family."

I was still trying to process the information of Brendon's second mistress, so I very nearly missed that last little bit.

"Wait, what? What do you mean it 'must run in the family'?"

Tessa waved off the question. "I'm through with

Brendon Lawyer and these questions. It sucks he died, but I can't say I'm overly upset by it. It's freed me up to do what I want, and I plan on keeping it that way. He wasn't my type. It took me a long time to realize that he, like most men, apparently, just didn't do it for me anymore." Her hand found her hip. "And that's all I'm going to say about the matter."

I really wanted to keep asking questions, but I realized she wasn't going to have any of it. Tessa was giving me a look that said if I kept pressing my luck, I'd be out on my butt in five seconds flat, without a dress to show for it.

Still, I couldn't stop my racing mind from coming up with various scenarios. Could the other woman have been married? Maybe her husband had killed Brendon in a fit of jealous rage? Then again, slipping peanut dust into food seemed like an odd way to kill someone who was sleeping with your wife. Jealous rages seem to be, I don't know, a little more "ragey."

I glanced at Tessa's finger, thinking that maybe she'd been the one to be married, but she wasn't wearing a ring on her ring finger and there was no mark there that said she ever had. In fact, it was probably the only finger that *didn't* have a ring.

I needed to figure out who this other woman was. Tessa claimed she didn't know, but maybe Heidi or her mother did. Maybe Mason or Raymond Lawyer knew more than either had so far let on and could point me in the right direction. If this other woman was the reason Brendon had died, then perhaps she had a connection to Lawyer's Insurance. It would be the only way she could have gotten peanut dust into his food and coffee.

"Was there something I could help you with?" Tessa asked, clearly impatient for me to be gone.

I just about jumped out of my shoes. I'd completely forgotten where I was. Sometimes, when my mind gets locked onto something, the rest of the world ceases to exist. One of these days, I was going to end up rear-ending someone or falling down a manhole because I was too busy playing "little miss detective" in my head.

It took me a moment to get my brain reoriented before I could answer. "A dress," I said after a slight pause. "I need a dress."

Tessa finally gave me a real smile. The prospect of a sale was enough to lift her spirits. "What exactly are you looking for?" She looked me up and down and pursed her lips. I couldn't tell if that was a good thing or a bad thing.

I spent the next half hour going through Tessa's Dresses and ended up choosing a dark blue dress that cinched with a black belt at the waist. I already had shoes that would match, thank God, because the dress itself cost more than I'd originally wanted to spend. There was a cheaper red dress I'd considered, but quickly dismissed it. I didn't want to seem desperate.

I paid for my dress and carried it back to Death by Coffee to show Vicki. She oohed and aahed over it and asked more questions about my plans for the night. I answered automatically, but I really wasn't listening. I kept thinking about what Tessa had told me about there being another woman, and I knew I had to find out who it was.

My eyes strayed over to the building across the street. I knew—absolutely *knew*—the answer was over there. I just had to find a way to get inside and get the information I needed, all before the police closed the case and Brendon Lawyer's killer walked away a free man.

Or, as I was beginning to believe, a free woman.

# 11

There is one thing that cat owners everywhere understand: no matter how hard you try, no matter how many times you lint-roll yourself off, you will always, *always,* have cat hair on your clothing.

I'm not sure how Misfit managed to get fur all over my new dress. I kept it in a bag from the moment I'd gotten home, carried it into my bathroom, and got dressed after a shower. It was like he found a way to shoot his fur like quills beneath the door and somehow managed to get them into the bag. It was almost like he had some sort of fabric radar.

"This is your fault," I said. I was standing outside on the front stoop, madly lint-rolling his fur off me. I swear I could have made a coat out of all of it. "I'm going to shave you bald, you know?"

Misfit stared at me through the screen door. I think he was grinning.

I finished my last swipe, turned in a circle as I tried to see if I got all the hair off my ass, and then stopped to frown at the door. My purse was inside, as were the shoes I planned on wearing. The moment I stepped inside that house, Misfit would be all over me, intentionally trying to coat me in a warm, fluffy blanket.

"Stay back," I warned, shaking the lint roller at him. "Or I'm going to run this thing over you until there's nothing left."

He eyed me warily before fluffing his tail and sauntering away.

Of course, I didn't trust the rascal. Just because I couldn't see him—it didn't mean he wasn't there. Chances were good I'd be ambushed the moment I let my guard down. I would *not* let that cat ruin my date even before it began.

I stepped into the house like I was entering a war zone. The living room was quiet, almost too quiet. I peered around the corner, half expecting Misfit to be crouched on the recliner closest to the door, ready to pounce. It was a favorite ambush spot of his.

I contorted my neck around, searching for any hint of tail, or perhaps ears pinned back above devious, glowing eyes.

But he wasn't there.

The dining room was likewise empty, as was the kitchen. A growing sense of dread crept over me as I moved through the house, toward my bedroom, where I'd dumbly left my shoes. I tiptoed as quietly as I could manage down the hall, into the room, and snatched my heels from the floor before rushing back out into the perceived safety of the dining room. I picked up my purse and scanned the immediate area.

No cat.

Irrationally, my heart was pounding. I couldn't remember the last time I'd been this nervous. Misfit still had his claws, so if he decided he wanted to shred my dress, he could do it faster than I could run. The cat—and he was bigger than the average cat—was a lot quicker than he looked.

A knock on the door startled a scream out of me. I spun around to face the door just as an orange streak came barreling out from behind the couch. He hit me hard on the legs, swishing his tail up and under the hem of the dress, coating the inside with his fur. He zoomed past me, into the hall, and vanished into the bedroom, where he was more than likely preparing for another sneak attack from beneath the bed.

"I'm going to kill you!" I screamed after him before regaining some of my composure and turning to answer the front door.

Officer Dalton stood on the stoop, eyes wide, hand hovering near his waist. Thankfully, he wasn't wearing his uniform, which meant he didn't have his gun. By the look on his face, I really think he would have drawn it if he'd had it.

"Is everything okay in there?" he asked slowly. He looked at me as if he thought he might have misjudged me and that he very well might be looking at someone capable of murder.

"My cat," I said, slipping on my shoes. There was nothing I could do about the fur now. I wasn't about to lift the hem in front of Paul to check the damage. *Here's hoping our date doesn't progress past the eating stage.* I blushed as my brain tried to turn the thought into something *far* different. "He's trying to kill me, I think."

Paul frowned. "A cat?" He gave a shudder. "I'm more of a dog person. I have two huskies."

"I like dogs, too," I said . . . like a dope. I glanced back toward the hall. There was a nervousness to my voice when I asked, "Can we get going now?" Who knew when the cat would make his next attempt on my life?

Paul stepped aside and I slipped out of the house before Misfit could make a bigger nuisance of himself. I closed the door firmly behind me and then turned to see Paul grinning at me.

"You look nice," he said, carefully keeping his eyes on my face, rather than scanning up and down my body like I knew he wanted to do. I mean, he was a guy, wasn't he?

"Thanks." It was then I noticed he was wearing a simple polo shirt and jeans. "You too." I felt my face flame. Boy, was I ever overdressed.

"I figured we could grab something to eat, if that's okay with you?" he asked as he led me to his car. "I probably should have mentioned it on the phone so you knew not to have dinner beforehand."

"It's okay," I said. "I figured you'd want to have something to eat." My mind flashed back to my earlier thought. I was thankful it was dark enough outside so that Paul couldn't see my blush. "I'm starving."

As if to prove the point, my stomach grumbled.

Paul laughed, opened the car door for me, and then went around to the driver's side. "I'm glad to hear it."

Neither of us seemed to have much to say as he backed out of my driveway and onto the road. I really wish I would have had time to run back in and get changed—preferably without getting assaulted by a demonic feline. As it was, I just had to make the best of things. It wasn't a sin to dress nicely on a date, even if I could have stuck with something a bit more comfortable.

"I hope you don't mind sandwiches," Paul said after

a few minutes. "I didn't know what you liked and, really, there isn't much selection in Pine Hills. I suppose we could have headed out of town to go to a real restaurant, but with everything that's happened lately, I wanted to be sure to stick close to home just in case I'm needed."

"Do you think you will be?"

Paul shrugged. "Chief Dalton can be pretty demanding when she wants to be."

I giggled. "You call your mom 'Chief.' That's cute."

We pulled into a mostly full parking lot as he answered. "It's best that way. We're a small force here. There's no real need for us to be any bigger. But that means we have to be careful so that the others don't think she's playing favorites. I sometimes wonder if maybe we're a little too casual and a little too small for our own good."

He parked in a space almost right in front of the door. My entire body groaned in protest when I saw the sign: *J&E's Banyon Tree*. Great.

"I hope this is okay?" Paul asked. He looked at me hopefully.

I gave him my warmest smile. "It's perfect."

We got out of the car and headed for the diner. When I'd first heard about the Banyon Tree from Rita, I'd assumed it would be this little place on the side of the road where the chairs were plastic and the food smelled of grease on top of more grease. When we entered the quaint little building, I found myself surprised to find sturdy wooden chairs placed around solid tables. The counter was long and barlike, with stools placed at regular intervals along its front. Rockabilly music played over the speakers overhead. Nearly every table was taken by smiling patrons.

A waitress met us at the door and led us to the last remaining booth. I kept my eyes peeled for Judith or Eddie Banyon, but if they were at the diner, they were keeping out of sight.

"The ham and Swiss is great here," Paul said as we sat down. He ordered a Coke to my Sprite.

The waitress gave us both a winning smile before winking at Paul. She then spun on her heel in a flurry of curls to grab our drinks. She glanced back once, quite obviously grinning at my date.

"Come here often?" I asked, feeling a little out of place. It wasn't the first time I felt like a square peg trying to fit into a round hole.

"Most every night," he said, but then hurriedly added, "but always alone. Until now." He looked shyly away.

I scanned the menu and found a variety of sandwiches and burgers. There were the usual chicken fingers and fish and chips as well. It was quite clearly diner food. However, if the smells coming from the back were any indication, it was *good* diner food.

The waitress returned and Paul ordered his ham and Swiss. I went ahead and got the same, trusting in his judgment.

"I really should have thought this out better," he said when our waitress—SHANNON, her nametag said—left. "It was sort of out of the blue, really."

"It's fine," I said. "I kind of like the place." I glanced around, hoping fate wouldn't come knock me upside the head in the form of Judith Banyon. It would have been just my luck for her to arrive to kick me out before

I'd had a chance to get to know whether or not I was making a mistake.

Paul smiled. "I'm glad. And I promise the food is worth the noise."

It was pretty loud, but I didn't mind. There was a coziness to the place you couldn't find much anywhere else. Back home you had to be careful how you acted, what you wore, when you went out. Here it felt like you could just be you and have a blast. No wonder Vicki had chosen to settle down in such an out-of-the-way town. It was nothing like the bustle of our former lives.

Our sandwiches arrived with a side of coleslaw. Shannon asked if we needed anything else, to which we both answered in the negative. Then she gave Paul a little finger wave and vanished back behind the counter.

I raised my eyebrows at him.

"She loves to tease me," he said. A ring of red crept up his neck. "Always asks me why I never bring a date. Now that I have, she isn't going to let me get through it without teasing me mercilessly."

I took a bite of my sandwich to keep from saying something stupid. I'd never known a place where you could go to eat and actually *know* the people serving you. I was used to everyone being strangers, even your neighbors. It was odd to think that if I stuck around town long enough, I might be treated just the same.

"Look," Paul said, setting down his ham and Swiss without taking a bite. "I have something to get off my chest."

"Okay." My hand shook as I picked up my Sprite. Was this going to be the big letdown? Had he only asked to go out with me because he thought that was what his mom would want? Was he already secretly engaged to a supermodel and was about to elope to Hawaii with her?

"When we first discovered your cup in Brendon's office, I instantly suspected that you might have been somehow involved in his death."

I very nearly choked on my Sprite. "What? You thought I'd actually kill a guy I didn't even know?"

"No," he said hurriedly. "I didn't think you did it on purpose, but thought that maybe you weren't careful and had accidently poisoned him. You were new. You didn't know about his allergy. Mistakes happen."

The last made me think of the conversation Mason and Heidi had had the day after Brendon's death. I almost brought it up, but decided against it. I had no proof either was involved. I didn't want to start pointing fingers and making things worse for the two of them. They were already having a hard-enough time as it was.

"Anyway," Paul went on, "I just wanted to get it off my chest. Ever since I talked to you the first time, it had been bothering me. I didn't want you to think I thought you were careless or a suspect or anything."

"It's fine," I said, and I meant it. "You didn't know me. I probably would have thought the same about you, especially if you owned a store called Death by Coffee and then someone had died after drinking said coffee."

Paul sighed as if a great weight had been lifted from his shoulders. He looked as if he was ready to drop the subject, but I wasn't about to let it end there. His bringing up Brendon made me think of my talk with Tessa and how I was sure all of the answers might very well be found within Brendon's closed-up office.

We might be on a date now, but what other chance, really, would I get to ask him?

"Did you know Brendon had a mistress?" I asked. I took a bite of coleslaw to hide my nervousness. Not surprisingly, it was fantastic.

"I did," he said. "I also know he had a second one." He leaned forward and grinned. "Turns out it was his secretary. How cliché can you get?"

Cliché or not, I found it interesting. I tried to remember anything I could about the secretary I'd seen when I'd chased Mason into Lawyer's Insurance, but I came up blank. I wasn't even sure what she looked like. Some detective I'd make.

"Do you know which one?" I asked, hoping I didn't sound like I was pumping him for information. I mean, that was exactly what I was doing, but I didn't want to make it *too* obvious.

"There's only the one," Paul said. "Beth Milner has been with the Lawyers for about a year now. I think she started seeing Brendon within a few months of getting the job." He glanced around to make sure no one else was listening before going on. "In fact, I think she got the job because he planned on sleeping with her from the start."

I was really starting to think that maybe Brendon's death wasn't such a bad thing. The guy was slime, yet I couldn't let it go. Whoever killed him—and I was pretty sure it was a murder—might not stop at one man.

With a sigh Paul finished off his own coleslaw and set his fork aside. "I really shouldn't be talking about this."

"I don't want to get you into trouble."

"It's not that. I don't know . . ." He frowned. "If this

was a bigger department, in a bigger city, I'd probably get fired for talking about an active case, even if we're thinking accident at the moment. This is mostly gossip and all, but still . . ."

I felt horrible for dragging out the conversation, but if there is one thing I'm not, it's a quitter. When I start something, I see it through until the end, even if it might ruin any chance I had with the hunkiest guy in town.

The next thing I said was probably the worst thing I could have asked of him, yet I couldn't stop myself. I had to know. The idea just sort of formed and lodged itself in my mouth. There was no way I could part my lips without it sneaking out.

"Do you think you could take me to Brendon's office?"

Paul stopped eating. He swallowed and took a long sip of Coke, studying me the entire time. The silence started to get to me so I began babbling.

"It's nothing, really," I said. "My dad is a writer and he wrote mysteries, so I sort of grew up interested in this sort of thing. I just want to go in and look around, see if I can figure out what happened, like all those great detectives you read about do. We don't have to touch anything, and I promise not to mess up the scene. I just want to see it."

"I don't know. . . ."

I hated myself, but I didn't want to lose this chance. I batted my eyes at him and leaned forward suggestively. I didn't run a finger over his cheek, or make "do me" eyes at him exactly, but it was a near thing.

*God, I'm such a jerk sometimes.*

"Please," I asked in my sweetest voice. "It would make me very, very happy if you would do this for me."

Paul sucked in a breath and a bead of sweat formed on his brow. He looked around the room, cleared his throat, and then smiled at me.

"Okay," he said, voice conspiratorially low. "Once we're done eating and it gets darker out, I'll take you."

"Thank you," I said. Deep down, I knew I'd have to make this up to him. In fact, I was probably going to have to say the Hail Mary a few hundred times. I could already feel the heat tickling at the soles of my feet.

Paul wiped the sweat from his brow and started eating. "I hope this doesn't come back to bite me on the ass." He said it with a smile, but I could tell he was nervous.

Not that I blamed him. I was thinking the same thing.

# 12

It's hard to walk quietly in high-heeled shoes.

I didn't want to walk in my bare feet, so I clacked along as quietly as I could. We weren't exactly sneaking, per se, but we didn't want anyone to notice us, either. There were a few other pedestrians walking the street, though most of them paid little attention to us. Pine Hills had a tendency to close down by seven o'clock precisely every night, meaning there wasn't much else to do but break in somewhere you aren't supposed to go.

The wait had been nearly unbearable. We'd finished our meals, sat around for a little while, nervously talking about nothing, before getting into his car and driving around for another hour. I think both of us were waiting for the other one to change his or her mind so we wouldn't actually have to go through with this. In the end neither he nor I was willing to voice these doubts out loud.

For a date it wasn't very fulfilling. We hardly talked and we didn't look at each other much at all. There was a nervous tension to the air that did all of our talking for us. We both knew that if someone saw us breaking in, our gooses would be cooked.

Of course, we weren't exactly breaking into the place. Paul had a key. The department had requested one from Raymond Lawyer, who had complied, though he did it loudly with a lot of yelling, if Paul was to be believed. Why he had the key on him was beyond me, but I was just thankful he did. I doubted Chief Dalton would have handed it over if we'd been forced to ask.

And you know what? I truly believe that Paul Dalton would have asked for it. He would have gone right up to his mom, his boss, and asked for something that would get us both into some serious trouble if anyone discovered what we were up to. What other guy would risk not only his job, but the wrath of his mother, *and* spending time in jail, all because a girl asked him?

What I really wanted to do was take his hand. It would look natural enough, though it would definitely start rumors. I was pretty sure any rumors that did get started would end up in Patricia Dalton's ear in about five minutes flat. With what we were about to do, I was hoping we'd fly completely under the radar, meaning I had to be on my best behavior.

We reached Lawyer's Insurance without anyone stopping us or asking us what we were up to. Across the street Death by Coffee was dark and empty. In fact, most of the buildings were dark by now. There were a few lights on in the rare apartments above some of the shops, and there were a few cars that coasted down the street. While no one appeared to be watching us, I knew appearances could be deceiving. Anyone could be sitting inside one of those dark buildings, watching and waiting. I didn't believe for a second that Eleanor Winthrow was the only nosy gossip in town.

Paul moved to the door while I kept watch. It was kind of exciting in a way. It was like we were in a movie, sneaking around in the dark while a killer was on the loose, more than likely watching us through the lens of a high-powered rifle. . . . Okay, maybe that wasn't *exciting* as much as it was *terrifying*.

The door clicked open. Paul ushered me inside before entering behind me. He closed the door and flicked on a flashlight he'd taken from his car. He shone it around before we headed for the door to Brendon Lawyer's office. It was closed and there was no yellow tape, further reminding me the police weren't actually considering his death anything more than an accident. Why bother preserving the scene if there was nothing to investigate?

Even if they had put up tape, I doubted Raymond Lawyer would have left it strung up all over his office building. He hadn't taken any time off after his son's death, so anything that interrupted his business would surely be unwelcome.

My hands were balled into fists as we approached the door. I really wished I had a flashlight of my own, but Paul had only had the one. I wanted something I could hold and maybe use as a weapon if the killer was lurking around the small office for some reason. I knew it was unlikely, yet I couldn't shake the feeling that we were walking into a trap of some kind.

The urge to reach over and grab Paul's hand was stronger than ever. From the way the light shook, I could tell he could use the support as well.

Paul was wearing black gloves, further increasing the

feeling we were doing something terribly wrong. He turned the knob and pushed the door open. The blinds were closed, leaving the room pitch-black. Paul shone the light around inside before stepping through the doorway.

I followed him in, wishing I had gloves of my own. They might have hidden the sweat glistening on my palms and kept me from digging my fingernails in too deep. To say I was nervous was a serious understatement.

The office looked as if no one had bothered cleaning the place up after the body had been removed. The office chair was pushed away from the desk, more than likely by the paramedics who had rushed in to save Brendon's life. The light played over a stain on the floor I instantly took for blood, but quickly realized was spilled coffee.

"I'm not sure there is much else to see." Paul spoke at a whisper as he shone the light around the room. "We took the coffee cup and his lunch from the room, but everything else should still be here."

I walked farther into the room, strengthened by his voice. Paul kept the light in my general direction as I moved through the office. I probably would have bounced off every table in the room without it.

"Do you think we should turn on the light?" I asked. The gloom was really getting to me, despite his flashlight. It felt like every shadow hid something horrible. Whether it was a murderer or a feral rat, I didn't know. I wasn't so sure I wanted to know.

"I don't think so," Paul said. "Someone would notice."

I didn't say that I thought people were just as likely to notice a flashlight beam passing over the windows of the office. In fact, they'd probably be more alarmed by that than they would if we'd simply turned on the overhead light.

But I wasn't the cop. I trusted Paul to know what he was doing.

"I want to take a look at his desk," I said, moving that way.

"Don't touch anything." Paul swung the light around to illuminate the large oak desk, which dominated the room.

I nodded absently as I approached. A stack of files sat on the corner of the desk beside a tray that held a few papers. I glanced at them, but the words meant nothing to me. Legalese was like another language to my eyes.

I moved around the side of the desk to stand where Brendon would have been sitting when he'd suffered the attack. The chair was pushed against the wall and had turned so that it faced the windows. A few crumbs lay on the floor from whatever he'd eaten. I was assuming toast.

My gaze moved from the floor to his desk. There, front and center, was a picture of Heidi Lawyer. She was smiling in the photo, which was something I had yet to see from her. The tired lines of her face vanished when she smiled, leaving her beautiful and young. I wondered if life with her husband had been what had washed most of her good looks away, or if it was something else, something that might have gotten Brendon killed.

"Hmm," I said, stepping a little closer. It seemed strange for him to have a picture on his desk of the woman he was about to divorce. I suppose he could have had it there for appearances. He wanted people to trust him, so having a picture of his family sitting in plain view might help ease their minds.

Then again, the picture faced Brendon fully. There was no way anyone sitting across from the desk would have been able to see it. Had he really left it there? Or perhaps the killer had placed it there so that the last thing he saw before he died was his wife's smiling face?

I was about to turn away when I noticed the faint dusting on the desk. It was almost invisible and I wouldn't have seen it at all if it hadn't been for a chance turn of the light. I wanted to run my finger through it like you'd see in the movies, but I didn't have gloves on and Paul had told me not to touch anything.

"What's this?" I asked, motioning to the dust.

He shrugged. "The room has sat empty for a few days now. It's not surprising there'd be dust."

I frowned. Dust accumulated, sure, but this seemed to be more than a normal amount. From what little I knew of Brendon Lawyer, he seemed like a man who would have had his office dusted every single day, meaning an awful lot would have had to build up in the short time since his death.

I turned and found myself looking at a filing cabinet beneath an air vent. There was something sitting on the cabinet. I walked over to it to find an open pack of Splenda sitting beside what looked like a ring a coffee cup might make. The entire cabinet top was covered in dust. Only the ring itself wasn't coated in it.

"Looks like Raymond didn't clean up here at all," I said, putting my hands behind my back so I wouldn't touch anything.

"Not surprising," Paul said. "No one would bother looking there when they came in."

Still, it looked like an awful lot of dust. With Brendon's job, he was probably in and out of this cabinet all of the time. And while there was dust in the ring, where he'd obviously set his coffee cup, it wasn't as thick as it was elsewhere on the cabinet top.

The click of the front door opening shattered my thoughts. I hissed in a breath and turned frightened eyes to Paul, who instantly turned off the flashlight, nearly leaving us in pitch-black darkness. There was the faintest trace of moonlight sifting in through one of the blinds behind me, so I moved away from them as not to give myself away.

The door to Brendon's office still hung open. Both Paul and I were too far away to close it without notice. Even if we'd been standing right there, it probably would have been a bad idea to push it closed. We had to hope that whoever had come in wasn't interested in Brendon's office.

A flashlight clicked on. Paul backed up against the wall so that he wouldn't be able to be seen from the doorway. I ducked down behind Brendon's desk, very nearly atop the coffee stain on the carpet.

My heart was pounding. Footsteps approached slowly. Light from the flashlight bobbed in time with the coming steps.

Had Raymond Lawyer come back to work? Had he planned on working from home and had forgotten something important? Could it be a Good Samaritan, checking to see who had entered the office so lafe at night?

Or perhaps it was the killer. He could have been watching the place, waiting for someone just like me to come along and interfere. I'd been asking questions. Maybe the killer knew I'd do something stupid like this and was going to put an end to my inquisitive ways for good.

God, I was as good as dead.

The flashlight lit up the room. I sucked in a breath and held it. I was trembling so much, I knew everyone in the room could hear my bones rattling. I could just make Paul out where he'd eased back behind the open door so that he'd be invisible unless the person with the light stepped into the room and turned around.

"I can see you." It was a strong male voice that had spoken. The light settled on the desk. "Stand up so I can get a better look at you."

Was this a trick? Could he actually see me, or was he trying to draw me out? I hunched my shoulders and ducked my head even more. Though if he could see me already, I didn't know what moving would accomplish, other than verify I was there.

Thankfully, I didn't have to find out. Paul cried out and leapt out from behind the door. He knocked the flashlight out of the man's hand. As he grabbed for the man's arms, Paul shouted, "Police!" I shot to my feet and tried to watch it all in the spiraling light of the fallen flashlight. "Stay where you are."

"No," the man with the deep voice said. "You stay where *you* are."

There was a moment of silence when no one moved.

"John?" Paul asked. The flashlight stopped spinning and illuminated the two men where they stood.

"Dalton?" the man—John—said. He was wearing a police uniform.

The two men stared at each other.

"Are you kidding me?" Officer John said with a disbelieving chuckle.

"Let me explain." Paul looked pale.

"No." A smile broke out over John's face. "I don't think so." He reached into a pocket and removed a pair of zip strips. "I'm placing both of you under arrest for breaking and entering."

Paul's shoulders sagged. He didn't fight back as his hands were zipped together. Then John turned on me.

"Please turn around," he said as he approached.

With little choice I did as he said. Our first date and I managed to get us both arrested. What were the chances?

Officer John jerked my hands behind my back. I could feel the satisfaction radiating off him.

"Hot damn," he said. "This is going to be fun."

# 13

Paul sat beside me in what I assumed was the interrogation room of the Pine Hills police station, though it looked like a lounge to me. There was the requisite table in the middle of the room, but the couch we were sitting on and the coffee machine across from us ruined the effect. Above our heads there was a dartboard, which looked well used. Unless they threatened to use our heads as targets, I doubted it was much use for interrogations.

Officer John Buchannan—I'd learned his last name on the way to the station—leaned against the wall by the door, grinning. When Paul tried to talk to him, John warned him to remain silent until Chief Dalton had arrived. He treated us like a couple of common criminals, which I suppose we were. Still, I didn't think he needed to go so far as to arrest us like we were going to make a run for it. We were still zip stripped up.

Officer Buchannan had that look about him that spoke of a need to prove himself. He knew who Paul was, knew his mom was the chief of police, which meant he knew that anything the prodigal son did would only hurt her position and elevate his own. He was relishing this far more than he would have if he'd caught real burglars at work. His grin threatened to cut his face in two.

The door opened. Officer Buchannan straightened, though his smug grin didn't leave his face. Patricia Dalton stepped inside the room to which he gave a sharp, "Ma'am," before he stepped back against the wall.

"What were you thinking?" Patricia said, closing the door. She was wearing her uniform, though it looked as if she'd thrown it on in a hurry. John had called her up at home and made her come all the way down here.

"Chief, I . . ." Paul trailed off at a sharp look from his mom.

"You were irresponsible," she said. "You made yourself look bad. You made *me* look bad." She turned to me. "And you . . . you managed to make yourself look guilty of something I know you didn't do. Why on earth would you two sneak in there like that?"

"It's my fault," I said before Paul could speak. All Chief Dalton could do to me was throw me in jail for a few days. She couldn't fire me, like she could her son. "I talked him into it. I wanted to see a real crime scene and asked him to take me."

"I didn't exactly resist," Paul said, doing himself no favors.

Patricia sighed. "The only crime scene is the one you created. Brendon Lawyer's death was an accident. There was nothing to see there because there wasn't a crime *until* you showed up!"

I clamped my mouth closed. I had my doubts about how much of an accident his death really was, and I assumed the police had to have the same doubts. However, to voice them now would only get me into more trouble than I was already in.

Patricia walked over to us, produced a knife, and then cut our bindings loose. Both Paul and I immediately began rubbing at our sore wrists. If it hadn't been so pathetic, it might have been cute.

"I never want to catch either of you doing something like this ever again. That building is privately owned. You have no business there, even though you might have a key." She stared hard at Paul. "Speaking of which . . ." She held out her hand.

Paul reached into his pocket and produced the key. He dropped it into her hand.

From where he stood by the wall, John smirked. He was thoroughly enjoying this. I gave him a good glare before turning back to Patricia.

"I'm sorry," I said. "This is all my fault. I didn't know we were doing anything wrong."

Before turning to face John, she gave me a look that said, "How stupid do you think I am?"

"Go take a walk, Buchannan," she said. John jumped at the sound of her voice and the smug grin faded.

He looked from where Paul and I sat, side by side on the couch, to the police chief. His face hardened as realization set in. He knew we were going to get away with this without much more than a slap on the wrist. I had a feeling he'd been hoping she would toss us both in a cell for a little while. He probably already had plans to post the pictures all over Facebook.

For a moment I thought he might actually argue. His face contorted, his mouth pressed into a thin line, and his eyes hardened. Then, with a huff, like a good little officer, he nodded once before he turned and stormed out of the room. He slammed the door behind him.

Patricia faced away from us for what seemed an eternity. She was rubbing her forehead with one hand while the other tapped lightly on the table. Paul shifted uncomfortably next to me as we awaited the next onslaught. I had no doubt we were in for a good long lecture.

"So," Patricia said, turning, "how did the date go?"

I'm pretty sure my jaw hit my chest. I wasn't too sure because Paul just about choked on his own tongue beside me and was sputtering out random gibber-jabber in an effort to come up with something to say. Whatever he'd expected to happen, this wasn't it.

"Come on," Patricia said. She sat down on the edge of the interrogation table, glancing toward the door as if to make sure Officer Buchannan was really gone. "Spill it."

"Well," Paul said carefully, "we went out to eat."

"The Banyon Tree?" she asked.

We both nodded.

She winced. "No wonder you decided to find something else to do. One of these days, I'm going to find a way to hit those two with enough violations, they'll be forced to pack up their grease bucket restaurant and find another town to poison."

I didn't want to mention that I'd actually liked the food there, so I simply twiddled my thumbs. Paul, likewise, only nodded, as if agreeing, though he'd said he went there every day.

"What could have possibly possessed you two to abandon a night out together and snoop around Lawyer's Insurance?" she asked, leaning forward. "Did you find anything to make the trouble you're in worth it?"

"No," Paul answered. "It was as we left it."

I clenched my teeth. If I were to bring up the picture and the dust, I'd just sound insane. I'm not sure why the police were so gung ho about classifying it as an accident, but I was pretty sure they wouldn't want me telling them they were wrong. Maybe once I had something more concrete, I could present it to them. Until then, I was on my own.

Patricia yawned and stretched. "Well, the next time you decide to finish off a date by breaking and entering, run it by me first." She stood. "There are far better ways to end a date, if you catch my meaning." She gave me an exaggerated wink.

I caught her meaning, all right, but I didn't want to. My face flushed about as red as Paul's did. We both stood to cover our embarrassment.

"I need to get some sleep." Patricia moved to the door. She rested her hand on the knob, but didn't turn it right away. "You two should probably get to bed soon." She winked again, this time with a grin, before opening the door and leaving the room.

I stood frozen beside Paul, not quite certain how I wanted to interpret his mom's words. I'm really not so sure there were too many ways to take them that weren't dirty. She was *far* too interested in her son's sex life—that was for sure.

"I'm sorry about that," Paul said, turning. He could hardly look me in the eye. "Looks like we're getting off with a warning, though I'm not so sure that makes this any better. First date and I get you arrested."

"I think it's the other way around," I said. "If I wouldn't have brought it up, we wouldn't have been there to get caught."

He gave me a wan smile, telling me he didn't quite agree. Men. Why can't they let a woman take responsibility once in a while?

"Let me get you home," he said after a brief, uncomfortable silence.

"Okay."

He led the way out of the interrogation room, into the station proper.

Just like the force, the Pine Hills police station wasn't very big. The front room held a reception desk up front and a few other desks farther in, where the officers did their paperwork. A door at the far end led to Chief Dalton's office. The bathrooms were across the room from that, and a stairwell was next to them. I assumed they led down to the jail cells.

John Buchannan stood by his desk, glowering. There was only one other officer in the room, but she was busy at a copy machine in the back. She didn't look up as we passed. Since Buchannan had been out on patrol earlier, I was assuming she was the night desk clerk.

I didn't breathe until we were out in the cool, clear night. A part of me had feared I'd never see the stars again. I imagined being dragged every hour from my cell to be interrogated brutally by Officer Buchannan, before being shoved back into my closet-sized cage. Clearly, I'd watched too many overly dramatic crime dramas in my time. I took a deep breath, let it out, and then practically sagged into Paul's car.

We rode in silence back to my place. It seemed like we did a lot of that when we were together. Was it a bad sign that we rarely had much to say to one another?

I was worried that just because we'd gotten off with a warning, it didn't mean we'd avoided a disaster. Paul would have to deal with the rest of the force poking fun at him, especially since he was the chief's son, and I had a feeling Raymond Lawyer wouldn't take too kindly to the fact we'd been snooping around. Not only that, but I was now going to be known as the girl who got arrested breaking into Lawyer's Insurance. I was under no illusions that the rumor patrol wouldn't pick up on the story within the hour.

Paul pulled his car up in front of my house. He didn't turn off the engine. He didn't even look at me as we sat there. It was clear he wasn't interested in coming in for a nightcap. I wasn't even sure he would ever want to see me again after this. It was my idea that had gotten him into trouble.

"I'm sorry about tonight," he said after a moment. "I'd envisioned things ending a little differently." He paused and frowned. "Of course, I didn't envision them ending quite like my mom did, either."

I laughed. As unpleasant as being zip stripped and being hauled downtown had been, I hadn't entirely hated my night. In a way the whole thing was sort of exciting.

"It's okay," I said. "I had fun." And strangely, I meant it.

He snorted. "Right," he said. "Getting arrested is part of every girl's dream of a perfect date."

"Really," I said to assure him. "It was an adventure. Dates are rarely this exciting, especially first ones." I said the last in a way that I hoped told him I was interested in there being more.

A small smile lit up his cheeks. There were those dimples I'd been missing. I'd been starting to worry I'd never see them again.

"I hope you won't hold it against me if I don't resort to criminal activity to impress you the next time?"

"I'll try not to."

There was a moment of silence wherein we both knew what was supposed to come next, but we weren't brave enough to take that step. I could feel eyes on us and knew Eleanor Winthrow was watching from her seat by the window. I'd left my outside light on and it shone right through the windshield, like a spotlight, illuminating us for the world to see.

And then it happened, witnesses be damned. Paul leaned over and gave me a peck on the side of the mouth. I think he'd been going for my cheek, but I'd turned into it. I wasn't sure if it was an accident or if I saw him coming and had been hoping for more. It was all kind of a blur.

"I'll talk to you soon," he said, sitting straight again.

"Yeah." I was leaning toward him like a dope. We weren't teenagers anymore. He wasn't going to push me into the seat and make out with me for the next hour.

Still, I was sort of depressed we didn't end our date with a little more flourish. The rest of the night had been over-the-top exciting, so why not end it that way?

"I should probably get back," Paul said, glancing into his rearview mirror like he expected to see John Buchannan back there, watching us. That, or perhaps his mom cheering us on, pom-poms and all. "I'll need to smooth things over back at the station. I'm hoping we can keep Mr. Lawyer from pressing charges."

"Do you think someone will tell him?"

Paul gave me a reassuring smile. "Even if they do, I'll make sure to spin it so that he thinks we saw something and had gone in to check it out. There was no harm done, so there is little reason to make a big deal about it." He shrugged. "This sort of thing often blows over here."

I really hoped he was right, though I did wonder if that was why they classified something that, to me, was clearly a murder as an accident. Were there so few crimes in Pine Hills that no one was willing to consider that an actual murder might have happened?

"Well, good night," he said when I didn't say something right away.

"Night."

I got out of the car and leaned in for one last kiss on the cheek. I closed the door and then stepped back as Paul pulled out of my driveway and drove away. I really hoped he managed to keep Officer Buchannan from smearing our names all over the place.

Then again, why would he need to? I was doing a good-enough job of that myself.

With a sigh I turned and headed inside for a good long cuddle with my cat.

# 14

I woke up the next morning with absolutely no desire to go to work. There was just something about the day that made me want to crawl right back into bed and sleep for a good ten hours. Perhaps it was my little brush with the law the night before that did it. Maybe it was Brendon Lawyer's death that was getting to me. Or it could just be the cloudy sky that gave no indication it was ever going to clear up.

Whatever the reason, it wasn't enough for me actually to stay in bed. Maybe by the time I finished my morning routine, I'd be in a much better mood and would be able to get to work with a smile on my face.

Yeah, right. Like that was ever going to happen.

By the time I was out of the shower, dressed, and working on my second cup of coffee, I was positive I wasn't going to be able to make it through the workday. Even the mushy cookie in the bottom of my mug couldn't cheer me up.

I glanced at the clock and grimaced. I was supposed to have been to work ten minutes ago. We weren't officially open, but by now, Vicki would have finished the morning setup. She was probably wondering where I was.

With a sigh I reluctantly picked up the phone and dialed the shop.

"Death by Coffee!" Vicki answered cheerfully. It sounded so sickeningly sweet—I wanted to stab her in her happy glands.

"Hi, Vicki, it's me," I said, squashing the thought. Homicidal tendencies weren't conducive to a long and happy life.

"Hey, what's up?"

"Do you think you'd be okay without me today?" I winced as I spoke, knowing how it had to sound. "I'm not feeling too hot and am afraid I might fall asleep in the middle of my shift."

"Oh no," she said, sounding genuinely concerned. "Is everything okay?"

How did I answer that one? I felt like a royal jerk for calling in sick. This was supposed to be our dream job together; and after only a few days, I was already making excuses as to why I couldn't come in. At least I was calling, I suppose. It's more than you can say about a lot of other people.

But what was I to tell her? That I got arrested last night on my date? That I was still thinking about Brendon Lawyer's death? Or that I was worried about how we never got any customers and I feared we were going to have to close the store by the end of the month?

I settled on "Yeah. I'm just feeling really tired." Sue me.

"Officer Hunky keep you out all night?"

Boy, I was glad I was home alone so no one could see the blush that instantly rushed up my neck. "Not really," I said, really hoping I didn't sound guilty. "I think it's just a combination of everything—new job, stress. I think I need a day to clear my head and then I'll be as good as new."

"Okay, sure." Vicki sounded just as chipper as she had when she'd answered the phone. "I can take care of things here. Just get better."

"Thanks, Vicki. I owe you one."

"Don't worry about it." There was a faint tinkle. "Oh! I'd better go. First customer of the day!"

I hung up, feeling a little better. Now that the pressure of actually having to work was gone, I felt as if I could face the day without breaking down into a sobbing puddle.

Misfit sauntered in from the laundry room just then. He plopped down next to me and gave me a look that quite clearly asked, "What are you still doing here?" I guess he'd already gotten used to this being his alone time.

"I'm taking a day off," I told him, which earned me an irritated tail swish. "Do you think I should get back into my pj's and veg out in front of the TV?"

His ears pinned back and he swished his tail a few more times. Clearly, he didn't like the idea as much as I did.

"You're probably right," I said with a sigh. If I wanted to break out of my little mental funk, daytime TV sure wasn't the way to do it.

I glanced over at the box sitting beside the island counter. I could always spend the day unpacking. In reality, I knew, I should have finished it up days ago, yet I just couldn't seem to find the energy for it. Unpacking meant going through all of my old things, which, in turn, meant bringing back all of the memories of things I'd prefer to forget.

Like Robert.

I ground my teeth together. Why should it matter to him where I was? We weren't together anymore. I had no intention of crawling back to him, no matter how lonely I might get.

Okay, so unpacking was out. It would just rile me up, or perhaps depress me even more. Maybe once I had another cup of coffee in me, I'd start to get motivated.

Misfit followed me across the room as I rinsed out my mug, put in a fresh chocolate chip cookie, and then filled the mug with the last of the coffee in the pot. I carried the mug—a white one with an orange cat snoozing on it—over to the counter, set it down, and removed a Sudoku puzzle. Misfit leapt up onto the counter, presumably to try to play with my pen as I worked.

Puzzles were my way of escaping. Whenever I had some deep thinking to do, out came a puzzle—any sort of puzzle. I could work on them, putting piece after piece together, whether it was words or numbers or actual puzzle pieces, and it was like my mind reacted, putting my thoughts in order. I got it from my dad, who believed writing was like a puzzle. He believed that as long as you carefully placed each piece of the story onto the page, no matter how little those pieces seemed to go together, you'd eventually get a complete story that made perfect sense.

And my life really was starting to feel like a giant puzzle. You have Death by Coffee. Then you add a little Brendon Lawyer, some peanut dust, and swirl them around, adding a mysterious death, a missing EpiPen,

d tried to break through my
eep into trying to piece things
background noise. I'd stopped
u puzzle, but was staring at the
e able to find the answer in the
*knew* Brendon hadn't accidentally
on the very day he'd forgotten his
tting a divorce. His mother-in-law
rother and father didn't seem too
his death. He'd had not one, but two
e seemed to be no end to the amount of
ght want him dead. I mean, the guy did
k for a living. How many people did he
his time on the job?

g sound picked up speed. I glanced over
to see an orange paw finish pushing the
coffee mug off the counter. I made a grab
was too slow. It hit the floor with a definite
shy cookie splattered everywhere.

it!" I shouted as he leapt gleefully from the
and bolted out of the room and down the hall
the laundry room. No wonder he hadn't played
hy pen; he wanted me to forget about him so he
take out a bigger, more satisfying target.

'm going to trade you in for a dog!" I shouted after
. I think I heard a kitty snicker from down the hall,
it was likely just my imagination.

With a groan I went to the sink for paper towels. This
asn't the first time I'd cleaned up a mess the cat had
caused on purpose and I seriously doubted it would be
the last. I was really starting to wonder if his entire
purpose in life was to make me miserable.

The cookie was ruined. It looked more like some-

and multi...
was a... ...to...
ce...

w...
his ...

I w...
determi...

With a...
found a pu...
pen—someth...
pencil, it mea...
right—and got to...

Misfit watched ...
thankfully didn't try ...
a few marks across my ...
a strike just right. I've ...
puzzles because I could no ...
written.

The coffee in my mug sl...
puzzle was falling into place, yo...
better. I'd made a few minor mista...
to no end, and was reduced to writin...
done countless number of these thi...
whenever I made a wrong mark. It wasn...

I drained the last of my coffee and ...
aside. I kept thinking of Paul and what we ...
Brendon's office. Why hadn't Heidi come t...
things? Why hadn't his father cleaned out the o...
the police were done? Or were they? Was this w...
"classifying it as an accident" thing some sort ...
smoke screen and they were closing in on the murdere...
even now?

A faint sliding soun...
thoughts, but I was so ...
together, it was only ...
working on the Sudo...
page as if I might b...
numbers somehow.
consumed peanuts ...
EpiPen. He was g...
hated him. His b...
broken up over ...
mistresses. Ther...
people who mi...
insurance wor...
screw over in ...
The slidi...
just in time ...
near-empt...
for it, but ...
crack. M...
"Mis...
counter...
toward ...
with ...
could ...
"...
him ...
bu...

thing a cat would hack up than anything I'd actually eat, spread across the floor as it was. I wiped it up, tossed the paper towels into the trash, and then carried the mug over to the sink. There was a crack that ran most of the way down the side, but other than that, it didn't look too damaged. A line of superglue might keep it sealed well enough to use again. It was one of my favorite mugs. I wasn't going to give up on it so easily.

I froze, mug hovering under the faucet, where I'd been about to rinse it out.

That was it. That was what I was missing.

I set the mug down and started pacing.

Brendon and Heidi Lawyer were getting a divorce because he'd cheated on her, not with only one woman, but two. Heidi was ready to break it off with him, but someone, perhaps her mother as Raymond believed, had interceded.

I glanced at the mug, mind racing. It was cracked, but still usable. I could put it back together and, really, it could be just as good as new.

Could their marriage have been the same?

I should have seen it before.

Brendon had kept a picture of his wife facing him, front and center, on his office desk so he'd look right into her eyes as he worked. Would you do that with a woman you were about to divorce? Raymond *had* said someone had interfered with them breaking up, but I'd dismissed it, thinking there was no way Regina Harper would have wanted her daughter to get back with her husband, but what if it wasn't because of her? What if someone else was involved in restoring the spark they'd once had?

I could see how it fit, even if I didn't have the entire

picture. Maybe Regina Harper decided to kill Brendon instead of letting her daughter go through with a divorce, not knowing the two had worked things out. If Heidi would have been left with nothing by leaving her husband, but inherited everything upon his death, instead, maybe she decided to stay with him so she wouldn't lose everything.

Or could they actually have come to some sort of understanding and someone decided to put an end to their reconciliation?

I needed to talk to Heidi Lawyer.

The problem was, I didn't know where she lived. The last time I'd seen her, she'd been at Death by Coffee. I seriously doubted she'd come strolling in for a cup of joe just because I wanted her to do so.

The phone book. I knew I had one around there somewhere. I'd been sure to pick it up the very day I'd arrived in Pine Hills, but I couldn't remember where I'd put it.

I rushed from the kitchen into the dining room. There were boxes stacked in here, just as they were everywhere else. Most of them were still taped shut. I passed by them and went to the nearly empty hutch. It was where I normally kept my phone book.

At first glance I didn't see it. Papers were tossed on the shelves—mostly bills, which had already found their way to me. I shoved them to the floor in my scramble to find the book. I feared that even if I found it, I would arrive too late, that Heidi would have up and left town. I needed to talk to her before something else happened.

And then there it was, lying askew at the back of the bottom shelf. I snatched up the phone book, flipped through the pages until I got to the *L*'s, and then ran my finger down the page.

There it was: *Brendon and Heidi Lawyer.*

I scrawled the address on the back of a bill envelope, grabbed my purse, and headed out the door.

# 15

Pine Hills was situated among a smattering of small hills dotted with many different types of trees, pine predominant among them. It was where the town got its name, obviously. Most of the residential areas were built near the hills, probably because of the view. Death by Coffee, like most of the other businesses, sat in the flatter valley portion of town.

Heidi Lawyer's house was nestled within the shadow of one of the small hills. It was clean, white, and was surrounded by well-tended hedges. The driveway was paved and looked to have been done recently. My tires made a pleasing hum as I pulled up behind a little blue Toyota parked in front of a two-car garage.

I didn't get out of the car immediately. I'd come here on a whim, and I really sort of expected her to have gone in to work or perhaps to be off talking to her lawyer in an attempt to get things settled. I mean, she had all of these details to take care of—the funeral among them—that it was highly unlikely I'd find her at home.

But I was here, and, apparently, so was Heidi. A

curtain moved and a face appeared and disappeared so quickly, I didn't get a good look at who had peeked out at me. Whoever was inside knew I was sitting there. So the only thing I could do—besides turning tail and running—was to get out and do what I'd come to do.

I shut off the engine and got out of my Focus, taking my purse with me. I didn't believe Heidi would attack me the moment I started asking questions, but you couldn't be too safe. If she really was the murderer and suspected I knew something, she might come at me. I didn't have a gun or anything, but ask any woman: Most purses have weight behind them. I was pretty sure I could fend her off with it long enough to get to my car.

A walkway led to the front door. Square stones had been placed a few inches apart rather than a solid sidewalk. The sound of my footsteps on the stones sounded loud to my ears and I kept wondering what Heidi might be doing inside. Was she getting a gun? Grabbing a knife? Or perhaps she was calling the police and they'd be here at any moment, ready to haul me right back down to the station, where I'd earn another reprimand from the mother of the guy I had the hots for.

*Ugh, my life . . .*

A ceramic frog by the front door held a sign: WELCOME! It was hard to imagine Brendon allowing such a thing, but I guess I really didn't know much about his life. He'd spoken all of six words to me, so it wasn't like I'd had a chance to get to know him and his tastes. He might enjoy sipping martinis while practicing ballet, for all I knew.

But none of that mattered now. The guy was dead. It was the murderer I had to watch out for, if indeed there *was* a murderer.

The front door opened before I could knock. Heidi peered out at me, face red and swollen. A tissue was balled in hands that visibly shook. She quite clearly had been crying.

"Excuse the intrusion," I said, hoping I sounded official. I had no idea how I was going to get anything out of Mrs. Lawyer. I wasn't a cop. She could slam the door in my face and there was nothing I could do about it. I just had to hope she didn't remember me from the coffee shop. "Could I ask you a couple of questions?"

Heidi looked me up and down, sniffed, and then stepped aside. I was thankful she didn't appear to recognize me because as I stepped inside the house, I noticed the baseball bat leaning just inside the door. If she'd killed her husband, I doubted she would have any reservations about clunking me upside the head with it.

She turned away and headed into the living room. I closed the door behind me and followed after her. I was so busy trying to come up with what to say, I didn't notice we weren't alone until the sharp bark of a voice next to my ear very nearly scared the life out of me.

"What in the *hell* are *you* doing here?"

I just about jumped right out of my shoes. Regina Harper was standing against the wall, tucked away in the corner near the window. I hadn't seen her when I'd come in, yet I was pretty sure she'd seen me. And from the way her foot tapped and her eyes bore into me, I was pretty sure she remembered me.

"Mrs. Harper, Mrs. Lawyer," I said, still trying to sound professional. I almost wished Vicki were here. She was a far better actress than I was.

"I asked you a question." Regina moved to put herself between Heidi and me. "What are you doing here?"

"I wanted to ask Heidi a few questions."

Regina snorted. "What business do you have here?" she demanded. "You are nothing more than a coffee shop girl." She made it sound like I was so far beneath her, I wasn't worth her time.

"Mom, it's okay."

"No, it isn't, Heidi." Regina glanced at her daughter, shot her a withering glare, and then turned back to me. "You can turn around and walk right out of here. We have nothing to say to you."

What I really wanted to do was slap the older woman. What right did she have to talk to me like that? Just because she had a better job—or, at least, I thought she did based on how she dressed and how she acted— it didn't mean she had the right to treat me like something she'd scraped off the bottom of her expensive shoes.

And I wasn't there to talk to her, anyway. I'd come to talk to Heidi and, darn it, that was exactly what I was going to do.

"I'd heard rumors that you were going to get a divorce from your now-late husband," I said, looking around Regina, who shifted from one foot to the other as if she thought she could block the words with her body. "Is that true?"

"Well . . . ," Heidi started. Her lower lip trembled. She wouldn't meet my eyes.

"Don't answer that," Regina cut in. "Her relationship is none of your business."

Of course, she was right. I had no business looking into this at all, but I couldn't help myself. The police might like to hear what I'd deduced. I'm pretty sure they hadn't looked too close at the Lawyers' relationship.

As much as I liked Paul Dalton, the department he worked for did seem a little on the Mayberry side.

"You were getting back together, weren't you?" I asked quickly so Regina wouldn't have a chance to stop me.

There was a moment of silence. Regina's face reddened in anger and her hands balled into tight little fists. I took a step back, afraid she might actually hit me.

Heidi groaned and sat heavily onto the couch. She covered her face with her hands as sobs wracked her body. After a moment, she nodded.

I stepped carefully around Regina, keeping myself out of punching range, and went to Heidi's side. I didn't have experience with this sort of thing, but I knew what to do. I rested a hand on her back and rubbed gently.

"This isn't your fault," I said, and I meant it. Something about the way she cried made me believe she could have had nothing to do with her husband's death. No one could fake misery like this.

She sniffled and looked up into my face. "I don't understand why this had to happen," she said. "Things were finally getting better for us. We'd come to terms with our mistakes and had just started putting our lives back together when . . ." She shook her head as more tears brimmed in her eyes. "It was no accident."

My blood ran cold. Was she confessing? Had I misjudged her tears? Was she crying, not because she missed her husband, but from a guilty conscience, instead?

"What do you mean?" I asked, carefully controlling my voice.

"Heidi . . ." Regina warned. She glared at me as if this was my fault.

"Mason agrees with me, Mom," Heidi said. "Brendon would never have forgotten his EpiPen. He's too careful for that. And I'm positive I saw it in his briefcase before he headed to work. You know I always double-check to be sure."

Regina stood stiffly in the middle of the room. She didn't nod or make any sign that she even heard what was said. She continued to glare in my general direction. Her eyes had taken on a glazed look, as if lost in thought.

"Someone killed him," Heidi all but whispered. "I know it."

"Do you have any idea who?" I asked. Could it really be this easy? I was almost positive Heidi hadn't talked to the police much about her suspicions. There was something about the way she talked to me that told me she was expressing her doubts to someone—outside of Mason—for the very first time.

Heidi shook her head. "I don't know. At first, I thought it might have been one of his girlfriends, but I . . ." She trailed off and then shrugged. "I just don't know anymore."

Was that why I'd caught her in Tessa's Dresses? Had she gone to accuse the other woman of murdering her husband? I mean, it sounded pretty feasible that Tessa could have killed Brendon after he'd broken things off with her. Then again, hadn't she said *she'd* been the one to break up with *him*? If she'd killed him, I wouldn't put it past her to fudge the facts to make herself look better.

My mind drifted to the other, *other* woman: Brendon's secretary, Beth Milner. Could she have killed him, instead? There were just too many variables, too many things that were unclear. I made it a point to talk to Beth before the day was out.

"It just isn't fair," Heidi said. Her eyes brimmed over, yet she fought hard to keep the tears from falling. "After my own indiscretion, I realized why he'd done what he'd done. It gave me insight into his mind that I never would have had before. I realized I truly wanted to be with him, that sometimes we all make mistakes." She looked at me, almost pleadingly, as if she desperately needed me to believe her. "We were going to be happy." She covered her face in her hands, once more overcome by her tears.

*"Indiscretion?"* I asked, almost to myself. Did Heidi mean what I thought she meant?

Heidi glanced up and her eyes widened. She gave a panicked look to Regina, telling me she hadn't meant to let that information slip.

I instantly thought of what Tessa had said about unfaithfulness running in the Lawyer family. Is this what she meant? Could Heidi have cheated on her husband with his brother?

It was like a lightbulb went on in my head. If Heidi had cheated with Mason and then suddenly realized she wanted to be back with her husband, it had to have devastated Mason. Could he have killed his own brother so he could have his wife?

"Get out." A hand clamped down on my wrist and jerked me away from the sobbing Heidi. "You've done enough damage."

Regina pushed me toward the door. I rubbed at my wrist and took an involuntary step backward. The look on Regina's face was enough to tell me that she was perfectly capable of murder and I was number one on her list.

"Who was it?" I tried to ask, but Regina shouted over me.

"Get out!" she roared. She took a couple of threatening steps my way and I scrambled back. I balled my purse strap in my hand, ready to swing if she whipped out a knife or perhaps an Uzi she had hidden away in her skirt somewhere.

"I just want to understand what happened," I said, still wanting to reach Heidi. If only I had a name, I was sure I could fit the rest of the puzzle together.

"Listen to me," Regina said, advancing slowly. "My daughter is devastated right now. Her husband just died. *You* are making it worse."

I bumped up against the door and yelped, but Regina didn't stop coming.

"She is better off without that *cheating asshole*." She almost hissed the words. "I'm glad he's dead. It might very well have saved my daughter's life."

I reached for the doorknob. I really wanted to ask Heidi who it was that she'd cheated with, but I knew I would never get past the dragon before me—with or without her Uzi. I turned the knob and was forced to take a step toward Regina to open it. Her hands were still balled into tight little fists, and I think she very well might have hit me this time if I hadn't scuttled out the door like a scorned puppy, purse held up to shield my face.

"Don't come back!" she shouted after me. "If I see you here again, I'm going to call the police." She slammed the door without waiting for a reply.

I slunk to my car and slipped inside, thankful Regina hadn't thrown anything at me. Or shot me. I started the engine and backed out of the driveway, still not quite certain she was done with me.

As soon as I was back out onto the road, my shoulder muscles eased and I could breathe again. I glanced back, half expecting the little blue Toyota to be barreling down on me, *Duel* style, but the road behind me was empty.

I considered calling it a day right then and there, but decided I had one more thing to do before I could go back home to my mug-breaking fluffball.

I just hoped Brendon Lawyer's secretary would be more willing to talk than Regina Harper had been.

# 16

I parked down the street from Lawyer's Insurance. I could have pulled right up front, but something told me not to be too obvious. Chances were good I was just being overly paranoid, yet I couldn't bring myself to drive any farther. It looked like I was going to walk.

A part of me felt bad for what I was doing. I could see Death by Coffee and knew Vicki was inside, working alone. I should have been there, standing at her side, praying for more customers. Yet here I was, going to confront a woman who very well might be a murderer.

It seemed as if I was doing that a lot lately.

I straightened my shoulders and faced forward as I walked briskly toward Lawyer's Insurance. Dad's books always had the detective moving as if he belonged wherever he went and I planned on doing the same. If I approached the secretary timidly, there was a good chance she would laugh in my face and call Raymond Lawyer to deal with me.

*I can do this,* I thought as I pulled open the door and stepped into the chilly office.

The secretary looked up as I entered. Her hair was

brown, streaked with bottled blond. It was pulled up into a bun that was supposed to look professional, but it made her look like a model pretending to be a secretary, instead. Her nails were polished and her makeup crisp and perfect. No wonder Brendon had hired her, especially if he'd planned on sleeping with her from the start.

She gave me one of those fake smiles that all people who hate their jobs seem to have. "Can I help you?" There was a hint of nervousness to her voice.

"Hi," I said, putting on my own fake smile and chipper voice. "Are you Beth Milner?"

Her eyes narrowed, though her name was right there on the plaque on her desk. "Why do you want to know?"

If that wasn't suspicious behavior, I didn't know what was.

Then again, who was I to come in and ask after her? She probably remembered me from when I'd come in chasing Mason Lawyer the other day. She would know who I was, that I wasn't really a cop.

"I'm just wondering how well you knew Brendon Lawyer," I said. "I talked to Tessa."

Beth's face darkened so much, I thought she might actually strike out at me. It was a good thing she spent so much time on her nails. There's no way she'd ruin a manicure like that.

"Tessa, huh?" she asked. "That tramp was all over Brendon, begging him to come back to her. And then when he told her he'd moved on, she got all up in his face." She glanced at the closed door of the office where Brendon had died. "They fought in there a week ago." She looked meaningfully at me before adopting an unconcerned air. "Not that I was listening or anything."

"Of course not," I said. "Tessa told me that Brendon was seeing another woman?" I made it a question.

Beth snorted in a very unladylike way. "*She* was the other woman. *She* was the one who was little more than a fling. What Brendon and I had together was special. He was going to leave that cow of a wife of his to be with me."

"Really?" I asked, sneaking a glance toward Raymond Lawyer's door. It was closed, but I was pretty sure he was inside. I only hoped he couldn't hear our conversation from there. "I thought he was going to get back together with Heidi?"

Beth's face did something I couldn't decipher. She looked disgusted, aghast, and sad—all at the same time. It made her lips dance around on her face in what might have appeared comical, if it wasn't so pitiful.

"He was, the bastard." She bit her lip, took a deep breath, and then glared at me like it was my fault. "I think she threatened to take him for everything he had. It's the only thing that makes sense. He didn't love her. He loved me. She had to have said or done something horrible to make him turn away from the love of his life." A tear slid down her cheek.

Good Lord, but this woman was a mess.

I fumbled into my purse for a tissue and handed it to her. She took it and mumbled, "Thanks."

Still, a few tears wouldn't deter me. "So he broke up with you?" I asked, making it sound as if I was siding with her. Really, it wasn't that hard, considering how unlikable Brendon had been.

She nodded. "He said he was doing the right thing

for his family or something like that." She shrugged.
"'What family?' I asked him, but he didn't talk about it
any further. I don't know what happened to make him
change his mind, but I do know he loved me more than
either Tessa or Heidi." Her fist tightened on the tissue
as she glanced back at the empty office. It looked like
she wanted to go in there and break something.

"Were you here on the day he died?" I asked, making
sure not to sound like I was accusing her of anything.
She might have loved the man, but you know what they
say about a woman scorned. I wouldn't have put it past
her to kill him in a jealous rage, though rages usually
aren't thought out ahead of time. Plus, most people
didn't have peanut dust lying around.

"I was," she said. "This is my job."

"Did you happen to see anyone enter Brendon's
office that day, before he died?"

Beth frowned in a thoughtful way. "Well, Raymond always went in for a morning meeting with
Brendon, and Mason had stopped by earlier that day.
Come to think of it, Heidi came in right before he
went to lunch . . ." She trailed off then, with her frown
deepening.

"And what about you?" I asked. "Did you go into his
office at all that day?"

Beth lowered her eyes and started tearing the tissue
into tiny little pieces. "I usually do when he wants
something. It's my job."

It was my turn to frown. "Why are you still here?" I
asked, more to myself than to Beth. Something was
starting to bother me.

"Excuse me?"

"Why did you stay here after what Brendon did to

you? Wasn't it hard to stick around and see him every day after he dumped you?" It wasn't the most delicate of wording, but it did the job.

Beth shrugged and tossed the remains of her tissue into a wastebasket by her desk. "I suppose," she said. "But where else was I supposed to go? If I quit, the Lawyers would have made sure I never worked in Pine Hills again. They are a vindictive bunch, in case you haven't noticed." She sighed. "I had to keep the job so I could pay my bills, you know?"

I nodded. It made sense. Beth didn't look as if she was the brightest of bulbs, though she wasn't stupid, either. She could have found another job in town if she really wanted, but I had a feeling this one paid better than working at the local grocery store ever would. It would be far easier to suffer the Lawyers than to find another job, hoping you could pay the bills in between.

There was no doubt about it: Beth Milner might have once loved Brendon Lawyer, but he'd hurt her pretty badly. A part of her probably still loved him, yet a bigger part of her hated and resented him for what he'd done to her. People have killed for a lot less.

And what if she'd decided to kill him as a way to equal the score? The easiest way to do it would be to stick close to where he worked. If she'd quit, she wouldn't have had access to his office. Stay here and she could go in and out as she pleased, possibly even contaminate his food while he wasn't watching. All she would have to do was wait until he had to go to the restroom, slip some crushed peanuts into his food or drink, grab his EpiPen, and then sneak out before he was back. It would take all of a minute, maybe two. It was almost too easy.

For whatever reason, I flashed to the dust in Brendon's office. It had been all over the place, especially under the vent. It might have been too much of a risk to try to sneak in there to contaminate his food while he was taking a leak. But what if she found a way to set something else up while he was out of the office, something that would cause the dust to get into his food while she was out of the room?

Before I could think things through any further, a door opened and Raymond Lawyer stepped out of his office. He froze when he saw me, mouth open as if he'd been just about ready to speak. Beth jumped, startled, and looked at him guiltily, as if talking to me was a crime in itself.

"Oh, hi," I said, plastering on the fakest smile I'd ever attempted in my life. Just looking at the man terrified me. He wouldn't have to kill anyone physically; he could just stare them to death. "I was just talking with Ms. Milner here."

"Out," Raymond said, face turning red. "I want you out of here before I call the cops and have them drag you out." He took a threatening step my way. "I might have been lenient on you before, but I'm done playing nice."

I backed toward the door. Apparently, someone had informed Mr. Lawyer about my late-night intrusion into his office building. Either that or this was a very, very angry man.

"I'm sorry," I said. "I just wanted to talk."

I glanced toward Beth in the hopes she'd take my side. Instead, she was doing her best to look as if I'd been torturing her. Long strands of hair had somehow come loose from her bun and hung around her face, which was swollen and red, as if she'd been crying for hours. She held her hands up close to her face, like she was afraid I was going to strike her.

"If I *ever* see you in here again, harassing my employees, I'll make sure you're locked away for good!"

I bumped up against the door with a yelp. I scrambled for the handle and pushed my way out onto the sidewalk, afraid that Raymond would follow me out and chase me clear across the street, trying to kill me with his glower. I took two quick steps back and watched the door. I knew that if he came storming outside, I was going to run screaming in the other direction, like a girl in a horror movie.

But the door stayed closed, meaning I could keep hold of what little dignity I had left. A few pedestrians gave me odd looks as they passed. I wiped the sweat from my brow, breathed a sigh of relief, and then fumbled for my cell phone with trembling hands. I walked a few buildings down, just in case Raymond decided to come outside to check on me before I made the call.

The phone rang twice before Paul answered with a quick "Yeah?"

"Officer Dalton?" I asked to be sure. It was his personal number, but sometimes you never could be sure. "It's Krissy."

"Oh yeah, hi!" he said, sounding oddly chipper. "I'm on duty," he added, almost as an afterthought.

"I know." I vaguely wondered why he was answering his cell phone while on duty, but I shook it off. This *was* a small town. They did things differently here. Outside of catching a killer, he probably didn't have much else to do.

"So, what can I do for you? Is this about last night?" He sounded almost sheepish.

"Sort of," I said. "Well, I guess a lot."

"I thought I'd taken care of everything," he said with a sigh. "Is Mr. Lawyer causing a problem for you?"

"Oh, not really." I glanced back at the Lawyer's Insurance building and grimaced. If anyone was causing problems, it was me. "But I did think about something on my way into work today." I made a mental note to stop by so Vicki could verify my presence.

"What's that?" Before I could answer, he cut me off. "Hold on a second."

The sound from the other side became muffled. I imagined him standing at his desk, phone pressed against his toned abs while he flexed and smiled for another officer who was asking him how he managed to be so damn cute in his uniform. Obviously, she'd melt into a slobbering puddle at the sight of his dimples.

"Are you there?" Paul asked. I realized I'd been hearing his voice for a few seconds now.

"Yeah, sorry," I said. "I got distracted."

"It's okay. What was it you wanted to tell me?"

I took a deep breath. Now that I was about to say it, it sounded kind of stupid. I wasn't a cop. I wasn't even a detective. I was the owner of a coffee shop who just so happened to have a father who wrote mystery novels for a living and who had a knack for getting herself into trouble.

"The dust in Brendon Lawyer's office," I said, figuring I best say it now, since I'd already started. "Have you tested it?"

"For?"

"To make sure it was real dust."

Silence. And then, "Real dust? What other kind is there?"

"I mean, did you test it to see if it was peanut dust?"

More silence. "I'm pretty sure there'd be some around, since it was in his drink. I don't think anyone checked for sure, but I can look into it. Why?"

"Before Officer Buchannan caught us, I'd noticed the dust was thicker beneath the air vent. There was a circle on the cabinet that could very well have been left by a coffee cup. It got me thinking. The Lawyer building is always freezing cold. It tells me they run the air nonstop. What if someone took advantage and put peanut dust in the vents so it would blow into the room?"

Paul was silent even longer. In fact, if it wasn't for the faint sounds in the background, I might have thought the call had dropped.

"Still there?" I asked after I couldn't take the silence any longer. My vision of him went from all muscles and dimples to him quietly laughing at me for having such a stupid idea. I almost told him to forget it, when he spoke.

"I'll look into it," he said. "I don't think anyone checked the vent because we'd already found the dust in the food. Everyone knew about his allergy." I think the last wasn't a comment for me, but more of a rumination about how anyone could have planned this because Brendon's allergy wasn't a secret.

"I also learned that Raymond, Mason, and Heidi all went into Brendon's office that morning. Beth was working the desk at the time. I'm almost positive one of them is our killer."

"Where did you hear this?" Paul asked.

My mind raced. I didn't want to tell him I'd barged into Lawyer's Insurance, making a nuisance of myself again.

"Beth told me," I said. "I ran into her on my way to work."

"Ah."

"I hope that helps."

"It does." He took a deep breath and huffed into the phone. "I'd better go. It's going to take some work to convince Raymond to let us in. He thinks this is over and can be obstinate when he wants to be."

*Among other things,* I thought. "Let me know if you find anything out, okay?" I asked, hoping he wouldn't laugh at the idea. Why would he tell me anything? I wasn't officially on the case. I wasn't even a real detective.

"I will," Paul said. He sounded distracted, so I'm not so sure he realized what he was agreeing to do.

"Talk to you soon?" I tried not to sound too hopeful, but I don't think I did a very good job. I really wanted to see him again, outside of work, and was afraid our arrest ruined any chance of that.

"Sure. Gotta run." He clicked off.

I stood there a moment more, wondering if I'd done the right thing. Brendon had hurt so many people, maybe it was better he was dead. If it wasn't for the fact that someone had actually killed him, meaning there was a murderer on the loose, I very well might have dropped it.

But no matter how uncomfortable I might get, I knew, in the end, I was definitely doing the right thing.

# 17

"Don't get involved."

"Haven't we had this conversation already?"

Vicki rolled her eyes and set a cup of coffee in front of me. Without me having to say anything, she'd added the chocolate chip cookie.

"We have," she said, sliding into the chair across from me. "But you aren't listening." She rested a hand on my own. "You've done all you can. Now let the police do their jobs."

Speaking of the police, I glanced out the window toward the building across the street. A cruiser was pulled up out front, but I couldn't tell whose. I'd missed the officer getting out of the car because a customer had spilled her coffee trying to get a better view. It had missed landing in my lap by inches.

I was dying to go over and see who was there. Had Paul followed up on my tip himself? Or was it someone else, someone like Officer Buchannan, who wouldn't take anything I said seriously, simply because I'd gone on a date with what appeared to be his rival within the force?

"See," Vicki said, cutting into my train of thought. "This is exactly what I mean. You're looking over there like you can't stand the thought of letting someone else do all the work. You don't have to know everything that goes on here. Relax!"

I forced myself to look away. "That's not true," I said. "I'm here, aren't I? I could be over there this very minute, but I'm sipping coffee here with you, instead."

"Yeah," Vicki said. "How is your coffee?"

I glanced down; I had yet to touch it.

"You might be here physically," she went on. "I'm not so sure about mentally. You're going to get yourself hurt if you keep at it."

I knew she was right, but I wasn't about to admit it. I finally took a sip of coffee and closed my eyes. It felt good going down. I think my favorite part of it was the little bits of cookie that floated around in the caffeinated goodness.

Death by Coffee, like usual, was dead. The name was sounding more and more ominous, the longer it took to figure out exactly what had happened to Brendon Lawyer. So far, he'd been the only person who'd died after drinking our coffee, but that didn't mean the rest of the town wanted to risk it. The only person I'd seen since I'd gotten there earlier was the woman who tried to scald me with her coffee. She'd left five minutes ago, leaving Vicki and me alone.

Well, Trouble was there, too, but he was up in the bookstore, where he belonged. Chances were good that he was quietly living up to his name somewhere.

"I just want to know what they've found," I said, poking at the cookie, which had floated to the top. It would eventually soak up a good portion of the caffeine and would await consumption at the bottom of the cup. If nothing else, I had that to live for.

"And you will," Vicki said, "when the rest of the world does. You don't need to go snooping around anymore."

I grumbled and took another sip. *Mmm, cookie.* "What else am I going to do with my time?"

Vicki smiled and propped her chin on the backs of her hands. "Well, you could, I don't know, come to work here, perhaps?"

"And after we fold in a couple of days?"

She sighed. "We're not going to fold. You'll see. Business will pick up."

"Seems like we've had this conversation, too."

"You know I'm right, Krissy. Things have a way of working out."

Unless you're Brendon Lawyer, apparently.

My gaze traveled back to the window. A few onlookers were doing their best not to appear as if they were, well, *onlooking.* They milled around outside, going up one way, and then back the other. A few women stood off to the side, whispering to each other. I thought I caught a glimpse of Eleanor Winthrow at one point, but she vanished into the pacing masses before I could be sure.

"So, how did it go, anyway?"

Apparently, Vicki had been talking. I turned back to her with a "Hmm?"

"The date," she said. "With Officer Studly."

I couldn't stop the grin from rising to my face. "It went okay . . . until we got arrested."

Vicki's eyes just about popped from her head as she leaned forward. "Are you serious? What did you do?"

"Nothing bad," I said. "We just sort of snuck into Lawyer's Insurance and had a look around."

"Wait . . ." Vicki looked stunned and amused at the same time. "You convinced a cop to let you go snooping around at what very well might be a crime scene?"

"Maybe," I said with a smile.

"What did you offer him?" Her eyes dropped and I instantly knew what she was thinking.

"Of course not!" I said, actually offended. What did she take me for? "I sort of just convinced him, that's all."

"Mmm-hmm," she said, as if she knew exactly how I managed it. "And you ended up getting yourself arrested."

"*We* did." I made sure to stress the "we" part.

"How?" She held up a hand before I could answer. "Wait. I don't want to know." She shook her head. "An enabler."

"What?"

"He's an enabler."

I didn't have to ask who it was that she was talking about. "He is not! Maybe he just likes me."

"Is that how you impress a girl these days? Get her arrested when you take her to a place where *somebody got murdered*!"

"It wasn't like that. . . ."

I was saved from further taunting when the bell above the door jingled. Both Vicki and I turned in the hopes we actually had a customer.

"Ladies," Officer Dalton said as he sauntered into the room.

Vicki snorted and rose. "I've got a few things to do. You two have fun." She started to walk away and then glanced back at me. "Try not to get arrested this time."

She hurried up the stairs before I could formulate a response.

Paul walked over to where I sat. He paid Vicki only a cursory glance before turning those blue eyes on me. "She's an odd one, isn't she?"

"Tell me about it," I mumbled. "Would you like to sit?" I indicated Vicki's recently vacated chair.

He looked like he might say no; then he heaved a sigh and sat heavily down. He looked troubled, which wasn't much of a surprise considering where he'd just come from. Paul was in full uniform; and I had to admit, it felt a lot warmer in the room now that he was here.

"Did you find anything?" I asked, nodding my head toward the window.

Paul frowned and looked down toward the table rather than meet my eyes. He started to say something, and then his frown deepened. He leaned forward and peered into my coffee cup.

"What the hell is that?"

By now, the chocolate chip cookie had turned into a black-and-brown lump of sugary, chocolaty goodness. It took all of my self-control not to slurp it up.

"A cookie."

"Why do you have a cookie in your coffee?"

"Because it is tasty and I like it and . . . ," I trailed off, and gave him a helpless shrug. Sometimes there are things you just can't explain.

Paul shook his head as if he didn't even want to know any longer. He turned his attention, instead, to the window and the building across the street.

"You were right," he said after a long moment. "It wasn't your usual dust."

"You've tested it already?"

"The pinky test. But the real tests won't be in for a while."

"'The pinky test'?"

He mimed running his finger along the table and licking it. "The pinky test."

I shuddered. What if it had been the guy's dandruff or something? I reminded myself to wait until he brushed his teeth a few dozen times before ever trying to kiss him again.

"So it was peanut?"

He nodded. "As far as I can tell. I suppose all dust could taste like that—I haven't tasted much dust to see—but I highly doubt it."

"So I'm totally off the hook then? It wasn't my coffee that killed him?"

Paul finally met my eyes and dazzled me with his dimples. "You never were on the hook."

My heart did a little pitter-patter and all my muscles eased at once. I didn't realize how tense I'd become over this. No matter how much I told myself that my coffee had nothing to do with Brendon Lawyer's death, I'd still harbored doubts. Having it confirmed both relieved and worried me at the same time. It meant there actually *was* a killer out there.

I tore my gaze away from Paul's dimples and focused on my own hands. I needed to focus here, not get lost in the man's facial features, no matter how dreamy they might be.

"Did you talk to Raymond Lawyer?" I asked. "And the secretary, Beth?"

"I have." I could hear the amusement in Paul's voice. "But I haven't said anything about the dust to them yet.

I don't want word getting around. If the killer still thinks we view this as an accident, they are less likely to make a run for it."

I'd never even thought of it that way. "Do you think the secretary might have done it?"

"Beth?" he asked with a laugh. "She couldn't have hurt a fly, let alone someone like Brendon Lawyer. He'd walk all over her first. She's just . . ." He shrugged as if that said it all.

"Oh. I see."

"So I went in and told Raymond I wanted to check on a few things before we let him clean out the place," Paul went on. "He grumbled a lot about it, but he let me in, anyway. I opened the vent and found a small amount of dust trapped up against the base. If the lip hadn't been there, all of the evidence would have blown away." He patted a bulge in his chest pocket, telling me he had some of the dust on him.

"Then it's definitely murder?" I dreaded the answer.

"I'm not ready to say that." Paul looked around the room as if one of the empty chairs might overhear. He frowned once more and then stood. "I should get the evidence in so we can run the proper tests," he said. "Though I'm pretty sure I already know what we'll find."

"Great." I stood. "Let me know."

"Even if it is peanut dust, I doubt we'll be able to use it as evidence in court."

"Why not?"

Paul sighed. "The room has sat open for a few days now. A good lawyer will say that anyone could have come in and planted the dust at any time. And really, it isn't like we're going to get fingerprints from the dust particles, even if we do prove that he was murdered. There were no fingerprints on the vent."

My stomach plummeted. "Oh."

He nodded distractedly. "But I will let you know what I find out." He turned toward the door.

My heart stopped its pitter-pattering and instead did a huge leap and a hiccup. "Paul?" I asked, too afraid to move his way, lest I scare him off.

He stopped and turned to me. "Yeah?"

"Is everything all right?"

He wiped a hand over his face, looking suddenly a lot more tired than he had before. "As much as it can be, I suppose. I just found out for sure our man was probably murdered. I'm going to have to log extra hours looking into this, especially at his wife."

"It's not her." It was out of my mouth before I could stop it.

"Why do you say that?" He didn't sound offended or overly interested. In fact, he just sounded weary.

"Just a hunch," I said. "I'd focus on her mom. And maybe the mistress." I paused. "Both of them."

Paul cracked the faintest of smiles, gave me one last nod, and then strode out of the building. I watched him go, wondering if I'd done something wrong. I would have thought he would have at least brought up our date, especially after Vicki's parting jab, but there'd been nothing. Had I already ruined my chance with him? Considering my usual luck with men, it wouldn't be much of a surprise.

Vicki came up beside me and watched Officer Dalton get into his car and drive off. Trouble was purring contentedly in her arms.

"You hear?" I asked, unable to look away from the dwindling shape of his car.

"I heard."

"Think it'll help business? We can advertise that our coffee doesn't actually cause death."

She snorted a laugh. "Where's the fun in that?"

Paul's car vanished around the corner and my world got just a bit darker. Trouble batted me once on the arm as if to tell me to forget about Paul; there were a lot of men in Pine Hills.

Of course, the little troublemaker was right. There *were* lots of men in Pine Hills. I just hoped that when I did find one, he wouldn't end up like Brendon Lawyer.

Or worse: like the person who had killed him.

# 18

I hung around the shop for a few hours more because, well, what else was I going to do? I wasn't really interested in going back home just so I could mope around. I was completely out of Rocky Road and didn't feel up to going to the store to get some more.

So, in the end, I chose to come to work, after all.

A few customers came in, bought coffee, and one elderly man bought a book. Lena appeared on her skateboard, bought a red eye, and then rolled down the sidewalk, sipping it. I hoped she was careful or she could add severe burns to her list of bodily injuries she'd sustained while riding that death trap.

I must have been moping a little too much, because after two hours of me wiping down tables and looking gloomily out the window, Vicki had had enough.

"Go," she said. "Find something to do."

"I have something to do," I said, indicating the thrice-washed table, which no one had sat at all day.

"Please," she said. "You're going to drive me crazy."

"I can't just leave you here alone," I protested weakly.

She gave me her movie star smile and shooed me

toward the door. "I can handle this. If we suddenly get busy, I'll call."

And out the door I went, still wearing the apron I'd put on. I considered taking it off and handing it to Vicki, but I was pretty sure any movements that didn't equate to me getting farther away from Death by Coffee would end up earning me another firm reprimand—and I was all reprimanded out.

I left the apron on as I crossed the street to where I'd left my car. I figured if nothing else, it might serve well as advertising. The apron *did* have DEATH BY COFFEE on the front.

It took monumental effort not to poke my head into Lawyer's Insurance as I passed. I had no idea what good it would do, considering Raymond would bite my head off the moment he saw me, and the police had once again been over the office. A part of me wanted to do it, anyway, just to irk the old man a little more before I headed home. But then again, if Raymond Lawyer had killed his son, he might kill me off, just to be rid of me.

I turned my back on the place just as the door flew open, nearly smashing into the wall. Mason Lawyer stormed out, face red. A few choice words hurled by his father chased after him. He stopped when he saw me, and the frown he already wore deepened.

"You again," he said, as if I'd been out here waiting for him on purpose.

"Sorry," I said. "I was just heading home." I gestured toward my car.

His eyes narrowed as if he didn't quite believe me, and then he gave a frustrated sigh. "Whatever."

And then, like magic, both our stomachs growled at the same exact instant.

Mason glared at me like I'd planned it, and I did my best to look like it had not happened at all. Despite my best efforts, I could feel my face reddening.

"I haven't eaten," I said. Coffee and cookies didn't count.

Mason ran his fingers through his hair. "Yeah, me either."

Okay. I might have restrained myself from rushing over the moment I'd seen the cop car pull up in front of Lawyer's Insurance, and I might have avoided begging Officer Dalton for every ounce of information he had about the case, and I'd even stopped myself from making matters worse by tweaking Raymond Lawyer's nose by sticking my own nose where it didn't belong, but there was absolutely no way on God's green earth that I could possibly pass up this opportunity.

"You know," I said, taking a step toward him, "I'm new in town. I'd love to sit down and talk for a little bit."

Mason looked at me as if I'd just sprung horns and pooped on the sidewalk.

"Really," I said hurriedly, before he could run screaming in the other direction. "I just want to talk."

Mason looked either way as if he was looking for someone to rescue him before he grudgingly turned back to me. I gave him the smile I'd learned from Vicki, the one that would have earned her any role she could ever want. Mason visibly melted at the sight.

"Okay, fine," he said. "At least take that thing off."

The apron left my waist in a flurry of arms and hair. I balled it up and hid it behind my back, like I thought he might forget about it because he could no longer see it.

"I'll drive," he said, walking toward his car.

There was a moment where that little voice in my head started screaming: *Mason Lawyer could be a murderer!* If I got into his car with him, he could drive off with me, kill me, and then leave me lying in a ditch somewhere. No one would know I'd gone with him. I knew—just *knew*—that anyone on the streets now wouldn't remember seeing me with him.

But I really did want to talk to him. If I turned him down now, or went to my car and followed him instead of riding with him, I'd lose a golden opportunity to get to know the man. Without me in his car, he might even change his mind and try to lose me. It wouldn't be hard; I barely knew my way around Pine Hills. A few quick turns down the right side streets and I'd be as lost as if I'd been dropped into the middle of Eastern Europe.

I smiled, hoping it didn't look too strained, and slid into his car, next to him.

There are some people you should never ride with: Mason Lawyer was one of them.

He clearly believed the rules of safety and sense didn't apply to him. He stomped on the gas the moment my door was closed. I was thrown into my seat with a huff of expelled breath. I scrambled for the seat belt as he turned the corner, and I just got it snapped into place as I slammed against the door. His engine revved and we blew through a light that had just turned red.

I have to admit, I spent most of the ride with my eyes closed and my hands gripping what I'd always lovingly referred to as the "Oh, shit" bar, instead of actually saying anything. By the time we screeched to a halt outside J&E's Banyon Tree, my hand felt as if it was locked into the claw position. I just about had to pry my fingers loose.

Mason didn't even wait for me to get out of the car before he was inside the diner. I closed the door and ran after him, knowing I looked a mess after my terrifying ride. The guy was a legitimate maniac.

A waitress fluttered over as soon as we were seated. She took our orders—I ordered the grilled cheese and a water, while Mason ordered something called the Tree Burger—and then whisked herself away as if she was going to float off into the clouds and marry the first man who looked at her twice. I had a feeling she needed to cut back on both the sugar and the caffeine.

"What do you want to talk to me about?" Mason asked, folding his napkin onto his lap.

"I know it's hard, but I thought we could discuss your family."

He scowled, but he didn't say anything. The waitress set our drinks onto the table and then vanished again without a word.

"Did you know your brother was cheating on his wife?" I blurted out the question both because I was afraid of him and because I hoped to catch him off guard. I wasn't sure what I'd learn from it—but, hey, I never said I was good at this.

Mason's scowl turned into something that would scare little kids. "I knew," he said. "Everyone did."

"Did you know he had more than one mistress?"

"Of course." He took a long drink of the tea he'd ordered and just about slammed the cup back down. Iced tea sloshed over the side and splattered onto the table. "Why does this matter?"

I bit my lip. I couldn't tell him the police suspected his brother had been murdered. If Mason had killed Brendon, I didn't want him to know I suspected anything, either. I really didn't want to end up stuffed in his trunk.

"I don't know," I said with what I hoped to be an indifferent shrug. "It happened so close to where I work—it was kind of shocking. And then there are the rumors . . ."

That caught Mason's attention. He tried not to show it, but I saw the way his eyes widened for a heartbeat, how his hand froze for an instant as he set his silverware onto the table in an orderly fashion.

"What kind of rumors?"

Before I could speak, the waitress returned. She placed a scorched thing that was supposed to be a grilled cheese in front of me and a strange concoction in front of Mason. The bun had been toasted to a dark brown and I was pretty sure it consisted of ham, bacon, hamburger, lettuce, maple syrup, and almond slices. My own heart cried out in protest.

"Anything else?" our waitress asked. Both Mason and I shook our heads and she vanished as if she'd just gone up in a poof of smoke.

I took a moment to think about how I was going to word what I was going to say next. I tried my grilled cheese and found that despite its blackened state, it wasn't half bad. The cheese might have been a little too gooey and the blackened bread a bit on the crunchy side, but it was still far better than anything I ever produced out of my own kitchen.

"You were saying something about rumors?" Mason prodded just before taking a bite out of his sandwich.

Surprisingly, he didn't keel over from heart failure right then and there.

"Well," I said, leaning forward, "I'd heard a rumor that Heidi was so upset with her husband, she chose to, well . . . ," I trailed off, suddenly uncertain I should go on. I was about to accuse this guy of something that some people view just as bad as murder. He might decide to dispense with the trying to kill me in a round-about way and instead force me to eat his heart attack on a bun.

But there was nothing I could do but go on. If I stopped now, then I might never get a straight answer from him ever again. And with the way everyone else had been treating me lately . . .

I glanced around the diner and lowered my voice. The place was actually pretty packed, making me feel worse about the state of my own store. If only a third of the people I saw drinking coffee here would go to Death by Coffee, we'd be set.

"I heard you and Heidi had gotten together."

Mason snorted as if dismissing the idea, but his hands squeezed on his sandwich, squirting maple syrup and almond slivers onto his plate.

"Where did you hear a thing like that?"

I shrugged, hoping he wouldn't kill me for bringing it up. "Around."

Mason ground his teeth together and looked at his Tree Burger like he might take his frustrations out on it instead of my head, which was a good thing in my book.

"It's a lie," he said, still staring into his toasted bun. "Nothing but a pack of lies."

"So you and Heidi never . . . ?"

"Of course not!" he roared. Everyone in the place turned to look at us. They stared for a few moments before turning back to their meals, though I could tell most of them were now leaning our way in the hopes of catching some juicy gossip of their own.

Mason glanced from side to side, set his Tree Burger down, and then leaned closer.

"Look," he said at a near whisper, "Heidi and I are friends. Brendon was a dick to her and she needed a shoulder to cry upon. I lent her that shoulder, but I would *never* take advantage of her. Everyone is so busy blaming each other for what happened to Brendon, no one is seeing how torn up Heidi is over his death. Maybe if more people cared about something other than themselves, they'd see it."

I cringed back into my chair. I detected nothing but honesty in Mason's voice. I felt like a royal jerk for even thinking he could have had anything to do with Heidi, outside friendship, let alone with Brendon's death.

"I'm sorry," I said. "I didn't mean to insinuate anything."

He smirked. "Of course, you did. Right now, that's pretty par for the course around here."

"What do you mean by that?"

Mason started to speak, but I never got to hear what he had to say.

"Out!"

I just about fell out of my chair. The command had been barked directly into my right ear. I managed to choke back my yelp of surprise as I turned into the furious face of Judith Banyon.

"I said, get out!"

"What did I do?" I asked. I snatched up my grilled cheese and held it up like a tiny blackened shield against the woman's rage.

"You opened up that dirty place downtown just to steal my customers," she all but shouted into my face. "I won't have you here advertising yourself."

My mouth fell open. I wasn't advertising myself. I wasn't a product. I'd even taken my apron off before coming. It was sitting in Mason's backseat.

"Judy, please." The soft voice came from behind her. Eddie stood there, looking chagrined.

*"Please, nothing,"* Judith snarled. "This woman is here to steal our customers. She wants to kill them with her poison coffee!"

"That wasn't my fault!"

"I don't care!" Judith roared. She bared her teeth at me. They looked strong enough to snap steel, so I stood, holding my flimsy shield protectively in front of me.

"We just came in for a bite to eat," Mason said, his voice full of reason. Out of all of the Lawyers I'd met, he sounded like he could actually have *been* a lawyer. He could talk a bear out of its cave, his voice was that smooth. "We aren't here to cause trouble."

Judith snorted. "If you knew what kind of person you were dining with, you wouldn't feel so secure, mister." She waved a finger in front of his face. "I have my sources, you know."

And I knew who that source was. She was probably sitting in front of her window even now, waiting for me to get home with her binoculars at the ready.

"I have it on good authority that this woman is nothing more than a harlot who can't even make coffee that doesn't kill anyone who drinks it." Judith glared at me. "She's even trying to seduce sweet Jules Phan!" That earned her a gasp from the crowd. "I've even heard rumors she screams about killing people while in her own home."

I was about to protest, but then I remembered how I'd threatened Misfit. I doubted anyone would care that I was referring to my cat, and not an actual human being.

Mason looked longingly at his Tree Burger. If anyone should be accused of trying to kill people with their food, it was Judith.

"Go," she snarled, her attention back to me. "Never come back."

With a sigh Mason rose. "Let's go," he said. "I've lost my appetite, anyway."

I took one last bite of my meal, tossed the remains onto my plate, and then hurried out of J&E's before Judith could strangle me with her apron. She looked mean enough to do it.

"Is everyone in this town insane?" I muttered, walking back to Mason's car.

To my surprise, right then, he laughed. "They might be." He opened his car door and ducked inside. "They very well might be."

# 19

Unpacking is a chore best left for someone else. I managed to unpack my clothes and Misfit's kitty treats before I called it a night. I couldn't focus on the job and, quite frankly, I was beginning to wonder if living out of boxes was really so bad. I could always get things out when I needed them and then put them away afterward.

Misfit was curled up on the couch, watching me with one eye as I sagged into my recliner. What I really wanted to do was talk to Heidi Lawyer to find out what man she'd been sleeping with. Once I had that bit of information, I was sure everything else would fall into place.

"What do you think?" I asked the half-comatose cat. He kicked out with one back foot and turned his head away from me.

"Fine," I said, rising. I couldn't sit there anymore, doing nothing. "I'll be back in a bit."

I made sure to fill Misfit's bowl with fresh water and sprinkled a few treats onto the counter for when he woke up. If I didn't, he'd tear into the box himself and I'd have a bigger mess to deal with later.

I was pretty sure Heidi would be home this time of night. It wasn't so late that she would be in bed, but not so early that she'd be out working—though to do that so soon after her husband's death would be pretty callous, if you asked me. It was odd how Pine Hills seemed to shut down earlier than the rest of the world. Is that what small-town living was all about?

I was about to get into my car when headlights from another vehicle came down the street. The car hesitated just in front of the Phan driveway before continuing down to my own, where the little car parked behind me. Jules Phan got out, wearing a startling pink suit with a polka-dotted tie.

"Hi, Krissy," he said as he approached. "You looked like you needed someone to talk to."

I raised my eyebrows at him. "You could see that from all the way over there?" I indicated the end of his driveway with a nod of my head.

He chuckled. "Well, I've seen you around town and you've looked . . . *upset?* I'm not sure that's the right word."

I sighed and leaned against my car. "I suppose I have been. A lot has been going on lately."

"About Brendon?"

I nodded. "I know I shouldn't get involved, but I'm positive someone killed him. This wasn't an accident. If I could just put all of the pieces together, I know I'd be able to crack this thing wide open."

Jules was giving me a wide-eyed look. "So you are positive he's been murdered? I haven't heard anything about it." He gave me an embarrassed smirk. "Well,

I've heard things around town, but you know how some of the ladies gossip." His gaze traveled to Eleanor's house. A curtain swished closed.

My jaw tightened as I remembered all the nice things Eleanor Winthrow had been telling the Banyons about me. I forced a smile and pushed my anger away. There was no use getting bent out of shape about it. It would all work out okay in the end.

"I'm pretty sure he was," I said. "He never would have forgotten his EpiPen." I paused. "But I don't have any proof, really."

Jules nodded slowly. He looked mildly uncomfortable. He kept looking back at his house like he thought it might be the only place he'd be safe.

Finally he sighed and gave me a sad smile. "It is terrible, no matter what happened," he said. He glanced once more at his house. "Well, I best get home. Maestro is probably having a fit right about now. He'll need to be let out."

"Sure," I said. I could tell what he really wanted to do was walk away from the conversation, but I let his excuse slide. If I wasn't so involved in the case already, I might feel the same.

Jules started to get into his car, but I stopped him as another thought hit me.

"Hey, Jules," I said.

"Hmm?"

"Do you happen to know if Heidi Lawyer was seeing anyone outside of her husband?" It was a stab in the dark, but Jules Phan seemed pretty in touch with the pulse of the town. It might save me a trip.

He thought about it a moment, tapping a finger on

his chin. I noted the nail was polished pink, with little yellow smiley faces.

"Sorry," he said with a shake of his head. "If she was, then she's kept it pretty secret. I've heard nothing of the sort."

"Thanks."

Jules got into his car as I slid into my own. He backed out, honked once, and then headed for his own driveway.

I sat there a moment longer, thinking. Heidi had done a pretty good job of concealing her relationship, which seemed to be a hard thing to do in a town like this. It was a wonder a memo hadn't been sent to the local gossip club. She'd been far more careful with her indiscretion than her husband had been.

I started up the car and backed down the drive. If the rumor mill didn't know whom she'd cheated with, then I'd just have to go and ask her.

Apprehension for what I was about to do built up as I got closer to the Lawyer residence. Heidi was a wreck—which was totally understandable—and I hated having to ask her more questions, but it seemed like I was the only person asking them. Sure, it would probably be best if I let the police handle it, but I'd seen nothing that led me to believe they would do anything about my theories.

By the time I pulled up in front of the Lawyer house, it was starting to get dark. A light was on inside and the driveway was clear. I got out of the car, mentally prepping myself to ask the hard questions as I strode toward the door. This was going to be difficult, to say the least.

I rapped on the door, forgoing the doorbell. A moment later the door opened and Regina Harper appeared. Her face instantly turned a deep shade of purple.

"I thought I told you to leave us alone," she said through clenched teeth.

"I just need to talk to Heidi for one second." I tried to look past her, but Regina moved to stand in my way.

"Go," she said. "If you ever come back here, I'll have you arrested."

It seemed like a lot of people were saying that lately. How could Raymond Lawyer hate this woman as much as he did when the two of them thought so much alike? Maybe getting the both of them together would be like an anger time bomb that increased in power the closer they were to one another.

"Please," I said. Then on a whim I shouted past her, "Heidi! Are you there?"

"Get out!" Regina shouted. She actually pushed me hard on the shoulder, which surprised me, considering how it could have damaged one of her nails. *"Now."*

"Mom . . . let her in. It's okay." Heidi sounded like she'd been crying. Again. With a mother like Regina Harper, I'd probably cry a lot, too.

Despite her daughter's words, Regina steadfastly refused to move. She lowered her voice and gave me a glare I was sure she'd used on her daughter a million times. It could have scared the bear Mason talked out right back into its cave, but I refused to be swayed.

"You've done enough," she hissed at me. "I'm tired of you snooping around, making my daughter's life miserable. Can't you just let it go?"

"No," I said. "I can't."

And then I went for broke.

Regina was wearing heels and wasn't a big woman

by any stretch of the imagination. I might not be in the best shape in the world, but I was wearing tennis shoes and was determined. I rushed forward and pushed past the older woman before she could stop me. She grabbed my arm with an insulted gasp. I jerked away, earning myself a couple of scrapes from her nails, though only one of them bled.

"Heidi?" I called, hurrying into the house. I found her sitting in the living room, red-faced. She looked so weary, I felt guilty for disturbing her, but I had to know.

"Get out! Get out! Get out!" Regina stormed into the room, took one look at the pleading eyes of her daughter, and then threw up her hands before storming right back out.

"I'm sorry about my mom," Heidi said. Her voice was husky from all of the crying. And probably some of the shouting she'd more than likely done lately. I couldn't imagine she'd sit back and let her mom treat her like that without ever fighting back. "She's only trying to look out for me."

I immediately wondered how far Regina would go to protect her daughter, but I didn't voice the thought. I didn't need to be pointing fingers when I didn't have any proof, especially while Heidi was so miserable. She didn't need to think her mother might have killed her husband, even if it was true.

"Heidi, I have to know. Who did you cheat on your husband with?" I spit it out fast, hoping the bluntness of the question would cause her to answer automatically.

She opened her mouth, but no sound came out. The look she gave me was one of a wild animal, trapped in a corner with no way out. Her eyes brimmed over with tears and she buried her face in her hands.

"I can't. Brendon . . . I'm so sorry." Sobs wracked her body.

I bit my lip. The right thing to do would be to go over and comfort her and then leave without asking any more painful questions. If I hadn't already dismissed Heidi as a suspect, I would have now. Sure, it could be guilt that was causing her to act like this, but I didn't believe it. She genuinely missed her husband.

"Heidi," I said, forcing myself to go on. Sometimes you just have to press forward, even if you don't want to. It might be the only chance I'd get. "Who was it? Could he have hurt Brendon?"

She shook her head and continued to sob. The woman was a total mess and I was only making it worse. I wasn't even sure she was shaking her head because she didn't think the guy could have hurt her husband or if she was simply refusing to answer. As far as I knew, she was no longer hearing anything I said.

I knelt in front of her and squeezed her knee. "I know it's hard," I said. "But if there is even a chance this person could have killed Brendon, I need to know." I paused. "The police need to know," I amended.

As if on cue, I heard sirens in the distance. Regina entered the room with a smile.

"I estimate you have about two minutes."

I shot her a glare and then turned back to Heidi. "Please," I said, "just tell me."

"Leave her alone. You've done enough."

Heidi covered her ears and continued to shake her head. There was no way I was going to get anything out of her, so I turned to her mother, instead.

"Who did she cheat on Brendon with?"

Regina showed me her teeth in a feral snarl. "I don't have to tell you anything."

"And if it solves the murder?"

"I don't care. Whoever killed the man deserves a medal."

"Mom!" Heidi sobbed even harder.

It was then I began to wonder what Regina had been saying to her daughter before I'd gotten there. The poor woman had already been in tears when I arrived, as if her mom had been doing or saying something Heidi didn't want to hear. Could she have been confessing to the murder? Had she been trying to force her daughter to forget about Brendon and run off and marry some rich guy who could support the both of them? I had no way of knowing, and asking would get me nowhere.

"I'll find out," I said. "Either from you or from someone else."

"It'll be hard from your jail cell." Regina glanced at the gold watch on her wrist. "Less than a minute."

I cursed silently and took one last imploring glance at Heidi. She was in no condition to acknowledge my presence anymore.

I started for the door, figuring I best cut my losses before the police arrived, but Regina stood in my way.

"I don't think so," she said.

The sirens were getting closer and were moving fast. I'm not sure what she'd told the cops to get them to hurry so much, but I imagine it couldn't have been good for my image. Despite the fact I was the one who was bleeding, I was pretty sure Regina would say I'd attacked her on my way in.

"Let me go," I said. I took a step to go past her and

she moved to stand in my way. I could easily shove her over, what with her small size and heels, but that would only put me in more hot water.

"No."

"Mom!"

*"Argh!"*

The sirens reached a crescendo and a cruiser tore into the driveway like the place was on fire. The car door opened and footsteps hurried to the door. I could hear the jangling of keys. I prayed the officer on duty would be Paul Dalton. He'd defuse the situation without arresting me for something I didn't do.

"Mrs. Harper? Mrs. Lawyer? Are you okay?"

I recognized the voice. It was definitely not Paul.

"She's still in here," Regina called. "The door's open. Hurry before she escapes."

*"Escapes?"* I gasped. I was just standing there, without a weapon, without any attempt to run. She was acting as if she'd caught me in the middle of ransacking the place.

The door opened and Officer Buchannan came in. He took one look at me and his face erupted into a savage grin.

"Well, well, well," he said. "Looks like you can't seem to stay out of trouble." He reached into a pocket and came out with a zip strip. "Please turn around." His smile was as victorious as Regina's.

I wanted to argue, to tell him what had really happened, but then again, what really happened was that I'd arrived uninvited, forced my way into the house, past the older woman, to ask Heidi painful questions about an active police case. Was there any possible way I could spin this and *not* make myself look like an idiot?

I turned and put my hands behind my back. Officer Buchannan read me my rights as he grabbed my wrists a little harder than he needed to and zipped me up. He leaned forward so that when he spoke, I could feel his hot breath on my neck. It smelled vaguely of tacos.

"Let's go," he said, spinning me around. And then, to himself more than me, he added. "Oh, I am *so* going to love this."

## 20

"I didn't do anything wrong," I said, shifting uncomfortably on the couch in the interrogation room. Officer Buchannan was leaning against the wall, leering at me, in almost the exact same position he had been in the last time I'd been here. Unfortunately, Paul wasn't at my side to make me feel better. Neither was his mother, though I had a feeling I was going to be seeing her soon enough.

Buchannan smiled at me, nodded once, and then continued to stare.

Grumbling to myself, I leaned back, hoping the wait wouldn't be too terribly long. Buchannan hadn't taken the zip strips off. That meant that by leaning against the back of the couch, I was putting pressure on my shoulders and wrists. Right then, though, I didn't care. If it had been any other cop, I probably would have been told to go home. But no . . . I got Buchannan, the man with a chip on his shoulder. His only purpose in life seemed to be causing me trouble, and all because I'd gone on a date with Officer Dalton.

I'd already tried to reason with him, but it was like

talking to a wall. Heidi had told me to come in and Regina had grabbed for *me*, not the other way around. There really wasn't anything they could charge me with.

Well, maybe obstruction. That one would be kind of hard to dodge.

The door opened and a tired-looking Chief Dalton entered. She looked me up and down, glanced over at Buchannan, who was grinning his head off, and then heaved a huge sigh.

"What now?" she asked. "Can't you stay out of trouble?"

"I didn't do anything wrong!" Maybe the claim would work on her, whereas it had been met with smugness by Buchannan.

"Mrs. Regina Harper claims you shoved her out of the way to enter the Lawyer residence uninvited in order to ask questions best left to the police."

"I didn't shove her," I said. "Heidi invited me in and Regina was in the way. I may have bumped her, but she grabbed for me!" I twisted around on the couch to show her my arm, where only one mark remained. The scratch looked so small, it could easily have come from my cat. "I swear I wasn't causing any trouble."

"Well," Patricia said, sitting down on the edge of the table. "Heidi Lawyer apparently agrees with you. Her mother doesn't like it and has tried to press charges, but her daughter won't have any of it." She glanced back at Buchannan. "Why am I here exactly?"

His smug smile slipped a little. "I thought you would want to know about this."

"I could have read the report." Patricia stood. "And

why is she still stripped? Why was it done at all? Did she try to resist?"

"Well, no. . . ."

"Goddamn it, Buchannan." She turned to me. "Stand up."

I stood so fast, it was as if I'd been shot. Patricia spun me around, whipped out a knife, and then cut away the zip strip. I immediately started rubbing at my wrists.

"I'm tired of this," she said, walking over to where Buchannan was now cowering. "Just because she's boffing my boy doesn't mean you need to make an example out of her."

"Wait!" I said. "I'm not . . . boffing him." If I hadn't already been blushing with embarrassment, I sure was now.

"Get out and do your job," Patricia said, stepping back so Buchannan could leave. He gave me a glare that could have melted steel before storming out.

"The man is intent on making me look bad," Patricia said, her voice much softer now. "He thinks I'm treating you differently just because of who you're with."

I didn't know what to say to that. Denying sleeping with her son seemed out of the question—she was going to believe what she wanted to believe—and I really didn't want to try to explain why I'd actually been over to the Lawyer place. I had no idea how Chief Dalton would react.

"You're lucky this time," she said. "Regina Harper isn't one to mess with. That woman will sue anyone who irritates her."

"Heidi told me I could come in." I sounded petulant. It probably wasn't the best way to win her over.

"Which is probably why you aren't sitting in a cell right now."

Okay, that was fair. I really needed to start thinking about my plans ahead of time. If I kept acting on a whim, I was either going to get myself into some serious trouble, or maybe end up as the murderer's next victim. Neither scenario was all that appealing.

"I don't want you going over there again," Patricia said, putting on her serious "I'm in charge" voice.

"But what if . . . ," I trailed off at the look she was giving me. There would be no *buts* here.

"No *buts*," she said, as if to prove the point. "You don't go over there. If you do, I'm going to have to stick you in the cell you've manage to avoid so far." She gave me a sympathetic look. "I'll have no choice."

I grumbled a bit at this, but I nodded. I'd just have to find another way to get the information from Heidi. Without getting arrested, of course.

"Now," Patricia said, standing, "I've had someone take your car from impound back to your house."

"What? How am I going to get home?"

Patricia smiled. "I got you a ride." She turned toward the door, paused, and then looked back at me. "It'll only be a few minutes more before you can go. Sit tight and please try to stay out of trouble."

I sat back down as she walked out, closing the door behind her.

I couldn't believe this was happening to me. *Again.* A few days in Pine Hills and I'd already made more trips to the local police department than I had in all my time back home. It was as if this little town was truly bad for me. It wouldn't surprise me in the slightest if I started forming hives or warts or something.

I just had to keep reminding myself that it would all work out in the end. As long as Death by Coffee survived, I would, too.

Then again, with the way things were going, I wasn't so sure I'd have a job in a few weeks. We could only keep going at our current rate for so long. If we didn't start pulling in customers soon, we'd be forced to give up the store, move back home with our parents, and more than likely have to start selling blood just so we could afford ramen noodles.

Could things possibly get any worse?

The door clicked open; and as if to prove that my night could indeed get worse, Paul Dalton walked in.

"Here again, I see," he said, coming inside.

"I take it you're my ride?"

He nodded. Of course, he was. His mother was still trying to play matchmaker, even though I'd been arrested twice already. Maybe she thought her son would be able to tame me.

"Mom told me what happened," he said, leaning on the same spot on the table where Patricia had just vacated. I wondered if that is where all of the cops leaned when they were about to lecture someone.

"It was blown out of proportion," I said. "Heidi told me I could go in. Regina just got in the way."

"You shouldn't have been over there, anyway."

"And why not?" I was getting angry about everyone telling me what I could and couldn't do. Sure, they might be right, but darn it, I wanted to make my own choices—no matter how dumb they might be.

"Because you are involving yourself in an active police investigation, perhaps?" He glanced down at my chest. "I don't see a badge. Do you?"

I looked away. "No." I crossed my arms and pouted. I felt sixteen again. If only I could recapture the smooth skin and trim body, then perhaps it wouldn't be so bad.

"It's too dangerous to go poking around on your own, okay?"

I nodded, frowned, and then turned to look at him, some of my stubbornness returning. "But I've learned some things *on my own*."

Paul looked interested, but he tried to hide it. I think he'd been told to make sure I understood not to get involved, yet he was part of the reason I *was* involved. If he hadn't taken me to Lawyer's Insurance that night, I might not have continued with my own private investigation. In a way . . . this was all sort of *his* fault.

*Yeah, keep telling yourself that, Krissy.*

"First, do you know for sure if the dust was peanut?"

He nodded. "It was."

"Okay. We know that Brendon Lawyer had two mistresses, one of them being his secretary, Beth."

"We do."

"And if the dust was placed inside the vent, then whoever killed him had to have access to the room, right?"

"Right."

"That could be anyone who worked there, as well as those who had gone in to see Brendon that day, correct?"

"Yeah." Paul's face was passive. He was listening intently, but I had a feeling I wasn't telling him anything he didn't already know.

"And maybe someone who managed to get into the office the night before could have planted it?"

"Perhaps."

I considered telling him about Heidi's mysterious boyfriend, but I decided against it. I wasn't sure it mattered. Just because she was seeing someone on the side didn't mean she, or the man she'd cheated with, had killed Brendon. Maybe once I knew more, I could tell Paul. Until then, I wanted to cause Heidi as little grief as possible. Regina had been right about something; I'd already done enough.

"Did you know Brendon and Heidi were going to get back together?"

Paul frowned. "Where did you hear this?"

"Rumors," I said with a shrug. "Heidi herself."

Paul's frown deepened. "She didn't tell me this."

"I don't think many people knew." I gave him a smug smile, one that told him I actually *was* being helpful. "But she told me." I didn't tell him that my interrogations had brought her to tears.

Paul scratched his head and then rubbed at his face. He looked tired, as if he'd been called in just after settling down for the night. Me being the reason he wasn't sitting snug in his favorite chair or lying shirtless in bed probably wasn't making much of a good impression.

I melted just a little. Paul Dalton. Shirtless. It sounded good to me.

"Krissy?"

"Hmm? What?" I came back to reality in a hurry. My traitor face flared red and I cleared my throat to hide the hitch in my voice. I knew he wouldn't know what I'd been thinking, but damn . . . he was right there. I didn't need to be daydreaming about him taking his clothes off, bit by bit, flashing those scrumptious dimples at me all the while. . . .

"Krissy." This time his voice was firm.

"Sorry," I said, rising. If I sat much longer, I'd probably drift off into dimple-filled dreams.

Paul sighed. "I said, I don't really see how the Lawyers getting back together is relevant. I suppose someone could have been jealous, like the mistresses, but . . ." He shrugged.

"It was Heidi's idea," I said. "She forgave him."

"Why's that?"

How could I answer that without smearing Heidi's name? "I don't know," I said, mentally punching myself for lying. He was *so* going to hate me when I finally told him the truth. "Maybe she just decided she couldn't live without him anymore."

"Uh-huh." He said it like he didn't believe it. I admit, the story was sort of hard to swallow after you'd met Brendon.

"It could be relevant," I said, hoping Paul wouldn't totally dismiss it. "Like you said, maybe one of the mistresses got angry after Brendon broke it off. Maybe she wanted him all for herself."

"Then why not go after Heidi?"

"Maybe she was just so mad at him, she figured that if she couldn't have him, no one would. Brendon wasn't exactly the nicest of guys. She could have been fed up with him."

"Maybe," Paul said. He glanced at his watch and yawned. "I think it'll be okay to take you out of here now. I'm to drive you home."

I gathered myself and followed Paul out the door. This time, when we walked through the station, all eyes were on me. There was suspicion there. I was getting the feeling that not everyone was certain of my innocence. I was beginning to wonder if Paul was starting to question whether or not I was involved in Brendon's death somehow.

He opened the car door for me and I got in. I barely even noticed when he slid in beside me, started the engine, and then backed out onto the road. My mind was elsewhere, sorting through everything that had happened. I was new in town. The day after I get there, someone died. While it was a coincidence, not everyone would see it that way.

Paul stared straight ahead as he drove. I could almost see the wheels spinning behind his eyes and wondered if he was thinking about me or about the case. Or both. I'd been the one to point out the dust. I was the one who kept poking her nose into everything. Could he really think I was responsible?

Then again, if I'd killed Brendon Lawyer, why would I have told him all of this stuff?

Before I knew it, we were sitting in my driveway. My Focus was parked askew, back wheels in the grass. I vaguely wondered if Officer Buchannan had driven the car here and done it on purpose.

"Here we are," I said. I didn't make a move to get out of the car.

"Yup." Paul didn't, either.

"Want to come in for a few minutes? I can make some coffee."

He was silent for a long moment before shaking his head. "I best go home and get some rest. I have an early morning ahead of me." He barely looked at me as he said it.

"Oh." I opened the car door and stepped out into the night. The air was cool on my flushed skin. I felt like a fool. "I'll see you soon then?"

Paul nodded, hesitated, and then leaned across the seat so he could see my face. "Krissy," he said.

For a moment I thought he might say something that would make everything better. He'd tell me he believed in me and that he had changed his mind and would come inside, not just for an hour or so, but for the night.

I leaned down, anticipating his smile, his dimples, and was instead rewarded with a concerned frown.

"Be careful."

He straightened and I closed the car door. A moment later he backed down the drive and drove off, leaving me standing there, alone. I waited in the driveway in the hopes he'd change his mind and turn around, but the only person who seemed interested in what I was doing now was Eleanor Winthrow. Did that woman ever leave her place by the window?

I turned away, hugged my arms to my chest, and then went inside for a long night alone with my cat.

# 21

Puzzles and ice cream weren't helping. It was still too early even to attempt to sleep, yet I wasn't sure what else to do. A bath would be nice and might help me work through a few things; but then again, did I really want to think anymore tonight? All it had done so far was to get me into trouble.

I kept hoping Paul would call and set my mind at ease. I ate my plain vanilla ice cream—I was still out of Rocky Road—chugged coffee, and then ate the cookie afterward, all while working through puzzle after puzzle, hoping for something that never came.

I knew I should simply drop my little investigation, but I was afraid the murderer might get away with it if I did. I seemed to be the only person making any headway in the case. Most of the police force seemed content to plod along and let whatever happened, happen.

A cynical part of me wondered if perhaps someone in the department was intentionally stalling the case. Could Officer Buchannan be the killer? Maybe he'd gotten a bad insurance deal from Brendon Lawyer and decided to kill him? He obviously could get into the place on his own. I almost hoped that was the case. I'd love to see the smug look fade from his face when I confronted him with the facts.

Sadly, though, it didn't quite ring true. As much as I would like to see Buchannan in trouble, I seriously doubted he would have killed Brendon Lawyer. He might be a jerk, but he was still an officer of the law.

I was back to my list of suspects—those that Beth had given me. Any of those people could have gone into Brendon's office and put the dust into the air vent while he wasn't looking. Sure, someone could have come in the night before and planted it, but if so, why hadn't Brendon suffered his attack earlier? And what had happened to his EpiPen?

With a sigh I pushed my empty bowl away. I needed to get away from the case. It was going to drive me insane if I let it.

Misfit immediately hopped up onto the counter and began to lick the bowl clean. He purred contentedly and even gave me a friendly glance as he ate. For the moment he accepted me. He'd go back to puking into my shoes as soon as the contentment wore off. I gave it about fifteen minutes.

"Hope you've enjoyed your time here," I told the purring cat. "I'm not sure how much longer it will last."

Death by Coffee was suffering. If I didn't find a way to bring in more customers, both Vicki and I would be going back home to California with our tails tucked between our legs. I don't think I could handle going back to retail, and I knew for a fact Vicki would rather jump off a bridge than go back to acting. Our families would take us in, sure, but at what cost?

Of course, thinking of home made me think of Dad.

Before I could change my mind, I picked up the phone and dialed. If nothing else, he would know what to do. He always did.

It rang only twice before he answered with a hearty "Kristina? Hello!"

"Hi, Dad."

"Why sound so glum? Aren't things working out in Pine Hills?"

He knew me so well. "Not so much," I said.

"Don't people drink coffee there?"

"They do." I sighed heavily into the phone. "But it looks like they prefer to drink it at a diner in town. No one seems to be interested in my place at all."

"Ah. It'll turn around."

"That's what Vicki keeps telling me."

He chuckled his dry, raspy chuckle. He'd never smoked, but he'd had problems with his throat a few years back, which now gave his voice a gravely sound. I think it only added to his mystique in most people's eyes.

"I'd listen to her, buttercup," he said, using the pet name he'd used for me since I was little. "Change happens, whether we want it to or not. Just because they don't come now, it doesn't mean they won't start popping in to investigate your wonderful coffee. They just need to get used to the idea of changing their routine. It's never easy."

"If we're not broke by then." I slumped in my seat. Misfit finished off the ice cream, licked his lips, and then whapped me in the face with his tail before leaping off the counter. Maybe fifteen minutes had been a little too generous for him.

"I'm sure everything will be okay."

And I knew he was right. Dad always was. He took

the "let things develop and see what happens" approach to life. I think that was why he was such a good mystery writer. He didn't rush things, didn't force them to happen just because he wanted them to. He sat back patiently, smiled, and let it wash over him. He claimed the characters wrote the story for him; he was just there to transcribe them.

"Is there something else bothering you?" he asked. I hadn't realized it, but I'd fallen silent in my ruminations.

*"Well . . ."* I drew out the word. Should I bother him with what I was starting to think of as a murder in a small town? He'd written countless books about this very thing. Maybe he'd have some insight that would lead me to the killer.

Then again, this was real life. Things didn't always fall neatly into place like they often did in books and movies.

"There's been a murder," I said, figuring I might as well tell him now. He'd more than likely hear about it eventually.

"I see." He paused. "Are you okay? Is Vicki?"

"We're fine," I said. "We didn't know the guy. He stopped over for coffee once." *And then went back to his office to die.* I didn't add the last.

Dad was silent for a long time. I could tell he was torn between asking for more information and driving down to Pine Hills to make sure I truly was okay. He'd always been protective of me, especially after Mom died five years ago from some genetic heart condition I couldn't pronounce the name of if I tried. It was hard on the both of us, considering how close we all were. Even though there was nothing Dad could have done to save her, he often blamed himself. Because of Mom, he would never let anything happen to me as long as he was able to prevent it.

"Tell me," he said eventually. "Tell me everything."

And so I did.

I started with how Brendon came in, rudely asked for coffee, and then started to drink it in the store before getting a call that sent him back to the office. I told him about how the police had first ruled it as an accident, but there was growing belief—mostly my own—that he'd actually been murdered. I told him about Regina Harper, about Heidi and Mason Lawyer, and all about the mistresses and the mystery man with whom Heidi had cheated on Brendon. What do they call that, anyway? A mister?

Dad listened in silence. He never interrupted, never asked for clarifications. He let me babble on and on. I could almost see him nodding thoughtfully as I spoke.

I felt oddly better when I finished. Having it laid out like that didn't make anything clearer, but it allowed me to just get it out and tell someone. I'd told him things I hadn't even told the police. He would know what to do.

"I don't know what to tell you, buttercup," he said after a slight pause.

*"What?"* I was shocked. Dad always knew what to do. "There's got to be an answer."

"There is, I'm sure," he said. "But you don't have all of the pieces yet, do you?"

I frowned. "What do you mean?"

I could hear him groan through the phone as he settled himself in. He was getting comfortable. It was the same sound he always made right before he'd open a book and begin reading, or when he was about to tell me a nighttime story. For the first time since I'd arrived in Pine Hills, I felt a little homesick.

"Well, for one, you don't know who this Heidi person was seeing. You also don't know who to trust, because you know so little about the people of the town. Just because someone is friendly doesn't mean he or she is a good person. The same could be said about some of the nastier people. Perhaps the reason Mrs. Harper was so angry with you was because she was upset that you kept bringing up the death of her daughter's husband. She might be happy he is gone, but she doesn't want to see her daughter upset. Make sense?"

"It does," I said. "I never really thought about it like that."

"And what else don't you know? What was Mr. Lawyer's last claim? Could he have shorted someone? Dropped them from their insurance? Could he have run a red light, dinged a car, and then driven off? Could he have discovered his wife's infidelity, confronted the other man, and then threatened his wife to stay with him or else he'd take her for all she had, while also revealing her indiscretions to the world?"

The questions swirled around me. Dad was right; I didn't know everything. There was no possible way I could find all of this out without going through Brendon's entire life. I didn't have the skill or energy to do it. I'd been running on the assumption his murder had something to do with his cheating ways this entire time without fully considering the fact the guy had his whole life to mess with people. It might even have been an old college rival who'd finally decided to pay up on an old debt who'd done him in.

"You're right," I said, feeling strangely lighter. With

it all put in front of me, I realized I never should have gotten involved. This simply should have been handled by the police and the families from the start.

"Now," Dad said, "I don't mean you should give up. I'm extremely proud of you for what you've done thus far. Not every person would have put herself in harm's way to put a killer behind bars."

"But I don't know what else I can do," I said. "I've tried to talk to the people involved, but they never tell me the whole story. I feel like everyone is hiding something—and no matter how many times I ask questions, I'll never get the truth."

"There is someone always willing to talk," he said sagely. "If you look hard enough and in the right places, someone will say something that will break the whole thing wide open. In fact, they might already have."

I frowned at that. I couldn't think of anything that anyone had said that would help me get to the bottom of Brendon Lawyer's murder.

"Just don't force it, okay?" Dad said. He sounded concerned. "I don't want you to stress yourself out over this. If you start to feel overwhelmed, then there is nothing wrong with stepping back and letting the legal system work. If you feel in danger, do the same. I'll never forgive myself if something happened to you."

"It won't," I said. "I promise."

"Good." I could hear the smile in his voice.

"I'd better go," I said, feeling much better. Dad had a way of making everything make sense, even if I still had no idea who'd killed Brendon. I was also pretty sure nothing could save Death by Coffee now. Still, the thought didn't bother me nearly as much as it had a moment ago.

"Okay. Get some rest. Think things over."

"Will do."

"Love you, buttercup."

"Love you, too, Dad."

We hung up at the same time.

I drifted away from the phone in something of a daze. He'd told me to step back when I felt overwhelmed. Well, I'd been feeling that way since the start. Maybe it was time I let things go and get back to work. I *did* have a life to manage.

I headed to the bathroom and ran myself a nice hot bath. It would wash away the rest of the stress, I hoped. I sank down into the bubble-free water and closed my eyes. Misfit jumped up and began drinking the bathwater like he always did. He would, of course, drink too much and gack all over the floor afterward. Right then, however, the sound of his lapping soothed me.

Brendon Lawyer might be dead, but I was still alive. It was time I put this whole thing behind me, like everyone kept telling me to do. I needed to get back to living my own life.

I just hoped that that life didn't end up getting me killed.

# 22

I felt energized and ready to face the world the next
morning. I sprang right out of bed, got showered,
dressed, and ate breakfast, all while humming to
myself. I even shared a few bits of my bacon with
Misfit, who gobbled up the pieces without leaving a
mess.

Vicki appeared surprised to see me when I arrived at
work an hour later. She was busy getting the cookies
baked for the morning, something that was supposed to
be my job, but I had slacked off doing it lately.

"Are you sure?" she asked when I took the mix
from her.

"Positive," I said. And I meant it.

I was done with the murder investigation. At some
point during the night, I realized I was just making my
life harder than it needed to be. I couldn't keep running
around, chasing after every little lead in the hopes it
would bring me closer to the killer. I mean, I was just a
little store owner. I wasn't a private investigator. I
should leave that sort of thing to the professionals.

Vicki and I finished with the morning prep in record

time and had ten minutes to lean against the counter and chat before we opened. Trouble was sitting on the counter—something I'd have to remedy before we opened the doors—and was purring contentedly as Vicki stroked his long black fur. Tufts floated to the floor to be swept up later.

"I think we should paint the place," I said, looking at the walls. They were the same off-white they'd been when we'd bought the building. "I'm thinking a cream color, something that might remind people of the foam on a really good cappuccino. It could make them thirsty enough to buy something."

"Maybe." Vicki sounded skeptical as she eyed me. "So you're really done?" she asked. "With all of this crime stuff, I mean?"

"I am. I feel like an idiot for how I've been acting. I should have been here helping you this entire time."

She shook her head sadly. "I don't think it would have mattered."

The tone of her voice caused me some alarm. Vicki looked defeated in a way I wasn't used to seeing from her. She was normally unshakably positive about everything, and yet here she was, looking as glum as could be.

"It'll work out," I said. "We just have to give it some more time."

"I suppose." She sighed. "But how much time do we have before we're forced to close?"

I looked toward the locked glass door. No one was lining up to be the first to sample the day's coffee. People walked past on the way to work—yet no one seemed interested in a morning shot of caffeine.

Then again, they'd probably already been to J&E's

Banyon Tree. By now, half the town already knew more about me than I did myself, thanks to Judith and her spy next door. It wouldn't surprise me in the slightest if she gave out a little piece of juicy "Krissy gossip" with every coffee purchase.

"It'll work out," I said again, not really feeling it. I joined her in sighing. "I thought I was supposed to be the pessimistic one here?"

Vicki laughed. "You are. I'm just trying to be a realist this time. We have a buffer, so it isn't like we're going to close down next week, but I've seen no signs of things ever picking up. It's been a lot slower than I anticipated, and I don't know what we could possibly do to make things better."

I could have kept trying to reassure her, but what was the point? I should have been here, trying my best to get people to come in, not chasing after would-be killers. This was my job, my life. I needed to focus on that.

I straightened. "We'll just have to come up with something that will bring more people in."

"And what would that be?" Vicki asked as she scooped Trouble off the counter and carried him up toward the bookstore, where he'd hopefully spend the rest of the day. "It's not like we can go door-to-door."

For an instant I was tempted. I could carry a stack of cups with me, take a pot of coffee, and hit up every business on the block. I was sure I could lure a few customers that way; and if they came in, maybe their friends and families would too.

But if I did that, I'd be coming face-to-face with people I was trying to avoid. There was no way I was going to let that happen—not today at least.

"I'll think of something," I said, moving toward the door. It was time to open.

The only thing that rushed through the door when I opened it was a warm breeze. I soaked it in for a few moments before returning to my place behind the counter. My morning coffee was down to the cookie and I munched on it contentedly as I waited. I tried hard not to let the imminent doom of Death by Coffee affect me.

The morning went as expected. A few customers came in, drank some coffee, and then left. Vicki managed to sell two books to an older woman who seemed to be becoming a regular, though I still didn't know her name. Where was Rita when you needed her?

Then, as if by magic, she appeared.

And she wasn't alone.

"Oh, hello, hello, hello!" Rita said, waving her arm at me. The flap of skin seemed especially jubilant this morning. "I missed you yesterday. We all did!"

Nearly the entire writers' group poured through the doors; only Patricia Dalton was missing. It was the most people I'd seen in the place since Brendon Lawyer had died. Had that really only happened a few days ago?

Rita came up to the counter, the rest of the group behind her like some sort of preschool class. They chittered and whispered among themselves, looking around like kids at a zoo. Only Lena met my eye. She gave me a wink, rolled her eyes, and then went to stand beside the silent Adam, who appeared asleep on his feet.

"I thought we could have something of an impromptu meeting here," Rita said, pressing against the counter. "It'll be fun, don't you think?"

"I wish I could join you, but I'm working," I said, indicating the apron around my neck. I glanced at Vicki for help. She smiled at me from her spot at the bookstore, Trouble in her arms. I think the cat was grinning at me.

"Oh, pah!" Rita waved her arm at me. "I know that! I wasn't implying you should abandon your job just so you could join us." She giggled in a way that made my eyes water. "We'll just get some coffee, find a seat, and have our meeting without you."

I plastered on a smile. While Rita was annoying me to no end, she *was* going to buy something. I couldn't turn away a customer, especially one who was quickly becoming a regular.

"What can I get you?" I asked in my best working-girl voice.

Rita, of course, got her usual plain black coffee and Lena her red eye. Adam asked for water, which didn't surprise me in the slightest. He might actually open his eyes and wake up if he were to jolt his system with caffeine.

"Do you have a French roast?" Andi asked. Georgina nodded behind her as if it was the most important question in the world.

"Of course," I said with a smile. "Would you each like one?"

"Oh no," Andi said. "I'd like an iced latte. I was just asking for a friend."

"Me too," Georgina said, which oddly caused Andi to giggle.

I wandered away to get their drinks. Those two were

a pair of very strange women. I couldn't imagine one without the other.

Once they were all served, the group took seats in the back of the store. Thankfully, they kept their voices down, though I could hear the occasional gasp from Andi. It seemed like every little thing shocked that woman.

Strangely, the longer I stood there, helping the rare guest, the more I wanted to go over and sit with them. I felt left out, as if the very act of them having a meeting without me shunned me from the group forever. I had to admit, I felt jealous they all were able to sit there during the middle of the day while I had to work.

Vicki kept mostly to the books. She had more customers than I did, which suited me fine. As long as people were buying something, I was happy, although I would have liked the company.

Eventually I couldn't take standing around anymore. I started a fresh pot of coffee and headed out onto the floor with a rag in hand. I could eavesdrop on their meeting while I cleaned off the tables. I was curious to hear what they were talking about, even if it was only bad poetry.

"Could be," Rita said. "It just seems so fantastic, doesn't it?"

Andi and Georgina readily agreed.

I glanced over at the table to find Adam apparently asleep and Lena looking as if she was considering joining him. She gave me a bored smile and then stood as Rita went on, though this time in a lower voice, as if she didn't want me to hear. She kept glancing at me out of the corner of her eye, telling me she very well might be talking about me.

"How's it going?" Lena asked. She leaned against the wall beside the table I was wiping down.

I shrugged. "It's going." I glanced at the others. "Interesting meeting?"

"Not at all." She sighed dramatically. "I was told we were going to discuss our writing, but all those women want to do is gossip about the dead guy."

My interest pinged.

*No, Krissy! Keep out of it!*

My brain battled with my interest. It wasn't a surprise as to which one won.

"What are they saying?" I led Lena away from the others so they wouldn't hear us talking about them. If they could do it . . . well, then, so could I.

Lena shrugged and picked at a scab on her elbow. "I don't know. I checked out pretty early, you know?"

A part of me felt overjoyed, while another was disappointed. I really shouldn't be getting involved. I swore to myself I'd keep out of this stuff. Yet, here I was, trying to pry information out of a teenage girl. What was wrong with me? I should just walk away and go about my day like it had never happened.

"I think one of the mistresses did it," Lena went on, dragging me right back into it.

"Really?"

She started picking at another scab. "I mean, isn't it always one of the mistresses? I don't think his wife could have done it. I've seen her around. She couldn't hurt much of anything, let alone that prick of a husband."

I nodded, mind turning it over. Hadn't Tessa seemed like she knew more than she'd let on? Could she have killed Brendon, or at least set it up?

"I think it's all a load of bullsh . . . ," Lena trailed off, and she lowered her eyes. "Sorry."

"It's okay."

"It's a load of crap," she amended. "The guy died. You shouldn't go around gossiping about it like it happened on some stupid TV show."

"I agree," I said, doing my best to keep my mind reined in. I really, really didn't want to get involved.

"But I do bet someone knows who did it," Lena said. "I mean, wouldn't they have to? I bet the police will talk to those girls he was sleeping with and they'll talk. Maybe it was one of their boyfriends and they've been trying to protect him or something."

*Or perhaps it could be the wife's boyfriend.*

Damn it! There was no way I was going to be able to walk away from this now. My mind was racing as I tried to come up with likely candidates for the man Heidi slept with. No one seemed to fit, but how well did I know anyone in town? Every single man in town could be a likely suspect.

"Lena?" Rita called. "Are you coming back to the group?" She blinked her eyes rapidly at the girl.

"I suppose." Lena gave me an eye roll and then went back to slump in her seat.

I carried my rag back behind the counter and dropped it onto a shelf without really paying attention to what I was doing. Could Tessa know whom Heidi was sleeping with? She'd made a comment about cheating running in the family. I'd assumed she'd been referring to Mason, or perhaps to Raymond. Could she have meant Heidi? Or perhaps there was some other member of the family I didn't know about, someone Lawyer

Senior had wiped completely from the books, a sort of black sheep.

There was only one way to find out.

I didn't quite slink up the stairs to where Vicki was waiting on a young man buying a graphic novel that looked a little too explicit for his age. Then again, who was I to judge? That was something his parents could deal with.

As soon as she finished ringing him up, Vicki turned to me. The smile she'd been wearing faltered the moment she saw the apologetic look on my face.

"You're going to go, aren't you?" she asked.

"I have to."

"That murder thing?"

I nodded.

Vicki sighed in mock exasperation and then gave me a huge smile. "You've got to do what you've got to do," she said, and then added, "I knew you wouldn't be able to put it behind you. It's just not your style."

"Thanks, Vicki." I gave her a quick hug. "I'll make this up to you."

She pointed a finger at me. "You'd better."

I turned and hurried back down the stairs before she could change her mind. I started for the door, and then veered off behind the counter. I filled a to-go cup with the freshly brewed coffee, grabbed a few packs of cream and sugar, and then carried them to the door. A bribe might get Tessa to open up.

I glanced back at the writers' group as I opened the door. Rita and her gossip girls barely looked up. Adam, as usual, looked asleep, but Lena was watching me. She gave me a sideways smile and then winked. She mouthed, "Good luck," before turning back to the group.

I had a strange feeling she'd known about my fascination with the case and my subsequent refusal to get involved. Had our entire conversation been a way to get me back on track? That girl was a lot smarter than I gave her credit for, if so.

I turned away and left the shop, mentally noting that from this point on, every red eye that girl wanted would be free.

# 23

An OUT TO LUNCH sign hung on the door to Tessa's Dresses. I tried the door, anyway, but found it to be locked up tight.

"Drat," I said, glancing up and down the sidewalk, hoping to catch a glimpse of Tessa. I couldn't have missed her by much more than a few minutes. It felt awfully early for lunch. There were a few people out and about, strolling casually up and down the sidewalk, but there was no sign of Tessa.

I checked my watch and was surprised to see it was just after twelve. Where had the time gone? It felt like only an hour ago that I'd rolled out of bed and had headed to work. I guess time actually does fly by when you are focused on your job, instead of wanting to be somewhere else.

I figured Tessa wouldn't be gone for more than a half hour, maybe forty-five minutes at the most. Actually, she might be sitting inside, snacking away on a burrito even now. I tried to peer in through the window, but couldn't see anything. The store looked dark and empty, as if Tessa hadn't been there at all.

The coffee in my hand was still hot and would be for a little longer, but not for thirty more minutes. I scanned the street one last time, but Tessa was nowhere to be seen.

My eyes fell on a store a little ways down the block. Bright pink lettering scattered with candy and chocolate hung above a door that was decorated like a gingerbread house. The windows were frosted, but I could still read the colorful lettering, even from as far away as I was: PHANTASTIC CANDIES.

Not wanting to wait around for Tessa, or worse, slink back to Death by Coffee without accomplishing anything, I headed for Jules Phan's candy store. If nothing else, I could give him the coffee and hope it would add one more customer to our meager regulars.

As I entered, the door made a strange crinkling sound that reminded me of a really large piece of candy being unwrapped from plastic. The smell of sugar and sweets was nearly overpowering. My eyes watered and my stomach grumbled at the assault on my nose. I hadn't craved a piece of chocolate-covered caramel so badly in my life.

Jules was in the middle of the store, dancing for a little girl whose mom was watching him with just as much adoration as the child. His tap shoes made a pleasing sound on the floor and I found myself wanting to join him, though I'd probably end up tripping over my own two feet and ruining the whole dance. He was wearing one of his bright suits—this one blue—and had on a striped top hat, which would have looked outlandish anywhere else.

Jules spun, clicked his shoes together, and landed in

a crouch in front of the girl, a sucker in his hand. She took it with a giggle.

The girl's mother clapped and thanked Jules warmly before leading the girl away. She'd already removed the wrapper and was sucking happily on the sucker as they left the shop.

"That was wonderful," I said, approaching.

"It was nothing," Jules said with a wide smile. "It's so good to see you, Krissy." He removed his hat, wiped the sweat from his brow with a polka-dotted handkerchief, and then replaced his top hat. "What brings you my way today?"

"I was in the neighborhood and thought I'd stop by. I brought you this." I held out the coffee.

Jules took it with a grin. "Thank you," he said. "I was thinking of stopping down there when I got a moment. Always so busy, but you know how that is."

Oh, how I wished I did. "Sure," I said, handing over the creamer and sugar. He took them and set them on the counter beside some taffy.

As Jules went about adding his condiments to his coffee, I looked around the shop in something akin to wonder. Candy in bins lined every wall all the way to the ceiling. Glass chutes gave the kids a view of the candy as it rolled and tumbled down, once they put in their quarters. Wrapped candies sat in boxes on shelves in the middle of the room. Just looking at all of the candy made my teeth ache.

"It's a bit much when you first see it, isn't it?" Jules said, stirring his coffee. "Lance and I weren't sure if we should go so extravagant, but then when I thought of the kiddies, I realized they would love it. It might be garish for you or me, but to see the smiles on their faces"—he somehow managed to clasp both hands over his heart without spilling his coffee—"is worth it."

It might be worth it to Jules, who was slim and fit. Me? I would be toothless within a month of working in a place like this. I didn't even want to think what would happen to my waistline. The coffee and the cookies were bad enough.

"It's nice," I said, and I meant it. Just because I wouldn't want to work here didn't mean I didn't like the atmosphere. If I had a son, I'd definitely bring him here once a week for a little candy. The place was too fun not to visit.

The door opened and about a dozen kids swarmed inside, led by a harried-looking teenager. She smiled at me as she breezed past, calling after a little boy named Joey, who was busy trying to shove his arm up a chute to reach the bubble gum there.

"I best get back to work," Jules said. He took a sip of his coffee. "Thank you for this. It's very good." He snatched a sucker that was bigger than my fist from the counter. "Take this," he said before rushing off after the kids.

I looked at the sucker and considered putting it back. There was no way I was going to even attempt that thing. The bellyache would put me down for days if I tried.

Thankfully, the thing was wrapped, meaning I could shove it in my purse and worry about it later. I didn't want to insult Jules by declining his gift. Maybe sometime later I'd need the comforts of sugar.

I turned toward the door, sucker in hand, and stepped outside without paying attention to where I was going.

Someone bumped into me, but didn't slow down to apologize in the rush past me.

"Excuse me," I grumbled, righting myself. I'd very nearly dropped the sucker. I looked up to find Tessa walking briskly away.

I stood there a moment, frozen in surprise, before I gathered myself and called after her. "Tessa!" I hurried away from Phantastic Candies, toward the retreating woman.

Tessa hesitated and glanced back when I called to her the second time. I caught a glimpse of wide-eyed worry and maybe a little guilt before she realized who I was. Her face then morphed to an irritated scowl.

"What do you want?"

Boy, did it seem like I was getting asked that a lot these days or what?

"I just wanted to ask you a couple of quick questions." I looked at the sucker in my hand and then held it out to her as a sort of peace offering.

She looked at it like it was poison on a stick. "No, thank you," she said. "I've got to get back to work." She made as if to turn away.

"Please," I said. "Just one minute?"

She heaved a sigh, and then glanced past my shoulder. She looked worried that someone might be coming down the walk at any moment and would see us together. Was my reputation really that bad?

"Can we at least get inside?" she asked, eyes flickering to me. "I might have customers waiting."

I somehow doubted it, but I agreed.

I followed Tessa to her shop. She unlocked the door and slipped inside after one more look over her shoulder. She was definitely worried about something. Could she have just come from a meeting with someone, perhaps Mason Lawyer? Or was she really that worried about being caught talking to me?

"So, what is this about?" she asked once we were inside. She relaxed visibly as the door closed and no one came bursting in. She tossed her purse behind the counter before removing the OUT TO LUNCH sign.

I watched her silently as she went through the routine. Tessa's hair was a mess and she kept running her fingers through it as if to tame it. Her lips were a bright red, telling me she'd either had a cherry smoothie for lunch, or had been doing something that involved pressing her lips firmly against something else. It wasn't too hard to figure out what that might be.

"Is everything all right?" I asked, glancing toward the door. She was staring at it again. I half expected it to burst inward and the police to come rushing in to arrest her. She appeared *that* nervous.

"What do you mean? I'm fine."

"You seem worried about something." I took a chance that she would just clam up and went on. "Are you hiding from someone?"

"Hiding?" She snorted. "As if."

"Then why were you so anxious to get inside?"

"I have a business to run," she said. Her face was darkening in what I took to be anger. "I needed to get back."

"There was more to it than that." I moved closer to the counter and she backed up a step. "Where were you?"

"It's personal."

I took in her mussed hair, the way her dress hung on her body slightly askew, as if she'd gotten into a fight or perhaps put it on in a hurry.

"Who were you with?"

Her jaw clenched. "That's none of your business."

I took a stab in the dark. "Was it Mason Lawyer?"

"What?" She sounded genuinely shocked. "No. Why would I be with him?" She heaved a sigh. "If you must know, I was meeting with a friend."

"A close friend."

"What should it matter?"

"I don't know, should it?"

She gave me a flat stare. "Is this what you wanted to talk to me about? I'm not in the habit of sharing every detail of my personal life with people, strangers especially."

"So you weren't seeing Mason then?"

"God!" She threw up her hands in frustration. "I really wish you people would stop asking me about the Lawyer family. I'm done with them. Brendon is dead. I had nothing to do with it. I want to be left alone, okay?"

"Who else has been asking you about him?" Vague thoughts about the killer coming in and milking her for information floated to mind.

"The police, you nitwit. Who else?"

I reddened. Of course.

Tessa huffed and opened her purse. I tensed, but all she pulled out was a mirror. She checked her hair and makeup, doing her best to fix it. She did a reasonably good job of it and I wondered if she learned to do that after many tumultuous lunch breaks with Brendon.

I decided to press on, knowing she was probably going to yell at me for not dropping it. I knew, just *knew,* she knew more than she was letting on.

"The last time we met, you said something about cheating running in the Lawyer family," I said. "Were you talking about Mason? Do you think he could have slept with Heidi?"

Tessa actually laughed. "Mason? God, no. That man is far too conservative for something like that." She gave herself one last look-over and then snapped the mirror closed and shoved it back into her purse.

"Were you referring to Raymond, then? Another family member?" And then I asked what I'd been thinking the entire time. "Or were you referring to Heidi?"

Tessa's eyes narrowed and she looked at her watch. "I really should be working right now," she said.

I wondered what she could possibly be doing without customers. Rearranging the racks? There didn't appear to be a place for new stock. Unless she was dusting the shelves, there really wasn't much else she could do.

Which told me she was hiding something. It was obvious she didn't like me asking these questions. She wanted to get rid of me. Why would she do that if she had nothing to hide?

Of course, I had to ignore the fact I was poking my nose where it didn't belong, and it was probably irritating to no end, but darn it, I was positive she knew more than she was saying.

"Just tell me who you meant," I said. "Who's the cheater? That's all I want to know. I'll leave you alone afterward. I promise."

Tessa glared at me. I could hear her foot tapping behind the counter. I didn't know if she was considering her answer carefully or if she was contemplating calling the police.

"Raymond," she said after a long moment. "I was talking about Raymond."

The gears in my head started spinning. "You don't think Heidi could have cheated on her husband with his *father,* do you?" It actually made my stomach twist to think such a thing. I mean, *ew!*

Tessa shrugged it off. "Who knows?" she said. "I honestly wouldn't put it past the old letch to try. He thinks he can get anything he wants just because he pretends to be a big shot around town." She shuddered. "I wouldn't touch the man myself. I have more dignity than that."

I seriously wondered about that, but I didn't say it out loud.

Tessa sighed and leaned onto the counter, visibly softening. "Look," she said. "Heidi is a good woman. I doubt she ever would do anything with someone like Raymond. She would have better taste than that." She straightened. "I really do have stuff to do. So if you would . . ." She motioned toward the door.

"Yeah," I said absently. "Okay." I turned and walked out of Tessa's Dresses in a daze, sucker still clutched in my hand.

Raymond Lawyer. How could I never have considered him when I was trying to come up with people Heidi might have slept with? He'd been right there in front of me this entire time, yelling at me to stop poking around. He had all the opportunity in the world—not only to sleep with Heidi, but to kill Brendon when things didn't work out the way he hoped.

But to sleep with his son's wife? That was low. I couldn't imagine someone stooping to that level, even if he didn't much care for his son. It was just so . . . icky.

I knew I'd never get the truth from Raymond Lawyer himself. The guy would probably have me arrested for even thinking about walking into his building. I tried to imagine Heidi with Raymond and just about puked on my shoes.

I just didn't see it. No matter how many ways I looked at it, I couldn't imagine a young woman like Heidi doing such a thing, especially with her husband's father. The guy was a total ass, much like his son.

But then again, revenge did make people do strange things.

Could she have cheated on Brendon with Raymond just to get back at him? People have done worse, I was sure, though to go that far . . . it defied belief.

I'd been walking aimlessly back toward Death by Coffee, turning it all slowly over in my head. No matter how many ways I looked at it, I just couldn't bring myself to believe Heidi would have slept with Raymond Lawyer. Even Tessa didn't think Heidi would have done it.

But if not Raymond, then who?

A crash brought me out of my reverie. It was followed by a startled scream.

I looked up, worried, as another crash sounded, this one louder than the first. It was followed by an ear-splitting scream that just about stopped my heart. I was only a few yards away from Death by Coffee. The sounds had come from there.

Dropping the sucker Jules had given me, I broke into a run, certain my entire world was about to come crashing down around my head.

# 24

I had to push my way through the front door, which was hanging open. People were crowding around, trying to see inside. Where did all these people come from? They sure as heck weren't buying coffee at the time.

Heart hammering, I shoved past a woman who was taking up the entire doorway. She grunted as I elbowed past her and then pushed me hard on the back shoulder. I lost my balance and staggered inside to crash against a table. A chair toppled over, just as another crash sounded from the bookstore portion of the store.

There were only a handful of people actually *in* Death by Coffee. They were all on their feet, looking up toward where the crashes were coming from. There was a growl, followed by a scream that had me scrambling back to my feet.

I was terrified at what I'd find, once up those few stairs. Would Vicki be lying there, mouth frothing from some poison the killer had managed to spread across the pages of a book? Or perhaps she'd have a bookmark shoved through her eye or balled up pages in her mouth.

Instead of helping, the people of Pine Hills were standing around and laughing.

I slowed halfway to the stairs. *They're laughing?*

It took me a moment to realize the screams I heard weren't agonizing. There was a howl, followed by a hiss, and then Vicki yelping in pain. "Trouble!" she shouted at the top of her lungs.

My heart, which had just about thumped its way clear through my chest, settled to a more manageable speed. No one was lying dead upstairs—at least, not yet. I had a feeling if Vicki caught hold of her cat, there very well might be a feline fatality soon enough.

I hurried up the couple of stairs and froze as I scanned the mess. Bookshelves lay toppled to the floor. Books were scattered every which way, many open with pages bent beneath them. An older woman stood by the stairs, one hand over her mouth, the other over her heart. She looked at me wide-eyed as I came to a stop next to her.

"What happened?" I asked, out of breath after my short run.

"The cat," the woman said. "It's gone crazy!"

That didn't tell me anything. Both Trouble and Misfit were born crazy.

"Vicki?" I called. I thought I saw her head duck down, which was followed by a howl and a hiss. A black-and-white shape darted across the room, causing a couple more books to fall from their shelves.

*"Argh!"* Vicki cried. "I'm going to rip off your claws, you demon!"

"Sorry," I told the old lady. "If you were interested in buying a book, I'd come back tomorrow." I smiled at her before turning back toward the destruction. I picked my way through the scattered books, mentally calculating how much damage the cat had caused. My initial tallies weren't pretty.

"Vicki?" She hadn't come up from where I'd last seen her.

"Over here," she grumbled. A hand fluttered up between a pair of fallen shelves and then fell back to the floor with a thump.

I stepped over an old Western, which was now missing its cover, and found Vicki lying facedown on the floor. Her arms were covered in tiny little scratches. There was little blood, thank goodness, but the marks would show for days.

"You okay?" I asked, scanning the area. The cat must have gone completely bonkers. A half-dozen shelves were toppled and two more were leaning against one another, their books spilled out between them. Only the two wire racks by the stairs had managed to remain upright. The rest were buried beneath the bookshelves somewhere.

Vicki grumbled something into the floorboards before pushing her way to her feet. She had a scratch across her chin, yet it didn't detract from her beauty. I swear, that girl could run full force into a wall, shatter her nose and bust her lip, and she would still be the prettiest girl in the room.

Jealous? Me? Never.

"What happened?" I asked, surveying the room. "How could one cat do so much damage?"

She huffed. "It wasn't just Trouble," she said, wiping herself down. She looked around with a grimace. "Do you remember that guy who complained about cat allergies a few days ago?"

"Yeah."

"He came back."

I glanced around, but didn't see him. "Did he sneeze the shelves over?"

Vicki gave me a flat look. "Of course not. He came in for a book, started complaining about cats, which only caused Trouble to rub up against his leg. I swear cats know. The guy jumped like he'd been electrocuted, landed on Trouble's tail, and then began flailing all over the place like he'd stepped on a land mine. He knocked over the first shelf, which sent Trouble into panic mode. Between trying to settle the guy down and catch the damn cat, this happened." She spread her arms as if to encompass the store.

"Wow," I said, trying hard not to laugh. "Of all things . . . Really? Wow."

"Shut up."

I snorted. "What happened to Allergy Man?"

"He started squawking about never coming back, tripped over his own two feet, and went headfirst down the stairs, where he wailed about suing." Vicki sighed. "I suppose we'll be hearing from his lawyer soon enough."

That wiped the smile from my face. As if times weren't hard enough already—now this!

"Is Trouble okay?" He'd gotten lost in the mess somewhere, presumably to lick his wounds.

Vicki shrugged and picked up a few books to reshelve them. "I don't know. That's why I was trying to catch him. Besides, I don't want him scratching up the pages. You know how he gets with paper lying around."

Oh, how I knew. Misfit was the same. If you left a

bare page lying around the house, he'd be on it in a second, either napping or ripping it into tiny little shreds. I could only imagine what he'd do in a place like this with books everywhere.

"You go find the cat," I said, picking up a few books of my own. "I'll take care of this."

Vicki hesitated, then nodded. "Thanks," she said. "I really screwed up this time." She slunk away to find Trouble before I could respond.

Thankfully, the bookshelves weren't that heavy. I went about righting them before worrying about the books. The shelves were made from cheap plywood and stood only four feet tall. We'd saved some money by going with the cheaper bookshelves. Maybe if we'd spent more and had gone with the more expensive, heavier shelves, they wouldn't have gone crashing down like dominoes.

I only had to stop twice to wait on someone while I worked. While people had gathered to watch the scene, they weren't all that interested in getting something to drink afterward. Even Rita and the writing group were gone, leaving the place depressingly empty.

I was replacing books in the sci-fi section when Vicki returned, petting Trouble. The cat actually looked contented, like this was the sort of thing he lived for. I could hear his purr coming from across the room and considered throwing a book at him just to make him stop. There was nothing funny about this anymore.

"This is a disaster," Vicki said, leaning carefully on a recently righted shelf. It wobbled ever so slightly. "I'm really starting to think you were right this entire time. This was a bad idea."

"We'll get through this," I said, though I really didn't

feel it. It seemed like everything was falling apart around us. Plus, no matter what we did to stop it, things kept getting worse.

Vicki sniffed, causing me to straighten, stunned. She was actually crying. I don't think I'd ever seen her cry before. She was always so good at keeping on the smiling face, even when things were at their worst. I wasn't quite sure how to handle it.

"It'll be okay," I said. I shoved the book I was holding absently onto a shelf and went over to stand next to her. "It's just a few books."

"I know." She wiped angrily at her eyes. "I just keep thinking that if things don't get better soon, I'm going to have to go back to California. My parents will force me to get an acting job and I'll have to go on some special diet, get Botox, maybe a boob job, and then make some vapid friends, who really don't care a thing about me, just so I can impress some Hollywood producer." A terrified look passed over her face. "Do you think those rumors about having to sleep your way to the top are true? I really don't want to have to go through that."

"You won't," I said. "We'll make this work."

She snorted a laugh, somehow making it sound sexy. "Funny how we've sort of swapped places. Didn't I say something like that just the other day?"

I smiled. "You did." The smile slipped away quickly. "And I still am worried."

"Gee, thanks." She gave me a crooked grin. "That makes me feel *so* much better."

I ran a hand over Trouble's head. He glared at me and stopped purring. I think I actually saw him flex his claws. I returned my hand to myself.

"I'm just being honest," I said, eyeing the cat warily. "But it's okay to be worried. We'll muddle through this, and things will work out. Even if I have to take another loan from Dad, or ask him to come down to do some event, we'll get through this."

I shuddered at the thought of asking my dad for anything else. I'd rather live on the streets, alone and dirty, than beg from him, though I knew he'd leap to help. I'd much rather go to Raymond Lawyer and ask him for some money than impose on my dad any more than I already had.

Of course, thinking of Mr. Lawyer made me think of what Tessa had said. Could Heidi really have slept with her husband's father? It was just so icky and yucky and vomit worthy. I couldn't imagine it. . . .

"We best get this cleaned up before someone actually wants to come in and buy something." Vicki set Trouble onto the floor. He wound his way around her legs and then darted off, presumably to find something new to destroy. "I hope there isn't too much damage."

Turned out, the damage to the books was lighter than I'd expected. Only eight books were beyond repair. Two dozen had bent pages, but they'd be fine tucked back onto the shelves. Five were bent up enough that we set them onto the counter with a CLEARANCE sign over them. All in all, we weren't out much money and maybe the excitement caused by the cat would bring a few people back in the hopes of catching a replay.

It took most of the day to put everything to rights. Every now and again, I'd think of Raymond or Heidi or one of the other unfriendly people involved in Brendon's death, but I never got past the initial thoughts. I had too much to do.

By the time we were done and Trouble was back to licking his privates on the tables, it was near closing time. How could such a big mess happen from such a small incident? It had looked like a stampede of elephants had rushed through the place, followed by a handful of mischievous monkeys.

Vicki and I slumped behind the counter, actually happy we weren't any busier than usual. I don't think either of us had the energy to wait on someone, let alone fill an order. Physical labor was not my thing; even Vicki looked exhausted and a little disheveled.

Of course, she still looked the part of a beauty queen. I, on the other hand, looked as haggard as I felt.

"Think we should close up early?" Vicki asked. She looked down at her nails. They were perfect, as always. Only the tiny cat scratches detracted from her hands in any way.

I winced as I picked at a splinter I'd managed to get from one of the shelves. One of my nails had bent and I had at least a dozen paper cuts. I might as well have stuck my hand in a shredder. It might have done less damage.

"I suppose," I said with a sigh. There were only two people left in the store. Even they looked tired and bored as they sipped their coffee.

It didn't take much wrangling to clear the room and lock up. Vicki had a much easier time catching Trouble and getting him into his carrier than she'd had earlier. It wasn't quite five, but it was close enough.

"See you tomorrow?" she asked as we stepped outside. She sounded genuinely curious, as if she didn't quite believe I'd show. That, of course, made me feel bad.

"Bright and early." I tried on a smile, decided it didn't feel right, and let it fall away with a yawn. "If I can drag myself out of bed, that is."

Vicki laughed. "Well, I'll see you then."

She sauntered away and I felt a pang of regret. Was I holding her back? If it wasn't for me, she might be a star right now, rich and famous with a super sexy husband and millions of fans screaming her name everywhere she went. It was a life I'd never live. Without me, she might soar to heights she never believed possible.

I quickly realized I was just being dumb. This was the life Vicki wanted. Just because I was failing at it so spectacularly didn't mean she would want to change anything.

I finished locking up, determined I'd work harder at making things right. No matter what happened, I swore to myself I wouldn't let my best friend down.

# 25

"What is a six-letter word for 'pest'?" I glanced over at Misfit, who was busy spreading crumbs across the countertop. I penciled in "misfit," but I quickly erased it. I'd already tried to squeeze in "trouble" twice.

I'd thought I'd go straight to bed when I'd gotten home an hour before. However, as soon as I stepped through the doorway, my mind started to race. I really wanted to know whether or not Heidi had slept with Raymond Lawyer or if I was just grasping at rather weak straws. I wasn't so sure I'd be able to sleep unless I knew.

But I wasn't going to find out tonight. It might still be early, but I was pretty sure Regina Harper would be hovering around Heidi at home. The older woman would surely call the police the moment I showed my face and I doubted Chief Dalton would be able to keep me out of a jail cell this time.

So puzzles it was. I'd chosen crossword, thinking it would get my mind off things, yet it just wasn't helping. At least I'd been smart enough to grab a pencil instead

of a pen this time. I penciled in "Krissy" where I'd
erased "misfit" and sighed.

Was that really what I was? I'd been making a pest
of myself ever since I arrived in Pine Hills. By just
being there, I'd irritated Judith and Eddie Banyon.
Well, at least Judith. Eddie seemed okay with me—
not that he'd ever show it in front of his wife. From
first meeting I'd gotten on everyone else's nerves in one
way or the other. Was there anyone in town I hadn't
annoyed?

I put down my pencil and stood. My back ached
from cleaning up Trouble's mess earlier, and sitting at
the counter wasn't helping. I looked at the mess Misfit
had left me and turned away. I didn't have the energy to
clean anything else up tonight. Maybe I'd get lucky and
he'd actually decide to eat some of the treat crumbs if I
left them there long enough.

Picking up my cell phone, I went to sit down on the
couch. I sank down with a near-contented sigh. I
clicked on the Facebook app, even though I'd much
rather use the full site. I had yet to unpack my laptop,
so it was either this or nothing.

I poked at the STATUS button and stared at the
prompt: What's on your mind?

"A whole lot of things, Mr. Phone," I said, wearily. I
thought about what to say for a few minutes and then
carefully tapped in, Hope things work themselves out
soon. I hit ENTER.

The post was vague, but vague was good. I liked
vague. Vague would earn me a few kind words from
friends I never see anymore, as well as people I've
never met in my life. I'd once been addicted to a few

Facebook games a couple of years back and never bothered to remove any of the "friends" I'd earned from it when I quit. Maybe I'd take care of it sometime later if I ran out of mindless things to do.

I started to close the app when a thought hit me.

*Does Heidi Lawyer use Facebook?*

Thoughts began zooming though my head. What about Raymond Lawyer? Would he be so dumb as to put Dating my son's daughter as his relationship status? What about Mason? I very well might learn a lot about the family if I looked them up on Facebook. People weren't always careful about what they put there.

I sat staring at the tiny screen, contemplating the ramifications of what I was thinking of doing. There was no way they'd know I was looking. What harm could there be in simply typing in their names and looking at their info? It wasn't like I was looking at anything others couldn't see. If they didn't want me to know something about themselves, then they shouldn't have put it on Facebook, where anyone in the world could access it.

"Come on, phone, don't fail me now."

I started with Raymond Lawyer, since he was the head of the family. Unsurprisingly, the old man didn't seem to be on Facebook. While my dad and grandparents were connected online, not everyone in the older generations was. It appeared Raymond was one of those who didn't view social media as a necessary part of his life. Or at least, he couldn't be bothered with it.

I moved on to Mason Lawyer. He had a page, but he

had all of two friends and hadn't appeared ever to have made a post, let alone filled in any of his info. I'm guessing someone talked him into joining—one of those two friends, perhaps—and he lost interest almost as soon as he got started.

Brendon came next. Maybe there was some evidence on the dead man's account that would point to his killer. Could I really be so lucky that he'd made some posts about how he feared someone might be trying to kill him? Or better, named that person?

No such luck. There were men named Brendon Lawyer, but as far as I could tell, none of them were from Pine Hills.

"What's wrong with these people?" I asked Misfit, who'd jumped up on the couch to curl up at my feet. He glanced at me with one eye and then resumed his slumber.

Didn't the Lawyers believe in technology and staying connected with the rest of the world? They really should get up with the times.

I decided I'd try one more name in the hopes of coming up with something useful. I typed in Heidi Lawyer and there she was, the very first entry. I clicked her name, excited, but my hopes were dashed when I saw the minimal information. It appeared she'd set her privacy settings to show only the most basic of information. I'd have to be her friend to see more.

Grumbling to myself, I considered what to do. There was no way I was going to see the information without her accepting me as a friend. I seriously doubted she'd want the woman who'd been hounding her about her husband's death stalking her online.

I happened to glance at her FRIENDS tab and clicked it on a whim. Maybe she was friends with her mother and I could check her page. Or perhaps I'd recognize a name that would trigger something that would put me on the tail of the actual killer.

As I began to scroll through the list, I began to realize something: There was no way Heidi could know all of these people. There had to be hundreds of friends on the list, many who didn't appear to speak English. It was as if she randomly accepted every friend invite that came her way.

Or, like I'd once been, she was addicted to Facebook games.

Could it really be that easy?

I went back and sent a friend invite to Heidi. I stared at my phone and willed it to update. If she was accepting anyone and everyone, perhaps she wouldn't even notice the latest person she'd accepted. Then again, did she even know my name? I didn't recall telling her, though I might have done it when we'd met face-to-face for the first time. And just because I'd told her my name, it didn't mean she'd remember it.

Time passed. No new friends were added.

I was about to give up and shut down the app when a new thought hit me—one that sent cold chills racing up and down my spine. My fingers trembled as I typed in another name, the most important of them all.

Paul Dalton

Sure enough, his face appeared, smiling at me from the tiny little box. I stared at it, heart pounding. Dare I click it? What if he left his site open so that anyone could see? I'd be able to look at every picture posted of him, read every post he'd made since he'd joined the site.

The thought of seeing vacation photos of Paul, shirtless, on the beach, tanned and grinning, had me sweating. There was no way I could resist that. I clicked his face with a trembling finger.

And there it was. Everything I could ever want to know about him, right there for me to see. I checked his ABOUT page and saw he'd lived his entire life in Pine Hills. His relationship status read SINGLE and I wondered how long ago a name had occupied that spot.

I thought of my own page and how Robert had once decorated my relationship status. Those days seemed so far away, it was almost as if it had happened to someone else. I kind of wished it had. That was another name that worked for pest, by the way: "Robert."

Pushing the thought away, I began skimming Paul's recent posts, hoping I'd see something about me there that wasn't in relation to Brendon Lawyer's murder. With the way things had been going lately, it wouldn't have surprised me in the slightest if I found a list of suspects—consisting of my name only—somewhere on his page.

I needn't have worried about that. Apparently, Paul Dalton kept his work life separate from his online life. There wasn't a mention of a single case or crime anywhere on the page. I wondered if perhaps there was a law against cops posting stuff like that on Facebook. I was pretty sure there had to be.

But while I didn't see anything about Brendon's death

or any subsequent cases he might have been involved in, I did see one line that had my heart hammering, despite its vague nature.

**Had fun tonight, though it ended sort of oddly.**

That had to be about me, didn't it? I quickly checked the date and time on the post and saw that it indeed was posted about the time he would have gotten home after our little jaunt into the Lawyer's Insurance building.

Did that mean he liked me? If so, why hadn't he searched me out as a friend on Facebook? I started panicking then, wondering if he'd made that post only to make his mom feel good. He might have hated every second he'd spent with me; and once I quit poking my nose into the Lawyer case, he'd never want to see me again.

*Stop it,* I reprimanded myself. I wasn't a teenage girl anymore.

Calmly I clicked the FRIEND REQUEST button on Paul's page. Almost immediately I got a notification that a request had been accepted.

"He likes me!" I shouted at Misfit. The cat put a paw over his face and turned his head away from me, but I didn't care. Paul Dalton actually liked me!

It was then I realized the little button still said: FRIEND REQUEST SENT. I clicked the notification button and found that no, it wasn't Paul who'd accepted my request.

It was Heidi.

My excitement was replaced by a different sort of thrill. This was my chance at actually learning something about Heidi, something she might not have told me when we'd met. I clicked over to her page and started reading.

Every recent post was about her dead husband. She seemed genuinely upset about his death. She'd been flooded with sympathetic messages. People from Asia told her how sorry they were to hear of his passing; some from Germany wrote what I assumed were well wishes, though they were actually written in German. In a way it was touching, while scary at the same time. I didn't like the idea of someone from so far away, whom I didn't even know, knowing my personal information.

Then again, maybe she'd actually once traveled abroad and had met all of these people. I shouldn't rush to judgment just because I didn't understand or like something.

After skimming a few pages of posts, I turned to the one spot I hoped to learn something that would tell me more about her life. I doubted she was dumb enough to list the guy she cheated with under her relationship status, but it couldn't hurt to check.

I clicked her ABOUT page and was met with disappointment.

There was sparse information there, and nothing about any sort of relationship, outside of it still listed her as MARRIED. I skimmed the information, anyway, and was about to close Facebook down and give up for the night when something caught my eye.

I was looking directly at Heidi Lawyer's place of employment.

If I couldn't go to her house to talk to her without Regina interfering, then why not go to where she worked? I found it unlikely that her mom would follow her all the way there, though I suppose they could work in the same place.

But what if she wasn't at work when I went in? I was sure they'd given her time off after her husband's death. Would she be back to work already? I know if it had been me, I would have taken a week off, if not more.

Knowing her mother, I thought that yeah, she very well might have gone back in, if only to get away from Regina.

Smiling, I wrote down the name of the building, figuring I'd check the address tomorrow. I glanced at the MESSAGE tab and thought about sending her a private message, asking her who it was she'd slept with, or at least if she'd be at work in the morning, but I decided it would be too tacky. This was something I needed to do face-to-face.

Closing Facebook, I rose, feeling much better than I had earlier. I might not be any closer to figuring out who killed Brendon, but I was at least doing *something*. That had to count for something, right?

"Come on, Misfit," I said, stretching. I glanced at the clock and saw it was only ten till eight, but I was beat. "Time for bed."

The orange fluffball leapt off the couch and raced into the bedroom ahead of me. I was excited about what I'd found, but couldn't do anything about it until the morning. I needed a good night's sleep, though I doubted I would get it. I was too wired for that.

Misfit was curled up, right where I normally slept. I considered pushing him to the side, but I decided I didn't want to deal with the scratches that would earn me. I got changed for bed, slid in next to him, and then, surprising myself, drifted off into a restful sleep.

# 26

What I really wanted to do the moment the sun rose and the birds started singing was to rush straight to Heidi's workplace and confront her about her cheating ways. I'd get her to confess that she'd cheated on her husband with his father—who I was now pretty sure was the culprit in this because nothing else really made sense. When I passed the information over to the police, they'd arrest the old man, who'd confess to killing his own son. I mean, the guy had the motive *and* the opportunity. He owned the building. It would have been easy enough to slip the peanut dust into the vent before anyone else came to work.

Instead of rushing off to save the day, I got up, showered, put on my morning coffee, and prepared to head to work.

No one else had died since Brendon, telling me it was unlikely anyone else was going to. I needed to at least make an appearance at Death by Coffee, help get the store open, and then I could head on down to where Heidi worked, in the hope she was there.

I headed out, coffee and cookie ready, mind full of

plans. I gave Jules Phan a quick wave as he got into his own car, and then I gave one to Eleanor Winthrow, for good measure. The curtain didn't twitch, but that didn't mean she wasn't there, watching.

What I should have done was call Paul Dalton the moment I'd woken up. He could have gone to talk to Heidi for me. I could tell him everything I'd learned, as well as everything I'd suspected. I had a feeling she would give in if confronted directly. The girl was a mess.

But then again, Paul had yet to accept my Facebook friend request. I'd fully expected to receive a notification when I woke up, but there was nothing. I wasn't sure I was ready to talk to him yet.

What bothered me most about the whole situation was that I was pretty sure Heidi knew who killed her husband, or at least suspected. There was something in her eye that told me she knew, a glint of misery that could mean only one thing: the person she'd slept with had done it.

But if her lover had killed Brendon, why was she protecting him? It was clear she loved her husband, no matter how much of an ass he might have been. So, why not go to the police and tell them everything she knew?

The answer was, of course, she was still close to the killer, maybe even still sleeping with him. While I suppose it could have been Regina who did the deed, I really did believe it was someone who had more to gain by Brendon's death. If Heidi was going to go back to her husband, then that meant she would be leaving the new guy. He couldn't have liked that, especially if that meant she was going back to her lover's son.

I parked down the street from Death by Coffee, got out, and headed straight into work. I'd actually beaten Vicki in, which was surprising. She was always the first through the door in the morning, but I suppose I did have a little bit more motivation propelling me.

I went about setting up for the day, mind elsewhere. I mixed up the cookie batter, threw a few dozen into the small oven in the back, and then went about getting the coffee machines started. Pleasant aromas of all sorts lifted my spirits. This was going to be a good day. I just knew it.

"Oh!" Vicki said as she entered. She held Trouble's carrier in one hand, her own travel mug of coffee in the other. "You're here."

"Where else would I be?"

A smirk creased the side of her mouth. "It's going to be a good day," she said, echoing my own thoughts.

She sauntered past and released the terrible feline into the wild. He darted across the room, black tail fluffed, and vanished somewhere into the stacks of books.

"Do you think keeping him here is such a good idea after our little incident the other day?" I asked. Morning prep was nearly done. All I had to do was wait on the cookies and we'd be good to go.

Vicki grimaced and somehow still made it look lovely. "Do you really think I should leave him at home? The little guy loves it here."

I caught a glimpse of Trouble as he leapt onto a bookshelf. There was nothing little about him. Well, I suppose that wasn't entirely true. If you were to soak him with water, he'd look like a giant rat with huge paws. The cat, like Misfit, was more fur than anything.

"You know," I said, watching him as he began the morning cleansing of his private parts, "I think I'd miss him. We definitely could use a mascot around here."

The timer on the oven dinged and I left to get the cookies, while Vicki started work on the registers. She handled all of the money because, quite frankly, I was terrible with it. If I was forced to manage the books, we'd be in quite a lot of trouble with the banks, and probably the government as well.

The morning went as anticipated. A few customers came in and then vanished like smoke after they received their coffee. I cleaned the tables a few times, and started a new pot of coffee whenever one grew low or too old. Then, finally, after about an hour of work, I decided it was time to go.

"Do you think it would be okay if I took a quick break?" I asked Vicki, trying to sound as innocent as possible.

She glanced at me, sighed dramatically, and then laughed. "It's okay," she said. "I can't stop you from being you."

"Thanks."

I tossed her my apron and rushed for the door.

I dialed Paul's number as I went, figuring I best give him a heads-up. I might be irritated about the Facebook thing, but he still was a cop. He'd need to arrest Raymond when this thing was all said and done.

The phone rang seemingly forever before it went to voice mail. I frowned, but waited, anyway. I wanted him and him alone. There was no way I was going to risk having Officer Buchannan show up if I called the station. He'd probably arrest me before I could even tell him why I'd called.

"Hey, Paul," I said at the beep. "I think I have things figured out. You need to look into Raymond Lawyer. I think he was sleeping with his son's wife. When he found out they weren't getting a divorce, he decided to end their relationship prematurely. Gotta go."

I clicked off and headed down the walk.

This was it. I was going to break the case wide open. I'd be the talk of the town. Officer Buchannan would be humiliated that he'd interfered with me; he'd possibly be deported to Iowa or some other far, out-of-the-way place for his trouble.

And Paul Dalton would sweep me up in his arms, tell me how brilliant I was, and then we'd ride off into the sunset to get married and have a half-dozen babies who would all have dimples to die for. . . .

I was so lost in my fantasies, I very nearly walked past Too Le Fit to Quit—Heidi's workplace. I stopped outside the squat building and shook my head. I really, *really* didn't understand why every store in this town had to be named something totally off-the-wall. It was embarrassing to think Death by Coffee fit the bill as well.

I pushed open the door to the fitness shop. I could worry about naming later. No bell tolled my coming, which, in a way, was a disappointment. I felt I needed the sound effects to make the moment perfect.

Heidi turned to face me with a smile, but the look froze on her face when she saw who had entered. She was wearing something that was a cross between exercise wear and casual dress. The pants were tight and stretchy, but they didn't have that "expose everything" look to them that yoga pants had. Her shirt was just as tight and showed exactly why Brendon had chosen her.

Her "assets" were pressed perkily against the thin fabric. Despite that, however, the tennis shoes on her feet looked somehow out of place, like the clothes she was wearing were solely for show, not exercise. Maybe that was the point.

"Can I help you?" Heidi asked as I approached. She glanced around the store nervously, like she was afraid someone shopping for supplements might see us together.

"Is your mother around?" I asked. I wouldn't put it past that woman to be lurking around every corner, waiting to leap out at anyone who so much as looked at her daughter funny.

Heidi actually smiled. "No, she's not. This is the one place I can be sure she won't come."

"Good," I said with a sigh of relief. I took her by the arm and led her deeper into the store. I didn't want her to stop talking if someone came in. This very well might be my last chance to get anything out of her.

"Is there something you need?" she asked, sounding nervous. I had a feeling she already knew what I was going to ask her.

"Remember when I was at your house?" She nodded. "I asked you a question, but you didn't get to answer."

She bit her lip and nodded again.

"Can you tell me now?" I asked, almost pleadingly. "It could be vitally important. Who were you cheating on Brendon with?"

Heidi paled. "I . . . I can't," she said in a whisper. She glanced toward an office at the back of the store. "Please. I just can't. If someone were to overhear . . ."

"He was your husband," I said, knowing how my

words would sting, but having no other choice. I *knew* she held the answer.

It did the trick. A tear slid down Heidi's cheek. She wiped it quickly away and sniffed. One more look to the back of the store, and then she led me to the side where a rack of insoles cut us off from view.

"Promise me you won't tell anyone," she said. "It's just so . . . so embarrassing. I don't know if I could take it if word got around."

"I'll only tell the police if I think it is important to the case," I said. "That's as good as I can do."

She appeared to think about it and then shook her head. "I can't," she whispered. I realized I was going to have to take the initiative. She was too nervous about someone else overhearing; she would never talk on her own.

"Was it Raymond Lawyer?"

Heidi's face did something I can't describe, let alone interpret. Disgust was mixed with shock, which was mixed with fear. It was like her cheeks and mouth were trying to do gymnastics on her face, while her eyes had decided it was time to pop on out for a quick drink.

Finally she seemed to gain some control over her features. She took a step away from me and her nose crinkled. "Oh, God! No," she said. "I'd never . . . How could you even think . . . . Just . . . *Ew!*"

*"Ew"* was right. It was both something of a relief and a disappointment that I'd been so wrong. I felt the need to apologize almost immediately. It was like accusing her of running off with somebody's demented grandpa.

"I'm sorry," I said. "Tessa said cheating ran in the

family, and when you revealed you'd cheated yourself, I'd just assumed . . ."

I trailed off as I realized the look on Heidi's face had changed. Color ran from the depths of her too-tight shirt and up her neck. She was soon so flushed, I was worried she might need help.

That was when the lightbulb in my head flashed to life. Who was the one person who'd dropped hints about Raymond Lawyer? Who had been the one person who had come to Heidi's defense when I mentioned the two might have gotten together?

"Tessa?" I asked, shocked. "You cheated on your husband with the woman he cheated on you with?"

It took all my self-control not to shout it.

Heidi nodded and then buried her face in her hands. "It was stupid," she said, "but it made so much sense at the time. I wanted to know what it was like, why she was so much better than me. I mean, why would he spend time with her when I was waiting for him at home, you know?"

My jaw unhinged and flapped in the breeze a few moments before I could manage to get it to work right. "Are you . . . I mean . . ." I took a deep breath. What did I mean? I finally settled on: "Are you still seeing her?"

Heidi lowered her gaze. "No," she said. "We had a fight yesterday."

Yesterday, as in when Tessa had looked rumpled and her lips looked as if she'd been making out with someone. Could she have tried to kiss Heidi and had her advances rebuffed?

It was like getting hit upside the head with a brick. It all made sense now. Too Le Fit to Quit was just down the street from Phantastic Candies, which was a few blocks down from Tessa's Dresses. If they'd had the fight here, it explained why she'd walked right past me without a second glance. And then when I started asking questions, it would explain why she'd gotten so nervous and wanted to get inside before someone could overhear our conversation.

Tessa had been misleading me this entire time. She'd wanted to throw me off, get me thinking about the other men in the family. She had to hate Brendon for what he'd done to her. How could I have been so blind?

"Heidi," I said, grabbing her by the arms. She gave me a startled look, but she didn't pull away. "Do you think Tessa could have killed Brendon?"

She started to shake her head and then broke down and nodded. "I don't want to believe it, but she'd been so angry with him." She started shaking with sobs and I let her go so she could wipe away her tears.

My mind was racing. I still couldn't figure out how Tessa could have done it. She wasn't on the list of people who'd arrived that day to see Brendon. Had she had someone else kill him? Or was I barking up the proverbial wrong tree?

"Don't tell anyone," Heidi begged. "*Please.* My mom doesn't know. No one does, not even the police. If this were to get out, people would start talking about me, about my . . . preferences."

I wished I could have told her I would keep her secret. However, if Tessa really was the killer, then the truth needed to come out.

"I'll do my best" was all I could promise before I spun away. I needed to confront Tessa. I couldn't let her get away with this.

I bolted out the door and ran straight for Tessa's

Dresses. I dialed Paul's number as I went, but it went to voice mail once again.

I didn't bother leaving a message this time. I didn't have time.

I had to catch a murderer.

# 27

A CLOSED sign hung in the window of Tessa's Dresses. I frowned at it and checked my watch. It was far too early for a lunch break and late enough that she should already have been there to open up. Had Tessa seen me coming and hurriedly closed up shop to avoid me?

I tried the door and found it to be locked. All of the lights inside were off, casting everything in shadows. The mannequins looked almost like real people in the gloom. Any one of them could be Tessa, hiding in plain sight.

"Tessa?" I called. I pressed my face against the glass and cupped my hands to block out the sun. There was no movement inside the store. If she was in there, she was holding extremely still or she was hiding in the back somewhere.

For an insane moment I considered breaking the glass and going in search of her. If Tessa was inside, hiding from me, I was even more positive she was the killer. Why go to all of this trouble if you are innocent?

Thoughts of the disappointed look Chief Dalton would give me if I were to end up in her interrogation room yet again kept me from doing it. Even if there were packs of dusted peanuts in the back room, I'd still get into trouble for forcing my way inside. There had to be a better way to do this.

"Damn it," I said, kicking the door's frame. There'd be no confronting Tessa today unless I figured out where she lived. I really didn't want to have to explain to Vicki why I kept leaving work so I could check to see if Tessa was in.

I started back to Death by Coffee, defeated. Maybe it wasn't such a bad thing she wasn't at work today. If she *had* killed Brendon Lawyer, she might come after me the moment I confronted her with what paltry evidence I had. I should leave the accusations to the police.

But a stubborn part of me wanted to break the case myself. If I brought the killer to them bound and gagged and ready to confess, they'd have to take me seriously. I wouldn't be the girl who convinced an officer to take me into a crime scene illegally, but rather the girl who caught a killer. It had a nice ring to it.

"I'd need handcuffs," I muttered, drawing a few eyes. I used to own a pair of handcuffs, but they weren't the sort you'd use to apprehend criminals.

My face flushed at the thought. Boy, were those days I'd like to forget. I'm pretty sure Robert still had the cuffs, which meant I never wanted to see them again, no matter how much fun they might have been.

Besides, I wasn't even sure the police still used

handcuffs anymore, so maybe all I needed to do was hit up the hardware store and pick me up some zip strips. I knew firsthand how well they worked.

There were five people in Death by Coffee when I returned. They glanced at me as I entered and then went back to their coffees, clearly bored. Maybe we needed to add some entertainment to the place? Setting up a Wi-Fi hub wouldn't be such a bad idea. People could get their work done while they enjoyed some coffee or maybe read a book.

I glanced at my phone and sighed. There'd be no criminal catching for me. I needed to focus on making this place a success first.

I dialed Officer Dalton, ready to tell him everything I knew. It rang a few times and then voice mail picked up. I growled in frustration and hung up without a message. If he wasn't going to answer his phone when I called—or add me as a Facebook friend—I wanted nothing to do with him, anyway. I thrust my phone angrily into my pocket.

Vicki was leaning against the wall behind the counter, watching me with a grin. The smell of fresh coffee was too much for me and I had to make myself a cup. I grabbed a cookie, plopped it in, and leaned beside her.

"Have a good break?" she asked, still grinning. She knew what I'd been doing and I had a feeling she could tell I hadn't accomplished everything I'd wanted.

"It was okay. You know, revelations and stuff."

"Ah."

"Have much trouble here?"

Vicki shrugged. "Nothing like yesterday."

"Good."

I chugged the coffee and instantly regretted it. I'd been so anxious to get to work today, I hadn't bothered to do much more than shower before coming in. The coffee was running through me in a bad way.

"Be right back," I said, setting the mug and soggy cookie aside.

Thankfully, the restroom was clean, probably because no one had come in all day. I suppose that's one good thing about not having a ton of customers; you don't have to clean the restrooms as regularly. Both stalls were empty, meaning I had my choice of thrones. I chose the farthest from the door because, well, why not?

I sat down, did my business, and then left to wash my hands. My cell was still in my pocket and I considered calling Paul again, but banished the idea before I could act on it. If he couldn't be bothered to pick up the first three times, then I wasn't going to give him a fourth. If he wanted to talk to me, well, he could just call.

I used the dryer on my dripping hands, checked to make sure my hair wasn't too disheveled, and then left the restroom, mind on Officer Paul Dalton and his inability to keep a girl happy. I was halfway across the room when I saw her.

Tessa was standing at the counter, waiting for her order. Her foot tapped impatiently and she kept looking out the window like she expected someone to come rushing in after her. Did nervous behavior like that prove her guilt?

Vicki was busy mixing what looked to be cappuccino

of some sort, completely oblivious to the fact that the
woman she was serving very well might be a killer. I
wanted to scream at her to be careful. Who knew what
kind of weapon Tessa might be packing?

But I simply stood there, uncertain what to do. Tessa
was right here, in my territory, where I could do what I
pleased. I could approach her, accuse her, and then
hope she gave herself up easily rather than attack me.
Or I could follow her, see where she went, and make
plans accordingly. Maybe she'd lead me directly to a
barrel of peanuts she was in the process of dusting so
she could kill someone else. Maybe she was looking
to become the Peanut Killer. She'd strike fear into each
and every person with a severe allergy.

Okay, maybe the last was a little far-fetched. Tessa
wasn't a serial killer—if she was a killer at all. She'd
been rejected by a man who she thought had loved her
and then proceeded to sleep with his wife as a form of
revenge.

My mind boggled a little at the last, but that didn't
change the fact that it had happened.

Vicki finished with the cappuccino and handed it to
Tessa, who paid and then turned toward the door.

I couldn't let her go.

"Tessa! Wait!" I shouted, running toward her.

She turned, saw me, and frowned. She glanced
toward the door as if considering just walking out. She
had no reason to talk to me.

"I know," I said, being purposefully vague. "I know
all about it."

That caught her attention. She turned, one hand on
her hip, the other holding the cappuccino.

"You have no idea," she said. "Just leave me alone."

I moved closer. I knew what I was doing was stupid. Didn't this sort of thing always end badly for the good guy? I really should have just called the police station and let whoever answered handle it, even if it was that jerk Buchannan.

But I didn't know for sure Tessa had anything to do with Brendon's death. For all I knew, Heidi had put me onto her trail because she realized I was getting too close. Maybe I'd been right when I'd thought Mason and Heidi had conspired together. Just because Tessa had slept with both of the Lawyers didn't mean she was a murderer.

"I know," I said again, stopping just outside of her reach, just in case.

"And what do you think you know?"

"I know about you and Heidi."

There was a collective gasp from the five customers scattered around the room. I could feel them pressing in on me, getting a better view. This was probably the most entertainment they'd had since, well, since the cat went on a rampage upstairs.

Tessa swallowed hard. She sucked in her cheeks and bit down, as if trying to keep from saying something she'd regret. From her wince I could tell it hurt.

"What of it?" she finally asked. "I don't see how it is any of your business what I do in my private time."

"Both of them?" I asked. The small crowd gave me strength to go on. She wouldn't do anything with the witnesses here. If I could get her to confess in front of these people, there was no way she could snake her way out of it later. "How could you?"

She snorted. "They were both . . ." She looked as if she was searching for the right word. "Lovely people," she concluded. "They were terrible for each other."

"But right for you?"

She shrugged. "It was their choice. I didn't force them into anything."

"At least until things started to fall apart for you."

Her eyes narrowed. "And what do you mean by that?"

I took a deep breath and looked around the room for support. All eyes were on me, including Vicki's. Word of the encounter would surely spread throughout Pine Hills within an hour. If I was wrong about her, I was going to be the laughingstock of the town. But if I was right . . . Visions of parades and maybe a medal or two swam through my head.

"You thought Brendon was going to leave his wife for you, but he cheated on you with Beth, instead." I nodded toward Lawyer's Insurance.

*Wait. Is that Paul Dalton's car over there?*

The thought that he might be close helped strengthen my resolve. If anything went wrong, I could scream for help and he'd burst in and rescue me.

"When that happened and Heidi came to confront you about it, you somehow convinced her to sleep with you, too. Maybe it was her idea. Maybe it was yours. I don't know. I have a feeling that you both thought it would be a good way to get back at Brendon, so you went through with it. Maybe in the end you actually cared about her. Maybe you still do."

Tessa glared at me, but she didn't speak. The hand on her hip kept tightening. It was a wonder her nails didn't pop right through the fabric of her dress and spear her.

"But when you learned Heidi and Brendon had called off the divorce and were getting back together, you realized you'd been dumped again. That had to infuriate you."

"What of it?" Tessa said, voice tight. "It sucks. I'm sure you've been dumped before."

"I have," I admitted. "But not like this, not by two people who were so close. It had to eat you up inside to see them together when you'd thought that they both loved you, instead."

Chairs scraped forward as our little crowd moved to get a better view. Even Vicki had come around the counter to watch.

Tessa ignored them all. She only had eyes for me.

"Everyone knew Brendon was allergic to peanuts. You somehow managed to steal his EpiPen, get into the office unseen, and plant the dust in the vent so that when the air kicked on, he'd breathe it in. Without his EpiPen, Brendon would stand no chance."

Tessa paled. "And how was I supposed to do that?" she asked, still trying to put on a strong front. She stuck out her chin and glared at me defiantly.

It was then I knew I had her. This woman had killed Brendon Lawyer, all because she felt humiliated by being dumped. I still wasn't positive how she'd pulled it off, but I figured the police could figure that part out. They had to be good for something, right?

"I don't know," I said. "But I'll find out." I took a chance and moved closer, like you'd see in a movie, crowding her space and lowering my voice. "Maybe you broke in. Maybe you entered his office while wearing a disguise or paid someone to do it for you."

She laughed, but it was strained. "You're insane."

"Am I?" I gave her my best "I've got you now" smile. "Am I really?"

Tessa looked around the room, seemingly noticing our audience for the first time. She licked her lips and then glanced back at Vicki, who had her hand over her mouth as she watched us. I could almost see the calculation in Tessa's eyes as she scanned the room, looking for a way to escape.

Finally she turned back to me and smiled. There was so much hate in that smile, I took an involuntary step back. So much for my tough-girl persona.

Tessa took a deep breath, looked to the ceiling as if hoping for rescue from Above, and then made her move.

I should have seen it coming. I mean, I'd seen enough TV and read enough novels to know the killer wouldn't simply turn herself in when confronted with her crimes.

No, the killers always tried to run and often used whatever they were holding as a weapon.

Tessa screeched at me and threw her coffee directly into my face. The lid popped off as I lifted my arm defensively to protect myself. Hot cappuccino splashed across my arm and face, but it didn't get into my eyes.

I yelped in pain and surprise and someone else screamed. There was a moment of confusion where I couldn't see, but I could hear the startled sounds of people getting to their feet and Vicki asking me frantically if I was all right.

And then my vision cleared. I caught a glimpse of

Tessa as she bolted out of Death by Coffee and turned to run down the sidewalk, toward Tessa's Dresses.

"I'm going after her!" I called, wiping coffee from my stinging face. "Call the police!"

I took off at a run.

The chase was on.

# 28

Have I ever mentioned how much I hate running?

Tessa easily pulled away from me while wearing a dress and flats. I was wearing my work tennis shoes and still couldn't make up any ground. She didn't appear much more athletic than I was, but she was definitely a lot faster.

I could only hope Vicki complied and called the police the moment I was out the door. Maybe they could pick me up and we could ride after her together. Of course, if Tessa got into a car while I waited for them, she could keep on driving until she was so far away from Pine Hills, we'd never find her again.

Pedestrians leapt out of our way as we ran down the sidewalk. Tessa glanced back at me a few times, sneering, which thankfully slowed her down or else I definitely would have lost her. I already had a stitch in my side and was just over a block down the road. I felt like I'd run a marathon.

I really do think she would have gotten away if she hadn't stopped. She pulled up short in front of Tessa's Dresses, a good ways ahead of me, and fumbled for something in her purse. She kept shooting glances my way, but unless she was actually trying to pick the lock with a toothpick, there was no way I was going to catch up with her before she was inside.

Fate, however, must have been on my side. Tessa pulled her keys from her purse, moved to shove the store key into the lock, and then dropped them. It was a move I'd seen in movies a million times, but I never thought it actually happened in real life.

I heard her curse from down the block as she scooped the keys up, sorted through them, and shoved one into the lock. She turned the key and pushed through the door just as I reached her. She tried to slam the door in my face, but I managed to get my arm through the doorway. The pain was nearly unbearable as she tried to squeeze my arm off with the door. After a moment of futile pushing, she cursed again, shoved one last time, and then ran for the counter.

Sucking air, I pushed the door open and entered Tessa's Dresses. My arm wasn't broken, but someone had forgotten to tell my nerves that. They were screaming for help, causing pain to shoot up and down my arm from elbow to shoulder. The door closed behind me, cutting off the gawking pedestrians who had watched the chase with no idea what was happening.

"It's over," I gasped, bending over to catch my breath. Boy, I really needed to work on my cardio if I was going to live here. All of this running was getting old, fast.

"I don't think so."

I looked up to find myself staring into the barrel of a gun. It was a tiny thing, something Tessa's small hands could handle without fumbling. Her hands were shaking, her hair was a mess, but I was the one who was in some serious trouble.

I raised my hands, palms outward, just like the movies showed me to do. The stitch in my side wailed and I winced, very nearly doubling over from it. However, I had a feeling if I did something like that, she'd shoot. I sucked in a pained breath and took a tentative step forward. Tessa's aim firmed and I stopped short.

"Tessa," I said. "You can't run forever."

She snorted, clearly laughing at my overused cliché. I was going on pure instinct now, and instinct told me to do what I knew. I'd never been in a situation like this before, but years of sitting on the couch, reading a book or staring at the television, gave me some indication of how to do this and survive.

"How did you know?" She brushed a strand of hair out of her face with her free hand. She was aiming at me one-handed, which I knew from my dad's books wasn't easy. It wouldn't be long before her arm would fatigue and she'd have to switch hands or go with a two-handed grip.

See what you can learn if you pay attention?

I licked my lips and slid a little to the side. Her gun followed me, but at least she didn't shoot or make any overly agitated movements that would cause the gun to go off accidently.

"I put the pieces together," I said, speaking slowly so as not to cause her alarm. "They were sitting right there in front of me. Eventually the police will figure it out as well, with or without me."

She wiped at her forehead with her arm. She was sweating heavily and her chest was rising and falling in a way that told me she was close to panic. What we both needed were a couple of comfy chairs and some iced tea. That would ease both of our minds. No one would get shot and I wouldn't keel over from exhaustion. I'd call that a win-win.

"I didn't mean to do it, you know?" she said. Her arm drooped and then rose again. Fatigue was definitely setting in.

"It doesn't matter," I said. "He's dead."

That was probably the wrong thing to say. She sneered and the muscles in her arm bunched. I winced, anticipating the bullet, but she didn't fire.

"I know that!" she shouted. Tears began pouring down her cheeks. "I didn't mean to kill him. It was an accident."

I wasn't sure how slipping peanut dust into a vent and stealing the man's EpiPen could be called an accident. However, since she was the woman holding the gun, I was willing to give her the benefit of the doubt.

"Okay," I said. "It was an accident. I believe you."

She sniffed and once more wiped at her forehead, this time with her gun hand. "I didn't mean it. I admit I went in with the dust, but I was just going to throw it in his face after confronting him, I swear."

My mind was racing, trying to put the last pieces together. I was also hoping I could keep her talking until someone arrived—the police, preferably. The door was unlocked, so it wasn't like they'd have to break in. All someone had to do was go over and tell Paul what happened and he'd come and save me.

"I went to see him during my lunch break, but when I saw him go into Raymond's office with Beth right beside him, I just sort of wigged out. I went into Brendon's office and thought about sprinkling the dust in his drink and then leaving, but I saw the vent and thought, 'What the hell?' I used a piece of paper to funnel it in, and on the way out, I grabbed his EpiPen because it was lying right there."

"And he died because of it."

She nodded. Her arm was seriously drooping now. The gun was still aimed in my general direction, but at least if it went off, the bullet would hit the floor rather than me.

Or so I hoped.

"I thought he'd choke for a little while and then call for help. I didn't know he'd die from it." The tears were really running down her face now. "No one told me how bad his allergy was. I thought he'd just break out, have some trouble breathing, and that would be it."

"I believe you." And the funny thing was, I did. When people think of allergies, they often think of normal, everyday allergies where your eyes water and you sneeze a lot. They don't think about the bad ones, the ones that kill. Unless you actually saw someone suffering an attack, it wasn't something you thought about.

"But he deserved it," Tessa snarled, wiping away the last of her tears. "He was going to ruin me. Heidi and I . . . we were in love!"

The gun rose and I could see her resolve firming. She actually thought she was still going to get away with this. I had no idea how she would explain away the encounter in the coffee shop or explain my body, outside of maybe claiming I'd broken in and attacked her. There were so many witnesses, no one would believe her, though.

But then again, I wouldn't be around to see it. That wasn't exactly reassuring.

"Tessa," I said, borrowing more from the books I've read. "Think about what you're doing."

"I can't go to jail," she said. "Brendon has ruined my life in more than one way, but I won't let him ruin this." She took a deep breath. "You're going to have to die. I'll tell everyone how you accused me of things that weren't true, how I tried to get away from you, and then how you came in here and threatened me. I'll tell them you were the one who killed Brendon, that the whole reason you came to Pine Hills was to sleep with him. They'll believe me." A look of doubt passed across her face and the next was spoken at a whisper. "They'll believe me."

"Tessa . . ." I had no idea what I could say that would calm her down. She truly believed she was the victim here. She might have killed Brendon accidently, but what she was doing now was no accident.

"You should have stayed out of it." Her second hand came up to steady the gun and I knew she was going to shoot.

And that's when an angel appeared.

There was a crash as the door to Tessa's Dresses flew open. Sun bathed Officer Paul Dalton where he stood, his own gun raised and aimed at Tessa. I swear I could hear the sound of angels singing as he shouted, "Drop it!"

Tessa stared at him, her gun hovering somewhere between Paul and me. She was watching him so closely, she didn't notice me as I started to move.

"I can't," she said. "I can't go to jail. It would be the end of my life."

"Just lower the weapon," Paul said. He kept his aim

on her, but his eyes flickered my way. He shook his head almost imperceptibly, but when was the last time I ever listened to reason?

I moved slowly around the room, hopefully putting myself out of Tessa's line of sight. My heart was hammering so loud, I was afraid she might hear me coming. A half-dozen more steps and I'd be there.

"You don't understand." Her voice had gone pleading, as if she thought she might convince him that none of this was her fault. "Brendon made me do it when he cheated on me and then tried to steal Heidi from me. He'd made his decision. He wanted someone else and he should have stayed with her. Why did he have to try to take everything from me?"

My foot kicked a hanger that had been lying on the floor. Tessa's head spun around to face me. Her mouth was open in an *O* of surprise as I leapt at her.

A gun went off as I crashed into her. Pain seared through my elbow, causing me to cry out. There was a clatter as Tessa's gun fell to the floor. We collapsed atop each other—me trying to keep from whimpering about my arm, Tessa scrambling to get away.

And then firm hands grabbed me from behind and pulled me from her. As soon as I was on my feet, I sank right back down to the floor, dizzy and sick. Paul was on Tessa and had her zip stripped before either of us knew what had happened.

The world did a few loop de loops and I leaned back against the counter, cradling my injured arm against my chest. I vaguely wondered if I was going to bleed to death.

"You all right?" Paul asked from somewhere a million miles away.

"Yeah," I said dreamily. My angel had saved me. "Peachy keen."

And then, just to prove that my life was indeed something out of a movie, the lights in my head flashed a few times before fading entirely. Then, with barely a whimper, I passed out.

# 29

Sweat poured down my face as I rushed from table to table, trying to get it clean before the next customer was seated. There was a line at the counter and Vicki was doing her best to keep up with it while not neglecting her duties upstairs.

Death by Coffee was buzzing. After my not-so-heroic chase and apprehension of Tessa Belkenni—I'd learned her last name earlier in the week—the store had suddenly picked up. Not surprisingly, people were interested in dining in a place where a hero worked. Even Judith Banyon had made an appearance, though she didn't look too happy about it and had left within two minutes. Baby steps, right?

I finished wiping down my tables and hurried back to Vicki.

"I told you it would pick up," she said with a grin.

"Now I just hope it slows down."

She laughed and scurried up the stairs to the bookstore, where Trouble was watching the flood of people from atop a bookshelf, his fluffy tail firmly wrapped around his body so no one could step on it.

Eventually the rush died down enough to where I could breathe. I leaned against the counter, pooped beyond belief, and closed my eyes.

"Time for a break?"

I just about jumped clear out of my shoes. Paul Dalton stood there, smiling at me, dazzling me with his dimples.

"Go," Vicki said, coming down to take my place. "I've got this."

Who was I to argue?

Paul led me to one of the few empty tables. I practically fell into my chair. My feet hurt so badly, I wanted to rub them, but I didn't think it would be seemly to pull off my shoes in the middle of the store. Maybe if Paul was interested in doing the job for me, I'd be willing. A good foot rub never hurt anyone.

"Getting busy, I see," he said with a smile.

"It is."

"How's your arm?" Did I detect real concern in his voice?

I flexed my arm a few times and smiled. "Good as new."

"Good."

Tessa's shot hadn't hit anything but the ceiling, much to my amazement. When we'd fallen, I'd managed to catch my elbow on the corner of the counter and jammed it pretty good. The bruise was immense, but I wasn't going to bleed to death from that. I'd take a bruise over a hole in the arm any day.

"It was pretty stupid what you did, you know?" He said it with a smile, though I could tell he meant it.

"What do you mean?" I asked, all innocence. "I stopped her, didn't I?"

"You did." He laughed, showing me his dimples

again. "But I had everything under control. You didn't need to put yourself in harm's way like that. It was dangerous. You could have been hurt."

"I was," I said, lifting my arm to show him, as if he'd forgotten.

He sighed. "Well, it could have been worse."

"What's happening with Tessa?" I asked, trying to change the subject from my near-death experience.

Paul leaned back in his chair and stretched. He was in his uniform, which I noted was just a tad bit snug. He should buy all of his clothes that size.

"She's being charged with Brendon Lawyer's murder, among other things. She's given in and pleaded guilty, though she still insists it was an accident."

I nodded. So far, no one had asked me to give much more than a statement. I was hoping I wouldn't have to go to court to testify against her or anything. In a way I did feel bad for the girl; she'd had her heart broken pretty badly.

"I still don't get it," I said. "She timed everything so well. I keep thinking Raymond knew something and asked Beth and Brendon into his office so Tessa could sneak in unseen. He had to have been involved."

"No, he wasn't," Paul said. "When I got your message that he might have killed his son, I headed in to talk with him to see if I missed anything the first time I was there."

My face reddened. Boy, had I been wrong about that or what?

"He was understandably upset about being implicated in Brendon's death." Paul chuckled. "But he did tell me a few things he'd left out before."

"Such as?"

"Turns out Raymond didn't know Brendon was

sleeping with Beth until earlier that day. He wasn't happy about it, so he called both of them into his office to yell at them. He wanted them to break it off. Little did he know, Brendon had already broken up with Beth, but the secretary hadn't let on. She was still telling her friends they were seeing each other, which, by the way, was how Raymond found out."

"So it was just a coincidence that Tessa showed up at the exact moment Brendon wasn't there?"

"Well, she knew when he took his lunch and had gone in to see him then. When they'd been together, she'd often visit him and they'd do more than just eat behind closed doors."

I reddened slightly, my mind going places it probably shouldn't.

"She figured she'd stop by like she used to, attack him, and then leave," Paul went on, oblivious to my embarrassment. "When no one was there, she did just what she said she did." He sighed. "Really, it all could have been avoided if Brendon didn't treat women like they were there simply to be used and discarded. I would never do something like that."

Was that a glimmer I saw in his eye? I couldn't stop the smile.

"Raymond blames himself," Paul said, glancing toward the building across the street. "It's why he wasn't willing to help before. He thought we'd find some way to blame him for his son's death, or shut down his business. The man is pretty self-centered, which didn't help matters one bit."

"At least it's over," I said.

Paul only nodded.

We sat in silence a moment, each mulling over the last

few days. It's hard to believe everything had happened in such a short amount of time.

Suddenly I remembered something that had been bothering me.

"Hey, Paul," I asked, drawing his attention back to me. "Do you use Facebook?"

"Sure, why?"

"Well, I sort of sent you a request and . . ." My face flushed. Now that I was asking, it sounded stupid.

"Sorry." He grinned. "I've been so busy, I haven't checked it in a few days."

"So you aren't mad at me or anything?"

For an answer he pulled out his cell phone, brought up the Facebook app, and clicked a button. A moment later I received the notification that I had a new friend.

"Not at all."

The bell above the door jangled and a familiar sound met my ears.

"Oh, my Lordy-Lou!" Rita cried. She saw where I was sitting and rushed over, Andi and Georgina right behind her. "You're a celebrity!" she said. "You're just like your father."

I groaned, which only caused Paul to laugh.

"I'll let you get back to work," he said. "I just wanted to make sure you were still doing okay." He rose, tipped an imaginary hat, and then headed out the door. Rita immediately took his place.

"I heard all about it," she said. "I mean, to catch a killer in your very own store." She hugged herself in delight. "This is my favorite place in all of the world. I'm going to come here every day, spend all my time writing in this very spot." She tapped the table and looked around the room like she'd never seen the place before. "This is perfect."

*Kill me now,* I thought, but instead smiled. "Great," I said. "I can always reserve a place for you." I didn't tell her I planned on making it in the back of the room, as far away from the counter as possible.

"That would be lovely!" she said. "Won't it, ladies?"

Both Andi and Georgina readily agreed.

I got to my feet, which protested at being used so soon after such a short rest. "I best get back to work," I said with a smile. "Busy, you know? I might actually have to hire someone if it keeps up."

"You do that," Rita said. I started to walk away, but she stopped me. "By the way," she said, "do you think you'll be coming to another meeting soon? You missed the last."

I almost told her "no," just so I could get back to work, but I stopped myself.

"You know," I said thoughtfully, "I think I might." I looked around Death by Coffee, at all of the patrons who were now crowding the place. They'd been drawn here by what I'd done, even if I shouldn't have risked my life in such a way. They appreciated it and were showing me how much by coming here.

Either that, or they were waiting for the next disaster. I really didn't care which, as long as they were coming.

And what about those who didn't live in Pine Hills? Wouldn't they be interested in hearing about how I solved a crime in my very first week in town? It wasn't every day a simple working girl solved a murder mystery on her own.

I gave Rita a big smile, eyes twinkling. "Turns out, I might actually have a story in me, after all."

Please turn the page for an exciting sneak peek of
Alex Erickson's next Krissy Hancock Mystery

**DEATH BY TEA,**

coming in December 2015!

# 1

A steady beeping tried to drown out the gunfire and pounding of my own heart. Officer Paul Dalton lay atop me—fully dressed, unfortunately—as he shielded me from some unknown assailant who seemed to have an endless supply of ammo. I knew I should have been scared; but with him that close to me, I couldn't think about anything but his firm muscles flexing as he held me, and those wonderful dimples of his that were even now creasing his cheeks. Even in the heart of danger, he could still find time to smile at me.

The beeping continued, louder, more insistent than before.

"Do you think it's a bomb?" I asked as I dreamily stroked Paul's bicep.

"No, Krissy, my love." His smile was enough to make my head swim. "I think it's an alarm."

"An alarm?"

Panic flared through me as I surged from the dream and into the waking world, arms and legs flailing. My cat, Misfit, who had been sleeping next to me, was uncenremoniously dumped onto the floor as I sat up, eyes darting to the clock, which read an alarming 8:31.

"Crapcicle!"

I practically fell out of the bed as I scrambled to my feet. There was no time for a shower, so I went straight for my closet, where I grabbed the first thing my hand fell upon. I was supposed to be at work at half past eight. Somehow I'd managed to oversleep my alarm by a good hour.

"Stupid dream," I grumbled as I ripped off my pj's, tossed them onto the floor, and scrambled into my clothes. I hopped my way into the kitchen on one foot as I tried to walk and slip on my shoes at the same time. Misfit was sitting next to his food bowl, watching me with a kitty grin.

"Enjoying this, are you?" I asked him. "Next time I'll let you starve." I filled his dish and he promptly buried his face in his bowl. The cat normally woke me up well before my alarm; yet this time I knew he'd intentionally let me sleep, more than likely because of something I'd done to him. He's devious like that.

I looked longingly at my coffeepot before darting back down the hall and into the bathroom. My hair was sticking up in every which direction in massive tangles that would take hours to fix. Either I'd spent the night twisting and turning my head on the pillow, or Misfit had been at my hair with his tongue and claws again, kneading away. I swear that cat has it in for me.

I grabbed my brush from the drawer and yanked it through my hair a few times. When that didn't work, I snatched up a hair tie and did my best to tame the mess on my head into a ponytail. It was uneven and lumpy, but it would have to do.

Next came a quick once-over with my toothbrush— there was no way on God's green earth that I was going to go out without at least making an attempt at brushing my teeth—and then it was back to the kitchen, where I grabbed my purse and keys and headed out the door. The curtains next door swished open as my neighbor Eleanor Winthrow leaned forward at her window seat to watch me. It was becoming a regular routine. The woman probably knew my schedule better than I did. She really needed a hobby other than spying on me.

I paid her little mind as I got into my black Focus, started the car, and backed wildly out of my driveway in a spray of dusty pavement. And then it was a mad rush to work, praying I didn't come across one of the local cops along the way.

At least I wasn't scheduled to open Death by Coffee today. My best friend, Vicki Patterson, and one of our new hires, Lena Allison, were scheduled for that, so the doors should already be open, but that didn't make me feel any better. I didn't like to be late, especially on a day like today when we were finally going to have Wi-Fi connectivity for our customers. It was a big day for us and I was going to show up for it smelling like I hadn't showered—which I hadn't.

I found a parking space just down the road from our shop. I made one last futile attempt to tame my hair and then headed down the sidewalk. I could see Lena hanging something on the front of the store. When she glanced up, I gave her an apologetic wave.

"Sorry," I said, hurrying over. "My alarm didn't go off." A little white lie never hurt anyone.

"It's cool." Lena gave me a crooked smile. A fresh scrape on her chin told me she'd crashed her skateboard again. The poor girl was practically a living scab. She'd recently cut her hair short and dyed it from dark brown to something a little more wild. I had to admit, the purple really did bring out her eyes. "Everything's taken care of." She motioned to the FREE WI-FI sign now hanging in the window.

"Good." I breathed deep, cringed at my pungent odor, and then hurried past Lena into Death by Coffee.

The combination bookstore and coffee shop was doing much better after a slow start. There'd been a murder and I'd somehow managed to solve it. Apparently, the people of Pine Hills enjoyed a little excitement every now and again, and I was viewed as something of a minor celebrity. It was the reason we were finally able to hire a couple of new employees rather than close up like I thought we would have to do. The money coming in wasn't as good as I thought it would be, but at least it was enough so the workday wasn't left totally up to Vicki and me.

I barely paid the nearly packed store any mind as I hurried behind the counter and into the office. My apron was hanging from a hook just inside the door. I grabbed it, threw it on around my neck, and then grabbed a spare bottle of cleaner. I sprayed the front of my apron a few times and sniffed. Satisfied it made me smell a little less ripe, I headed out to face the world.

Vicki was busy ringing up a book order upstairs. She gave me a quick wave before turning back to the customer, dazzling him with her million-dollar smile. She really should have been an actress—something her parents had pressed on her since she was little—but she'd chosen the life of a store owner, instead. She was wearing shorts today, showing off those legs of hers. I sighed and turned away, feeling even worse about myself than I had before, and found myself looking right into my dad's smiling face.

Something akin to *"Gah!"* garbled its way out of my mouth. My hand went reflexively to my hair to smooth it down as I staggered back a couple of steps. I was about to start babbling explanations for my appearance and late arrival when I noticed Dad's body was shiny and decidedly flat.

"Oh, I knew you'd approve!" Rita Jablonski, the resident gossip, said. She stepped around what was apparently a life-sized cardboard cutout of my dad.

"Approve of what?" My heart slowed down from its rapid pounding as I leaned on the counter. I loved my dad, I really did, but I didn't want him showing up in Pine Hills unannounced, especially with Rita lurking about. He is a retired writer and Rita considers herself his number one fan. I didn't want her to go all *Misery* on him.

Rita patted the fake James Hancock on the shoulder. "Of having him as your store mascot!" She just about swooned. "I hate not having him in my bedroom looking out for me at night, but I think he belongs here, don't you?"

"He was in your bedroom?"

"Of course, dear." She giggled in a way that made my stomach do a flip. It sounded bubbly, lustful, and just a little crazy. I *so* didn't want to think about what she did with the cardboard cutout. "I was lying there this morning, looking at him, when I realized how fitting it would be to bring him in here. I mean, the store *is* named after one of his books, right? He belongs here. And what with having the book club meetings here, and us reading one of his books, it just made sense."

"Wait, what?" My mind was unsuccessfully trying to catch up. I was still stuck on the fact she kept him in her bedroom. I mean, *ew.* "What book club?" And where had she gotten a cardboard cutout of my dad? I didn't even know such a thing existed.

Rita waved a hand at me. "Oh, it's no matter." She glanced over her shoulder. Andi Caldwell and Georgina McCully—Rita's elderly gossip buddies—were standing near the two stairs that led up to the bookstore portion of the store. They were beside a man and woman I didn't know. "I best get over there," she said. "It's the first day, you know!"

She carried my dad over to the plate glass window and set him up so he could look out into the street before she walked over to where the others waited. Together they went upstairs, with me and my confusion forgotten.

I stood at the counter, staring dumbly at the cardboard cutout. "What just happened?"

"Rita happened." Lena rolled her eyes as she stepped behind the counter. She walked over to the register to take an order.

Vicki came sauntering down the stairs and walked over to me then. "Are you feeling okay?" she asked. "You're looking a little pale."

"I'm not sure." I tore my eyes away from the cardboard Dad. "What's going on?" I nodded toward where

Rita and the others were talking with another group of five strangers.

Vicki glanced back before turning to me with a grin. "Rita asked if they could have their book club meeting here and I told her it would be okay. I figured it couldn't hurt business. In fact, it will probably help. She brought a few chairs to set up in the bookstore so they won't disrupt anything down here." Vicki paused and frowned at my expression. "That's okay, isn't it?"

"I . . . Yeah." I was still reeling from Rita's assault and didn't know what else to say. I mean, it wasn't like having more people in the building was a bad thing. If they ordered coffee for their meetings, that could only help, right?

"Okay, good." Vicki breathed a sigh of relief as she tucked a strand of blond hair behind her ear. "She asked me on your day off and I didn't want to call you and bother you with it. It seemed harmless enough, especially since you are a part of her writers' group and all."

"It's okay." And really, outside the cardboard Dad in the window, I didn't mind it all that much. Rita practically lived here, anyway. She spent a large portion of her day, sitting in the corner of the store, typing away at her little pink notebook, torturing innocent prose.

Rita's arms suddenly flew up into the air and she stamped her foot. She said something harsh to the man in front of her, who responded in kind. Georgina and Andi stood beside the two strangers behind Rita, while another four people I didn't know stood behind the man Rita was yelling at. They were leaning forward as they argued, fists clenched, eyebrows bunched. It looked like a scene out of one of those movies where a pair of street gangs would argue, right before breaking out into song and dance.

"I think I best go up there and see what's going on," I said, slipping around the corner. I doubted Rita and her crew would be dancing any time soon; this fight looked as if it might actually come to blows.

"I'll come with you," Vicki said.

We marched across the store, leaving Lena to handle the register. She didn't seem to mind. Ever since we hired her, she'd focused hard on her job. She might look like trouble with all of the scrapes and bruises, and now with the purple hair, but she was truly a good kid. I couldn't have asked for better.

"I don't see what the problem is," Rita said as we neared. "We agreed to the book months ago!" She waved a paperback copy of *Murder in Lovetown* in front of the man's face. It was one of my dad's earlier works, one that he was embarrassed of even today.

"We didn't know you'd be holding the thing in a store named after the author!" the man practically shouted. He was about five and a half feet tall, weighed no more than 120 pounds, and parted his hair right down the middle in a vain attempt to conceal his rapidly retreating hairline. "We believe another book should be chosen."

"Isn't it a bit late for that?" Rita asked with a smug smile. "We've already started reading and have had the first of our local discussions."

The man's jaw clenched as he leaned forward and grabbed a silver teapot from the table in front of him. His fingers went white where he gripped it and I had a sudden vision of him whacking Rita upside the head with it. I rushed forward and snatched it out of his hand before anything unseemly could happen.

"Calm down, everyone," I said, holding the teapot behind my back, out of everyone's reach. I looked from face to face. "Anyone want to tell me what is going on?"

Rita straightened and thrust her impressive bust outward, practically poking the man in the eye. "Albert here doesn't approve of where we are holding our meetings. He thinks we should read something else."

"It gives you an unfair advantage!" Albert said at a near whine.

"Why *don't* you read something else?" I asked. "Like Agatha Christie. She's pretty popular." And she wasn't my dad.

"Pah!" Rita waved a hand dismissively at me. "It's too late to make a change now." Her gaze moved past Albert, to a man standing behind him. He was closely holding a woman wearing a pearl necklace and diamonds on her fingers, as if protecting her. "Besides, *they* are the ones who should be ashamed. There are rules to membership and *he* hasn't lived in Cherry Valley long enough!" She nodded toward the man.

*"Rules? Cherry Valley?"* I was operating at a loss once again.

Rita sighed and gave me a pitying look. "It's simple, really. Each town's team can have five members, but the members have to be a citizen of the town for at least one year before they can be an official part of the book club competition."

*"Competition?"*

"We talk about the book and whoever understands it and can articulate it best, wins the prize for their town," Albert put in.

*"Prize?"* I wanted to break out of my rut of asking one-word questions, so I added, "What prize?"

"The silver teapot, silly!" Rita said with a gesture to the teapot in my hand.

I looked at Vicki, who simply shrugged. Who'd ever heard of a book club competition? Without having to ask, I knew Rita had been the one to come up with it. No one else would have thought of something so . . . odd.

I knew I was going to regret it, but I asked anyway. "How do you determine who the winner is?"

She gave me a look like I'd just asked her if the world was round. It was Albert who answered. "We hold a public discussion. We alternate towns, and Pine Hills has the honor of hosting the event this year. We discuss the book among ourselves during the evening for a week and then we have the big public discussion. Quite a lot of people turn out for it. The crowd votes for the winner."

I had a hard time believing what I was hearing. I mean, a book club competition. Really? I plowed on. "Doesn't that skew the results?" They both gave me a blank look. "Won't the people from Pine Hills vote for the Pine Hills team, and vice versa?"

"Oh no," Rita said. "This is much too important for that."

If she said so, I wasn't going to argue. None of this was making much sense to me.

"So you are going to have the meetings here?" I asked, still trying to feel my way through it.

"We are," Rita said. "We usually hold them at the library, but Jimmy has kindly agreed to move it here this year." She leaned toward me as if she was about to share some deep, dark secret. "He's the local librarian, you know."

Jimmy gave me something of an annoyed smile, telling me he wasn't all that happy with the move. He wore a sweater vest and brown slacks with loafers that just about screamed "librarian." His hair was buzzed short and his jaw square, juxtaposing the nerd with military. He was a good six feet tall and I caught a hint of muscle beneath his plaid shirt.

"It's nice to meet you," he said in a surprisingly nasal voice. "It's Jimmy Carlton." He put his arm around the short, round woman next to him. "And this is my wife, Cindy."

Since introductions were already started, I turned an expectant look on the Cherry Valley group.

"Vivian Flowers," the oldest member said with a shrug when my eyes landed on her. She looked to be at least eighty, and probably weighed not much more. Her dress was covered in white lilies. I wondered if she chose it because of her name or if she simply liked the pattern.

The next man in line squinted at me through black-rimmed thick glasses. "Orville Rush." He was clutching the paperback copy of his book close to his chest. Even then, his hands shook. His hair was but a wisp on his head.

The tall man Rita had indicated earlier smiled at me. He wore a fedora pulled down low over his eyes and an unbuttoned suit coat over a white shirt. "David Smith." He tipped his hat toward me and I nearly swooned. The man's voice did something strange to my insides. He was clearly from across the pond if his accent was any indication.

"Sara Huffington," the woman with the pearl neck-lace said in a bored tone of voice. She snuggled in closer to the Brit and promptly ignored the rest of us.

"And as you know, this is Krissy Hancock, daughter to our beloved author." Rita put an arm around me. "She has kindly agreed to host the event this year, so I do hope you can show her some respect." The last was aimed at Albert, who looked away, frustrated.

I tore my eyes from David and handed Rita the teapot. "I guess I should get back to work then." The argument seemed to be over, and I wanted to get as far away from these people as I could before another fight broke out. "It was nice to meet you all."

"Likewise," David said in his silky, smooth voice. It was followed by a wink.

I made a little squeak before spinning and hurrying away, Vicki hot on my heels.

"Cute, isn't he?" she asked as soon as we were back downstairs.

"Uh-huh." It was all I could manage. I fanned myself off.

"Do you think it will be okay to allow them to have their meetings here? If they argue like that all of the time . . ." Vicki looked worriedly back up the stairs.

"I think they'll be fine."

And if it meant I got to sit back and watch David Smith while I worked, I didn't think I'd mind a little arguing, either. I mean, what could possibly be the harm?